The Husband She Never Knew

Cynthia Thomason

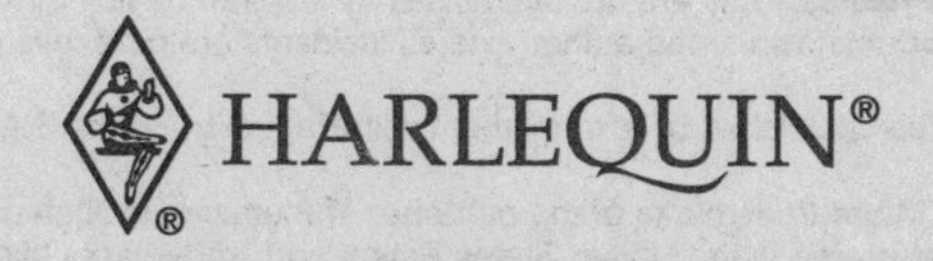

TORONTO • NEW YORK • LONDON
AMSTERDAM • PARIS • SYDNEY • HAMBURG
STOCKHOLM • ATHENS • TOKYO • MILAN • MADRID
PRAGUE • WARSAW • BUDAPEST • AUCKLAND

ISBN 0-373-71180-8

THE HUSBAND SHE NEVER KNEW

This edition published by arrangement with Harlequin Books S.A.

Visit us at www.eHarlequin.com

Printed in U.S.A.

"Does a man need a reason for wanting to see his wife?"

"He does when that wife is engaged to marry another man," Vicki replied.

Jamie froze. "He's proposed?"

"Well, no, not yet..." Vicki admitted. "But it wouldn't be fair to let you think that this relationship, or whatever it is that we shared for twenty-four hours, would ever amount to anything more than a night in a storm. You can't possibly believe this so-called marriage of ours is real."

"But it is. Otherwise you wouldn't need a divorce to end it."

Vicki exhaled her frustration in a long sigh. "Yes, it's real legally. But certainly not emotionally. We're two completely different people. We live completely different lifestyles. We have different goals. We enjoy different things."

"We both enjoyed kissing each other." Jamie's green eyes sparkled.

"That shouldn't have happened," Vicki insisted. "I'm attracted to another man. I'm going to *marry* another man as soon as you—"

"Yeah, I know. As soon as I sign the papers. A*nd*—" Jamie held back a grin "—as soon as he asks you..."

Dear Reader,

This book is about mistakes. Not the little social blunders that make us blush for a moment and are soon forgotten. No, this story is about a really big whopper, the kind we can only reveal to our best friend because if the rest of the world knew, we would suffer immeasurable humiliation.

Maybe you've suffered through one or two lapses in judgment in your life. I know I have, and a couple of those mistakes have come back to haunt me. But maybe you were one of the lucky ones—maybe fate exercised its fickle mastery over your future and saved you from the transgressions of your youth.

In this book you will meet Vicki Sorenson and experience the one big blunder from her past. Will it ultimately ruin her life or will it turn out to be one of those rare sublime moments of serendipity?

I love to hear from readers. You can write to me at P.O. Box 550068, Fort Lauderdale, FL 33355, e-mail me at cynthoma@aol.com or visit my Web site at www.cynthiathomason.com.

Sincerely,

Cynthia Thomason

To my talented brother, Doug, and his charming wife, Sal.
From different continents—
like the hero and heroine of this book—
they prove that second-chance love can be glorious.

Books by Cynthia Thomason

HARLEQUIN SUPERROMANCE

1120—THE MEN OF THORNE ISLAND

PROLOGUE

Orlando, Florida, 1990

VICKI SORENSON parked her ancient Ford Pinto a half block from the Orlando courthouse and stepped into the sweltering humidity. She plucked her blouse away from her damp back and pressed her lips together to blend the two quick swipes of Watermelon Ice she'd just applied in the rearview mirror. To make sure no lipstick had stuck on her teeth, she ran her tongue over them. A girl shouldn't have lipstick on her teeth on her wedding day.

She walked toward the courthouse, her shoulder bag thumping against her hip with each step. Kenny Corcoran, the short-order cook from the Orange Blossom Diner where she worked waved from the top of the stairs. At least there was some measure of comfort in seeing the friend who'd masterminded this plan today.

And then she had her first glimpse of the man she'd come to meet. The man she would marry just as soon as they could sign their names to the license and get an appointment with a justice of the peace. Her heart slammed against her ribs as she reached the first step. This man, this Jamie Malone, seemed to fill the courthouse entrance. Energy fairly radiated from him, and kept him in perpetual motion, arching his spine, rubbing the back of his neck, shifting his weight from one foot to the other.

Kenny twirled his hand in a hurry-up gesture. "Come on, Vicki. We've got a few minutes. You two can get acquainted."

Get acquainted. What a ridiculous thing to suggest to a bride and groom, but that was exactly what Vicki and Jamie needed to do if they were to have any hope of convincing immigration officials that this marriage was legitimate. She stopped two steps shy of Jamie Malone and resisted the urge to run. She had to remember why she was doing this, why she couldn't back out now.

Kenny, a shadowy figure himself with connections to a secret society of Irish brethren, introduced her. Jamie Malone smiled and extended his hand. She grasped it as she climbed the two steps, whereupon she noticed that he topped her five foot six by several inches. His fingers were long and lean, like the rest of him. Grease stains darkened his nails, though he appeared clean and freshly shaven. He was a workingman, this Irish immigrant, who needed a green card to stay in the United States.

"Hello, miss," he said. "It's a fine thing you're doin' today. You're probably savin' my sorry ass from a Belfast jail, you know."

She stared at Jamie a long moment and realized her ears were appraising him as much as her eyes were. His accented English, lilting and lyrical, flowed like the thick, damp waves of hair he'd tried to tame in a strip of leather at his nape.

''Don't thank me, Mr. Malone,'' she said. ''I have my reasons for agreeing to this, and you know what they are.''

His smile stayed in place, despite her curt response. ''Indeed I do, miss.'' He patted the pocket of his plaid shirt. ''I have the cash right here. But you'll not begrudge me the chance to express my gratitude. I can't imagine a thing like this would be easy for a girl.''

''No, it's not,'' she admitted. But at twenty-one Vicki found it hard to imagine that this one impulsive decision could affect the rest of her life. People got out of marriages all the time. Her biggest concern was seeing that wad of bills transferred from Jamie's shirt to her pocketbook and not getting caught by the immigration officials. The rest would work itself out in time.

''Well, then, let's go,'' Kenny urged. ''Jamie, hold her hand. And smile, both of you. It's your wedding day.'' He opened the courthouse door and let the soon-to-be newlyweds precede him inside.

CHAPTER ONE

Fort Lauderdale, 2003

VICTORIA SORENSON wasn't about to let the fact that she was a married woman spoil this night's celebration—not when she'd seen her husband of thirteen years for perhaps only ninety minutes in total. And not when she was anticipating becoming engaged to the man of her dreams in two weeks.

Louise Duncan leaned forward and looked at Vicki with unmasked skepticism. ''Okay, Vic,'' she said, ''that sparkle in your eye is about to blind me. What are we toasting?''

Vicki refilled her friend's wineglass with the better-than-average merlot she'd chosen for this occasion and smiled at her across the white linen tablecloth. ''It's that obvious?''

Louise speared another piece of shrimp scampi and lifted her fork to her mouth. ''This isn't a fast-food joint, my friend. This is a table with an ocean view at one of Fort Lauderdale's trendiest restaurants, and you're picking up the check. It isn't my birthday, so what's up?''

Enjoying the advantage of having information someone else didn't, Vicki folded her hands on the table and grinned at the woman who'd been her best friend for fifteen years. "Guess."

Louise smirked, a gesture she'd mastered to perfection. "I'll keep guessing as long as you keep buying the wine."

Vicki laughed, knowing she couldn't prolong the suspense another minute. "Graham's going to propose. I just know it."

Louise dropped her fork against the side of her china plate and gaped at Vicki. "Wow. That might have been my fiftieth guess. Do you think he's gotten the approval of all those people on the Townsend library walls?"

"I have Graham's approval, which is what really matters," Vicki answered. She tucked a strand of recently highlighted tawny hair behind her ear. "And he says I've progressed from probationary to acceptable on the Townsend-acquaintance meter."

"That must be a relief," Louise said with her usual sarcasm.

"It is, for Graham's sake," Vicki admitted. She knew it was important to him that his parents accept her as a member of the Townsend family tree, and it looked as if they finally had. Graham's Massachusetts pedigree had always been more of a problem than a blessing for Vicki. She'd constantly struggled to make Graham's relatives appreciate her better qualities, such as her work ethic and ambition, and pay less attention to her Midwestern immigrant background.

"What are you going to do about kids?" Louise

asked. ‘‘Have you told him your reservations about having children?’’

‘‘Not yet, but I will.’’ It was definitely a topic Vicki would have to deal with, and soon. There was nothing essentially wrong with the *idea* of being a mother. She knew that lots of women handled the job very well. But she doubted she herself would ever be a good mother. How could she when her role models, her own parents, used guilt and the threat of retribution as their primary child-rearing tools? Plus, Nils and Clara Sorenson had never shown the least delight in any aspect of maintaining a family. They viewed their responsibilities as parents as just another burden in a life of constant drudgery.

‘‘I’m sure Graham and I can come to a compromise on the matter of children,’’ she said when she realized Louise was still waiting for an explanation.

Louise laughed. ‘‘Oh, honey, you can’t make a compromise when it comes to kids. They’re either here or they aren’t. I don’t see much middle ground.’’

Louise dunked a bread stick into her wine and nibbled on her newly pink creation. ‘‘But enough about that. What exactly makes you think Graham’s going to propose?’’

Grateful to steer the conversation away from kids, Vicki said, ‘‘He’s been dropping obvious hints. Last night we were talking about my shop opening in two weeks and he said, ‘That’s going to be a really big night for you.’’’

‘‘And?’’

"And he said he was proud of me and he hoped our relationship lasted a long, *long* time."

"Well, Vic, he *is* your antique importer. Are you sure he wasn't referring to a successful business relationship?"

Vicki let a smug expression precede her answer. "I'm quite sure, my cynical friend, and you will be, too, when I tell you that last night I distinctly remember leaving my amethyst ring on the coffee table." Vicki wiggled her left hand at Louise. "The one I always wear on the third finger of this hand. When Graham left late last night the ring was gone. This afternoon he came by with a silly excuse about losing his business-card holder in the couch cushions. When he left, the ring was back on the coffee table."

Louise nodded slowly. "Ah. The old steal-the-ring-to-get-the-size ploy."

"Exactly. Now do you believe me?"

"Okay, now I believe you. So in two weeks you're going to be the proprietor of one of the most fashionable new shops on Las Olas Boulevard, and you just might have a Townsend-family diamond glittering on your ring finger."

Vicki laughed. "I don't know if the in-laws will actually sacrifice a diamond for me, but I'll be happy with a brand-new modest one." She didn't even try to squelch the tremor of delight that rippled through her. "After a year and a half, Lulu, it's finally all coming together."

Louise patted her hand fondly. "I'm happy for you, Vic, honestly." Oddly, Louise's expression did not reflect that happiness. "Look, I hope you'll forgive me," she said, "but somebody's got to point out the one little complication that you've avoided for thirteen years."

Vicki knew what was coming and was relieved that Louise had brought it up. "You're right," she said. "I should have handled the problem of Jamie Malone years ago, but until Graham, Jamie hadn't been a concern in my life."

Louise peered over the edge of her wine glass. "I'd call him more than a concern now, Vic. You can't begin a life with your second husband until you've done something about the first one."

Louise was right about that. And maybe she *had* avoided the man she'd married for cash after she'd moved to Florida. By the time she met Jamie, she'd used up her small savings and dropped out of college at the end of her junior year. Even after getting the money from Jamie, her life had been a constant struggle to survive on her own, and she hadn't had time to clear up past mistakes.

It wasn't until she discovered she had a knack for buying and selling antiques that her life finally got easier. She supported herself with enough profit left over each month to send money to her parents in Indiana. The gesture eased her guilt about leaving her family in financial straits while allowing her to keep a promise to herself never to go back to her humble, oppressive roots.

"You're thinking about your parents again, aren't you," Louise said.

A ramshackle farmhouse on the edge of an Indiana cornfield left Vicki's mind as Louise brought her back to the present. "Yeah, I was. I know you think I used my family as an excuse for letting those years slip away without taking care of my situation with Jamie Malone."

Louise sighed and attempted a smile. "I know you did, Vic, and I also know how hard you've worked to make a life for yourself away from your miserable, freeloading parents..."

The first hint of anger ignited in Vicki. "Don't start, Louise," she warned, feeling an irrational need to defend parents who probably didn't deserve it.

"Okay, sorry. But if Graham pops the question, what *are* you going to do about Malone?"

"That's where you come in," Vicki said.

"I was afraid of that."

"Come on, Louise, you're not just my best friend. You're also my lawyer. And I need your advice now more than I ever have. You've got to get me out of this."

Louise's smirk was back. "You should have asked for my advice thirteen years ago when you did this stupid thing."

Vicki rolled her eyes. "You weren't a lawyer then. And besides, I needed that money desperately."

Louise shook her head in frustration. "Yeah, I know. There was a drought in Indiana. The barn roof was falling in. Daddy needed false teeth—"

"Stop it, Louise. I've told you I felt obligated."

Louise pressed her lips together. "Okay, honey, I

know all about your big heart. But to put it more kindly this time, I've seen your parents take advantage of you over and over again, and what you did thirteen years ago went beyond what anyone should expect from you."

"Be fair, Louise. They didn't know how I got that money."

"True, but do you honestly think they would have cared?"

That hurt, but Vicki had to admit the truth in her friend's words. Louise had a gift for seeing the simple facts, pleasant or not. It was an ability that Vicki had never really developed. Even now she still couldn't judge her parents from an objective viewpoint. They were her parents, after all.

"Besides," Louise continued, "you could have gotten into big trouble. Malone was a stranger to you!"

"No, he wasn't. Not exactly. He was the friend of a friend."

"But you knew he was a criminal."

"He wasn't a criminal!" Vicki was tired of defending herself over this issue. Louise would never comprehend Vicki's motives for what she'd done that day, and why should she? Louise was the daughter of a pair of Orlando obstetricians who'd never demanded more of her than passing grades and weekly phone calls. But Vicki needed Louise's help desperately, so she tried once more to make her understand about Jamie Malone. "He left Ireland to avoid going to prison. He was innocent of any wrongdoing. It was a family-loyalty thing. I told you all this years ago."

"Yeah, I know," Louise drawled without enthusiasm. "The poor guy was in the wrong place at the wrong time."

"Exactly."

"So what do you want from me?"

"Get me a divorce. Or an annulment. Or make a case for abandonment. Whatever it takes. But do it quickly and quietly. When I get a ring in two weeks, I want to wear it as the respectable single woman the Townsends and Graham think I am."

"This won't be easy, you know that," Louise said.

"I know, but I'm putting my future in your hands."

Louise sighed. "Okay, our best chance is a divorce for the reason of abandonment. You'll have to run a newspaper ad for four consecutive weeks in the county of his last-known address. After that, you'll file papers with our court, and then you'll wait a prescribed amount of time for Mr. Malone to come forward. If he doesn't, and if the judge feels you have truly exhausted all reasonable efforts to locate him, he'll grant a divorce on the grounds of abandonment."

Vicki fought her escalating panic. "Four weeks? A prescribed amount of time? Lulu, I just told you I have to have this taken care of in two weeks."

Louise narrowed her eyes and spoke in low tones. "And that's not all. Your name will be in the newspaper, as will his, so you'd better hope that the issue of his green card and your fraudulent marriage in Orlando doesn't ring a bell with an overzealous immigration official."

Being accused of defrauding the U.S. Immigration

and Naturalization Service after all these years was enough to turn Vicki's blood to ice. And if Graham's family saw her name in the paper and investigated her background, they would do everything in their power to keep Vicki from becoming a Townsend. She didn't even want to *think* about Graham's reaction. She loved him, but he could be extremely opinionated about issues of respectability.

"You're scaring me, Louise," she said. "Surely there must be a statute of limitations on this sort of thing."

"I don't know, but even if there is and even if you get away with a clean divorce, it could be a very long and expensive process. Remember, Malone's in absentia. You're shouldering all the expenses."

Vicki pictured her dwindling savings account, and desperation crept into her voice. "I don't have a lot of money, but time is the most important issue. The process you described takes too long. What else can I do?"

Louise drummed her fingers on the table while she considered Vicki's question. Finally she said, "It's a long shot, but you actually might be able to find this guy and get him to sign uncontested divorce papers. That way, you see him one time, he signs, you're divorced in a Broward County court, and it's over like any other failed marriage with no assets, liabilities or children to argue over."

There was a ray of hope, after all. "So how do I find him?"

"Our firm uses a reliable detective agency. They

claim they can find anybody. I can have an investigator call you.''

Vicki poured another inch of wine into Louise's glass. ''You're an angel, Lulu. I'll owe you big time.''

Louise arched her trim black eyebrows. ''You bet you will.''

AT NINE O'CLOCK Monday morning Vicki met with her contractor and discussed the final decorative details for her shop. While they talked, a painter stenciled ''Tea and Antiquities'' in old-English script on the panels of the leaded-glass windows.

Vicki was pleased with the transformation of the two-thousand-square-foot store. After investing her life savings into this prime location of old-name insurance companies, law offices and upscale retail shops, she nervously anticipated the grand opening of Tea and Antiquities in twelve days. She hoped her shop would attract customers because of its originality. It was the only store on the street that offered the comfort and refinement of an English tearoom with the eye appeal of antiques she and Graham had personally selected.

The contractor had just left when Vicki's phone rang. She crossed to a mahogany Chippendale desk to answer it. ''Tea and Antiquities.''

''Miss Sorenson?''

She didn't recognize the male voice. ''Yes.''

''This is Russell Weaver from Insider Investigations. I got a call from Louise Duncan this morning advising me that you have a need for our services.''

Vicki set both elbows on the desk. Thank goodness. Louise hadn't forgotten. "That's right, Mr. Weaver. I need you to locate someone for me as quickly as possible."

"A former husband, is that right?"

Louise had obviously tried to be discreet, and Vicki saw no reason to correct the misconception by calling Malone her *current* husband. "Yes, that's correct."

"The man's name?"

"Jamie Malone."

"Last known address?"

"I'm not sure."

"Occupation?" Weaver asked questions as if following a script.

Unfortunately Vicki didn't know her lines. "I'm not positive of that, either. I think he used to work as a carpenter." She felt incredibly foolish. Certainly any woman would know more about a former husband.

"He changed jobs a lot," she said to cover her ignorance and tried to overlook the snort of skepticism that came from the earpiece. "I haven't seen him in thirteen years."

"His age?"

Vicki let out a breath of relief. She knew this one. There was four years' difference in their ages. "He's thirty-eight."

Mr. Weaver asked a few other pertinent questions to which Vicki responded with embarrassing ambiguity. Finally with a knowing smugness, he said, "Do you happen to have a description of your former husband, Miss Sorenson?"

"Well, of course." That was truly an honest answer. How could she forget seeing Jamie Malone for the first time on the steps of the Orlando courthouse? Her knees had been knocking. Her palms had been sweating. She'd been trembling like the last leaf in a windstorm on the day she'd agreed to marry him for the generous sum of five thousand dollars.

Besides his physical characteristics, which were still clear in her mind, she remembered the underlying brashness of the man—a trait that was intimidating to a shy twenty-one-year-old farm girl who only wanted to get the disagreeable task over with and collect her money. Even Jamie's quick smile and misplaced attempt at charm hadn't put her at ease.

She gave the detective a description of the way Jamie had looked thirteen years ago. Then, grateful that Mr. Weaver didn't ask more personal questions, she acknowledged his promise to call with information as soon as he had any.

That call came in the early afternoon of the same day.

"You've found Jamie Malone already?" Vicki asked.

"Sure have."

"How did you do that so quickly?"

The detective chuckled. "I'd like to tell you that I used some ultraspecialized procedure known only to the investigative trade, but the truth is, I found him on the Internet."

Vicki couldn't contain her surprise. "You're kidding!"

"Actually I found J.D. Malone. I had to do some

further searches to ensure that he was our man, but everything checked out. Turns out your ex is an artist living in a little town in North Carolina.''

Vicki's first reaction was to declare that she wasn't paying $150 an hour for this ridiculous, unfounded information. The Jamie Malone who'd persisted in invading her memory the past few hours could hardly be an artist. ''Oh, no, Mr. Weaver,'' she said. ''You must be mistaken.''

''Nope. No mistake here. This is definitely the man you're looking for.'' He read off a grocery list of Jamie's past. ''James Dillon Malone came from Ireland in 1988. Lived a year in Rhode Island on a work visa. Then moved to Florida where his visa was due to expire.'' The detective cleared his throat before introducing his next factual detail. ''And then it seems his immigration problems were miraculously over, Miss Sorenson. He got his green card after marrying you in 1990.''

Vicki felt a blush of mortification creep up her neck to her cheeks. ''I guess that's him,'' she admitted.

''You want his address?'' Weaver asked.

''Definitely.''

''It's simple enough. Jamie Malone, Pintail Point, Bayberry Cove, North Carolina. I looked on a map. It's in the extreme northern part of the state, on the coast.''

Vicki thanked the detective and told him to send her the bill. After disconnecting, she stared at the address she'd written in her day planner. Those few words abruptly connected her to Jamie Malone in a way she'd never expected to be again. She'd only seen him twice in 1990. Once at the courthouse and then again six months later at an INS office where they'd somehow managed to pass the required post-wedding interview. They'd exchanged extremely personal information over the phone a few days before the interview, and luckily, they'd memorized the very details the official that day had wanted to know.

Today Vicki recalled some of the particulars. Jamie had said he was an early riser. He slept in boxer shorts. As a child he'd had chicken pox and measles, nothing more serious. His mother lived in Ireland, but he hoped to bring her to America. He watched very little television, since soccer matches weren't broadcast much in the U.S. He didn't smoke, but appreciated his Guinness. He ate red meat and liked to run in the evenings before his shower. He had no political affiliation, and he wasn't religious, but if it turned out there was a God, it was okay with him.

Vicki also remembered that Jamie claimed he had a healthy sexual appetite, something Vicki had to admit, as well, in front of the INS agent. In fact, recalling how they'd professed to making love every day of the week made her face flush with heat even now.

At the INS interview, his hair had still been long and wild. There'd still been stains under his fingernails. And his smile had still been eager.

Vicki closed her planner and tucked it into her purse. She'd never have believed she could dredge up so many details about a man she'd only thought of over the years as a problem she'd have to address one day. Well, today was the day, she thought as she picked up the phone again and punched in Louise's number.

"What's up, Vic?" Louise asked.

"Draw up my divorce papers, Lulu. I'm heading to Bayberry Cove, North Carolina."

CHAPTER TWO

THE FIRST SNAG in Vicki's foolproof plan to obtain an uncontested divorce occurred two days later at the Norfolk, Virginia, airport. Minutes after her plane landed, Vicki and other passengers with schedules to return the next day were summoned by an airline representative. This woman calmly explained to the ticket holders that they should call the airline to confirm that their return flights weren't being affected by the approaching storm.

Storm? What storm? Vicki remembered a local TV weatherman's vague reference a couple of days before to a tropical storm in the Atlantic Ocean. But since it was October, near the end of hurricane season, and the system was well north of Florida, she hadn't paid much attention. Now, suddenly, *she* was well north of Florida and that feathery white ripple she'd seen on a meteorological radar screen had acquired a name and a circular motion. Unbelievably, Tropical Storm Imogene was targeting a still-unspecified patch of land somewhere along the North Carolina/Virginia coast.

Wonderful. Vicki slung her garment bag over her shoulder and made her way to the rental-car counter. She had a reservation at a hotel near the airport for tonight, but her flight back wasn't until noon tomorrow. She had more than twenty-four hours to sweat out Imogene's eventual landfall—at the same time she was sweating out her meeting with Jamie Malone.

After a thorough search, the rental-car agent found the small town of Bayberry Cove on a map. It was situated on the shore of Currituck Sound in the low-land marshes between the North Carolina mainland and the Outer Banks. A bird could have probably made the journey from Norfolk in about half an hour, but thanks to the narrow, twisting two-lane road Vicki had to take, she arrived at the town boundary sixty minutes later.

Now Vicki's problem was to find the even more elusive Pintail Point. And she didn't have time to waste driving aimlessly. She headed down Main Street, searching for a busy establishment where locals might direct her to where Jamie Malone lived. She chose the Bayberry Cove Kettle, a small, pleasant-looking café with ruffled curtains in the windows and an open parking space in front.

A hand-printed sign on the door reminded her of the approaching storm: "Closing at 3 p.m. Imogene's coming." Vicki entered the crowded restaurant and took the only available seat, a stool at the counter. Apparently the residents of Bayberry Cove were indulging in a last hearty lunch before holing up in their houses for the duration of the storm.

Most of the customers didn't seem too worried. In fact, several of them were concentrating on triangular-shaped puzzle boards spaced across the length of the counter. Each puzzle had a dozen wooden pegs sticking up from holes. Vicki remembered playing these leap-frog games when she was a little girl in Indiana.

These, like the ones she recalled, came with cardboard instruction sheets that described the participant's mental capacity according to the number of pegs left in the board when he ran out of moves. If the player left one peg, he was a genius. If he left five or more pegs, he was a blockhead.

A full-figured waitress with short platinum hair took Vicki's order. "What can I get you, honey?" she asked. Her voice was decidedly Southern. So was the name on her lapel badge. Bobbi Lee. Her smile was wide and friendly.

"Just coffee," Vicki said. "And directions, if you don't mind."

Bobbi Lee set a steaming mug of coffee on the counter. She slid a chrome pitcher of cream and two sugar packets toward Vicki. "I don't mind a bit. I probably know every address in this little town. Lived here all my life."

Vicki took a sip. It tasted better than Florida coffee, probably because there was a bit of October chill in the North Carolina air. "Do you know where Pintail Point is?"

Bobbi Lee's cherry-red lips tugged down at the corners. She leaned one well-rounded hip against the counter and stared at Vicki. "Pintail Point? Now why would you want to know where that is? It's way outta town in the marshes. There's nothing much out there but ducks."

"Maybe so," Vicki said, "but someone lives there I used to know. I need to find him."

Bobbi Lee tapped her pencil against her order pad. A bit too loudly and a bit too fast. "You just continue down Main Street till you hit Sandy Ridge Road. Turn right and in about three miles you'll see the causeway that'll take you to Pintail. It's only one lane, so make sure nobody's comin' the other way."

Vicki dug in her purse for her wallet. "I will. Thanks." She left two dollars on the counter. "By the way, do you know which house belongs to Jamie Malone?"

Bobbi Lee snorted and jabbed her pencil into a tight wave over her ear. "There aren't any houses out there," she said. "But Jamie won't be hard to find. He's the only man that lives on the point."

No houses? One lone resident? Vicki took a healthy swig of coffee.

"You do know a storm's comin'?" Bobbi Lee said. "Pintail's no place to be."

Vicki picked up her purse and headed for the exit. "I won't be there long," she responded. "Thanks again."

Bobbi Lee only nodded, but as Vicki went out the door, she distinctly heard the waitress say, "Now, why would that woman be lookin' for a married man?"

Married? Jamie Malone was married? Bobbi Lee had said Jamie was the only *man* on Pintail Point. She hadn't mentioned a woman at all. Vicki slid into the driver's seat of her small rental car. She took a moment before starting the engine to think about this latest shocking information. What kind of trouble was she heading into with the only man who lived on Pintail Point? Was she meeting with a bigamist? Jamie must have married another woman because surely he didn't still think of Vicki as his wife. Vicki definitely didn't think of him as her husband. Would she face an irate woman who knew nothing of Jamie's past?

And why did the waitress proclaim Jamie's marital status in a voice loud enough to ensure that she heard it? Was it a warning of some kind?

Vicki turned the key in the ignition, relieved to hear the steady hum of the engine. This little car would take her away from Pintail Point as reliably as it got her there.

"You've come this far, Vicki," she said. "Just get it over with." She pulled out of the parking space and headed in the direction of Sandy Ridge Road. In her rearview mirror she saw Bobbi Lee watching her departure from the open doorway of the Bayberry Cove Kettle.

ANY NOTION that the airline representative might have been wrong about the approaching storm vanished when Vicki left the town limits of Bayberry Cove and turned onto Sandy Ridge Road.

The two-lane paved road hugged the shore of Currituck Sound, and on a sunny day would have provided scenic glimpses of the protected waters between the North Carolina coast and the Outer Banks. But today the horizon was gray, leaving the far islands blanketed in charcoal shadows. White-capped waves crashed against the sea wall, spewing frothy streams of brackish water over the edge of the road.

Wind buffeted Vicki's little car. She gripped the steering wheel to maintain a straight course. The marshes were eerily void of wildlife, and there wasn't a boat in sight. Vicki imagined that on any other day, fishermen would be working these waters and cursing the many pleasure-boaters.

After three miles, she spotted the causeway Bobbi

Lee had mentioned and turned off Sandy Ridge. Her tires crunched on the gravel surface of the one-lane spit of land bordered by sloping rock embankments. The causeway appeared to be about half a mile long, and at the end, through a thickening haze, Vicki detected a couple of low buildings set amongst a copse of trees.

This path was more treacherous than Sandy Ridge. Currituck Sound attacked the causeway from both sides, sending churning waves onto the road and leaving the driving surface riddled with puddles, gravel and seaweed.

In the distance, clouds swirled in ashen bands heavy with moisture. The weather was deteriorating quickly, Vicki realized, and she would be wise to leave the causeway as soon as possible. Once Jamie signed the papers, she could wait out the storm in a hotel near the Norfolk airport.

The buildings on the point of the causeway were more recognizable now. Vicki slowed her car under the wind-whipped branches of a tall pine. Bobbi Lee had been right. There were no houses on Pintail Point. There was, however, a large metal shed with a tin roof. And a houseboat.

Vicki parked next to a pickup truck with a light film of sand on its metallic-blue panels. She removed her briefcase from a zippered compartment in her garment bag and examined the point, which was no more than two acres.

She didn't see anyone around the houseboat, a one-story structure with a sundeck occupying half the roof. The boat was painted forest green with tan trim around the windows and shake cedar shingles extending from the slightly peaked roof. Window boxes gave the compact place a whimsical look, almost like a mountain chalet.

Vicki closed her eyes and took a fortifying breath. A clear image of that other time she'd met Jamie Malone flooded her memory. She was even more anxious now than she'd been on the courthouse steps. On that day, however, she'd known what to expect. She and Jamie had followed the advice of a mutual friend who'd guided them through the marriage and green-card process. Now she had only herself to rely on. There was no intermediary to witness this odd reunion, except perhaps Jamie's wife.

Vicki shivered. She buttoned her jacket, stuffed her car keys inside the pocket and wrapped a trembling hand around the door handle. "Just go," she said to herself. "Find this man, get him to sign the papers, and you'll be on your way in a few minutes."

She opened the car door and stepped into a fierce wind that whipped her hair from its tortoiseshell clip and battered strands of it against her cheeks. For a moment she felt like the heroine of a gothic novel. All the elements were here. The wind, the threatening rain, the isolation of Pintail Point. And even worse, a man who was just as much a stranger to her today as he'd been thirteen years ago when she'd married him.

She approached the houseboat. "Mr. Malone?" she called, and realized her words had been swept up in a gust of wind. "Hello!" she hollered. "Mr. Malone, are you here?"

She heard a bang and a crack. She couldn't identify the sound, but it was repeated twice more before someone shouted back, "Yes, I am, though if the wind gets any stronger up here, I might be blown to the mainland.''

Up here? Vicki held the hair out of her eyes and stared at the top of the houseboat from where the voice with the hint of an Irish accent had originated. A man appeared on the roof. He braced his feet apart against the force of the wind and looked down at her. ''I can't imagine what you're doing on the point today, but as long as you've come, would you toss up a box of staples?''

Vicki followed the imaginary line from the tip of the man's index finger to a red metal toolbox on top of a large wooden picnic table. She went to the edge of the table and grasped the latch of the toolbox. She'd just opened the lid when a loud snuffling sound came from the ground. A second later a heavy weight landed on the toe of her loafer. Vicki screamed, jumped away from the table and leaned over to see what had attacked her shoe.

A large, pointed dome of patchy gray fur poked out from underneath. A pair of small amber eyes on each side of a long, grizzled snout looked up at her with an expression of casual canine interest. ''My God,'' she gasped, ''does he bite?''

The answer came from the top of the houseboat. ''Beasley? Only the occasional gnat. And it had better be flying low.''

Vicki shifted her attention from the strange-looking dog to the man. He wiggled his finger with an edge of impatience, reminding her of his request. He obviously had no idea who she was.

Vicki hadn't known what she would find on Pintail Point, but she'd half expected the past thirteen years would melt away and she'd recognize the ruddy face of the scruffy carpenter she'd married. The man giving her an expectant look from twelve feet above was Jamie Malone all right, but thirteen years had made a difference in him, as they no doubt had in her.

"The staples are in a red-and-white box," he said. "I'm up here with a roll of plastic and a staple gun that's just run out of staples. And a sky that tells me I'm running out of time."

"Oh, right." She rummaged through the toolbox and found the requested item.

Jamie approached the edge of the roof and bent slightly. "Just toss her up. I'll catch it."

The tail of a green flannel shirt flapped around worn denim jeans that accentuated long, lean legs. At the open yoke, a white T-shirt stretched across the tapered chest of a well-developed male, not the skin-and-bones frame of the young Irish immigrant who'd looked as if he'd survived on one meal a day.

He showed her his open palm. "Before I grow a beard, miss."

Beard? He hadn't had one thirteen years ago, at least not on his wedding day. Now he had the shadow of one, lending a nonchalant dignity to his face. His hair was still a tangle of coffee-brown waves, though it fell no longer than the edge of his collar. The wind played havoc with it, but Vicki had the notion that it would look pretty much the way it did right now even on the calmest of days. And Jamie's smile, the feature she remembered most, was still the solar center of his face. With a frown that said he didn't have time for conversation or even a serious inspection of his visitor, he held up his staple gun to bring her back to her senses.

She threw the box underhanded. It somehow defied the wind and landed in Jamie's grasp.

He opened the stapler, filled it and snapped it closed again. "Thanks. As soon as I get this tarp secured, I'll come down and see what brought you out here on this wicked day." He went down on his knees beyond the slight peak of his roof and she had only the sound effects of his work to identify where he was.

"Yes, please," she shouted to the general vicinity of the stapler. "I won't take much of your time, but I need to speak with you and be on my way as quickly as possible."

After another minute the stapling stopped. Jamie stood up again and looked toward the mainland. He shook his head once before returning his attention to her. "Doesn't look like you'll be going anywhere today," he said.

She stared across the sound. The waves had increased in size, but it wasn't as if Pintail Point was no longer connected to the mainland. She could simply drive away, couldn't she? "What are you talking about?"

"Causeway's washed out. You can't see it from where you're standing, but I can. The water's claimed the road about halfway between Pintail and the coast."

"That's impossible."

"I'm afraid not. It happens with every good storm. In a day or two it'll dry out." He looked over his shoulder toward the Outer Banks and frowned. "Though this storm seems a bit worse than most.

Come aboard and see for yourself.'' He gestured. ''The ladder's just at the bow there.''

After considering for a moment that only a lunatic would climb to the roof of a houseboat in a fiercely blowing wind, Vicki headed for the ladder. She had to see for herself if Jamie's assessment of the situation was correct. She crossed a narrow bridge from the ground to the boat, set her briefcase on the deck and moved around to an open porchlike space that spanned the front of the houseboat. The hull made a squeaking sound as it rocked against the rubber bumpers connecting it to the sturdy wooden dock.

Vicki had climbed nearly to the top of the ten rungs when Jamie appeared from above and offered his hand. When she looked up at him, his entire face changed. It was as if the sun had broken through a menacing layer of clouds. His green eyes sparkled and his wide grin produced a pair of distinctive dimples. ''Bless my soul,'' he said. ''I thought you looked familiar, Vicki. After all these years, my sainted wife has come to me.''

Startled by his enthusiastic greeting, Vicki grasped his hand and stepped onto the upper deck. ''I'm surprised you remember me.'' She tried to hide the strangely pleasing effect his recognition had produced behind a sober expression.

''A man never forgets his first, Vicki darlin','' he said. He was still holding her hand, she realized, and staring at her in an odd, almost familiar way. ''How did you find me?''

Omitting the detail of the detective, Vicki said, ''You were on the Internet.''

Jamie laughed. "I've achieved cyber-fame? Has the INS posted a Most Wanted list?"

The response, though meant to be humorous, still spawned an uncomfortable twinge of nerves in the pit of Vicki's stomach. "Let's hope not," she said. "Or if they have, let's assume they've got more desperate criminals to find than the two of us."

Jamie chuckled. "That's a good bet. Anyway, it's nice to see you again, Vicki. Even on a day such as this one."

"You've been on my mind lately, Mr. Malone."

The corner of his mouth lifted in amusement. "I'm flattered," he replied. "But it's 'Mr. Malone,' is it?"

She looked down before he could read her embarrassment in her face. It was, after all, a ridiculous way to address one's husband.

"Are you certain you've got your footing?" he asked. "The wind's blowing hard up here."

She nodded and he released her hand but stayed by her side. Vicki cleared her throat and spoke close to his ear so he could decipher her words in the wind. "As I said, I've been thinking about you. About what we did. That's why I've come. And I can't stay but a few minutes."

He pointed to the causeway. "You didn't believe me, but have a look for yourself."

Vicki stared across the sound from this improved vantage point and gasped. The mist was thickening, making visibility difficult. "I can hardly see anything," she said. He took her hand and guided her to where she could make out a stream of water surging in frothy ripples across several yards of the gravel surface she'd driven over not twenty minutes before.

"Do you see that?" Jamie asked.

It looked as though the causeway had broken in two. She dropped her forehead into her hand and fought a rising panic. "Maybe if I leave now, I can just make it."

"In that little car?" Jamie nodded toward her rental.

"Of course."

"You'd be swept off the road and into the sound like a teacup in a whirlwind. I wouldn't even attempt it in my truck." He shrugged one shoulder with matter-of-fact acceptance of her predicament. "Guess you're stuck here for the duration." He touched her arm, drawing her attention to a spot in the distance. "Do you see that man on the mainland?"

She did. Barely.

"I'm betting that's Deputy Blackwell putting up barricades like he does whenever the causeway's washed out."

Through the soupy mist she detected a figure on the coast, and suddenly a location a mere half mile distant seemed a continent away.

"It's official," Jamie said. "Luther's not letting anyone on or off now."

The deputy swept his arm in a huge arc over his head, and Jamie waved back. Then Luther Blackwell, the man who'd just decided Vicki's fate for the next several hours at least, climbed in his patrol car and headed on down Sandy Ridge Road.

"I can't miss my flight home," Vicki said.

"Maybe you won't," Jamie said. "When is it?"

"Tomorrow at noon."

He squinted at the darkening horizon. The first fat

drops of rain pelted them, driven by a sudden gust of wind. ''On the other hand, maybe you will.''

She was trapped on a virtual island with a man who was practically a stranger! Vicki couldn't imagine a worse outcome to what was supposed to have been an uncomplicated mission. She knew nothing about Jamie. He could be half-crazy living out here in the middle of nowhere. Or worse.

''Let's get down to ground level,'' he said. ''This roof's as secure as she's going to get, but we humans are tempting the elements.''

She tried to control a trembling that began in her legs and was working its way up. *And I'm tempting fate,* she thought.

Jamie helped her to the ladder. ''Are you cold, Vicki?''

''No, I'm fine.'' She scurried down and retrieved her briefcase while Jamie stowed his tools in the metal box. He whistled for his dog, who still lay in unperturbed comfort under the picnic table. By the time Jamie opened the door to the houseboat, the rain was hard and steady. Since escape was impossible, Vicki went inside. Jamie took her jacket, hung it on a hook by the door and handed her a towel. She dried off as best she could while watching the darkening sky through a large window over the kitchen sink.

''Maybe I should turn on CNN,'' Jamie said. ''We can get an update on the storm.''

Vicki stepped over Beasley, who was now sprawled in the middle of the floor and followed Jamie from the kitchen to a living area furnished with a beige leather sofa and two matching leather chairs. It certainly didn't look like the accommodations of a psychopath—not that she knew how psychopaths lived. He picked up a remote control from a glass coffee table with a ship's steering wheel as its base. The brass trim on the spokes shone as if they were polished regularly.

The rest of the room showed similar attention. A pine dining set occupied one corner of the room. Its top was clear of clutter, prompting Vicki to remember her own dining table, which was currently layered with unopened mail and magazines. Nautical paintings hung in groups around the walls of the houseboat. Remembering her surprise at hearing Jamie was an artist, Vicki wondered if he'd painted the canvases himself.

He pulled the chain on a dark metal lamp with a leaded-glass shade. The outside gloom was transformed into a soft amber glow. While Jamie selected the channel for CNN, Vicki surreptitiously inspected two of the paintings in hopes of discovering something about the man she was stuck with. Jamie Malone was not the artist of either.

When a reporter's voice caught her attention, Vicki looked at a twenty-five-inch television screen. The set had a built-in VHS and DVD player. Since the old Jamie hadn't been a TV watcher, at least according to the information they'd exchanged in order to fool the immigration officer, she wondered when this later version of the man had become inspired to buy a state-of-the-art model.

Within minutes the focus of a news story was a radar screen splattered with colorful images in blues, reds and yellows. A meteorologist was saying, "This one caught us by surprise, folks. Imogene is now a category-one hurricane. Residents along the North

Carolina coast should hunker down. The eye will pass near the Carolina/Virginia border by nightfall.''

Vicki stopped patting her hair dry and draped the towel over her shoulders. She gawked at the swirling mass in the center of the screen that had suddenly become even more terrifying than her runaway suspicions of Jamie. ''My God, a hurricane. And we're sitting on this narrow little spit of land in a houseboat! We might as well be a weathervane on top of a barn in a tornado.''

''We'll be all right,'' he said. ''It'll be a blow, and likely will claim some shingles.'' He patted the wall nearest him. ''But the *Bucket o' Luck* is a sturdy tub. She's withstood a good many storms in her thirty-five years.''

''Thirty-five years! This boat is that old?'' Vicki cringed at the thought. Certain that the *Bucket's* luck had run out, she pictured herself clinging to forest-green flotsam in twenty-foot waves.

''I'm just now getting her broken in,'' Jamie said. ''It took us a few years to get used to each other. But trust me. She'll come through this storm in fine style.''

''You speak of your boat as if it were a flesh-and-blood person,'' Vicki said. *A wife, for instance,* she added to herself, remembering Bobbi Lee's words.

He chuckled. ''I suppose there was that same sort of period of adjustment for the *Bucket,* and me, as there is for a pair of new roommates.''

The masculine furnishings of the houseboat did not suggest a woman's influence. But if Jamie had taken another wife at some time in his past, and if Vicki was going to weather a storm with him in this confined space, she had to know it now. ''May I ask you something?'' she said.

''Anything at all. There should be no secrets between husband and wife.''

She shook her head. ''Right. Are you married?''

Jamie's initial response was a bark of laughter, a most inappropriate reaction to a serious question. Vicki opened her mouth to tell him so, but his phone rang, prohibiting her from expressing her opinion.

Jamie picked up the receiver. ''Yeah, Ma,'' he said. ''I just heard it on CNN. Now don't you go worrying about me.''

Vicki relaxed a little. A man whose mother called to show her concern was probably not a homicidal maniac.

''Do you have everything you need in case you're holed for a day or two?'' he asked.

He sat back on the sofa. After a minute he looked at Vicki and touched his fingers to his thumb repeatedly in that gesture men use when a woman is talking too much. ''Sure, I'll be fine, Ma. Got plastic on the roof, and I'll be putting shutters at the windows just as soon as I can get off the phone.''

A long pause. ''Yes, plenty of food. I was at the supermarket yesterday.'' He moved his head up and down in time to his mother's conversation. ''I can't do that, Ma. Luther's already blockaded the road. I'll call you when it's over.''

He set the receiver back on its cradle and looked at Vicki. ''That was my mother,'' he offered unnecessarily. ''She lives in Bayberry Cove—another result of our wedding vows for which I owe you a debt of gratitude.''

''Me? Why?''

''When you married me, you cleared the way for me to bring my mother over from Ireland. I was able to get her an immigrant visa and apply for her permanent residence once she got here. It wouldn't have happened if I hadn't become a citizen first.'' He leaned forward and rested his elbows on his knees. ''So, does that answer your question about my state of wedded bliss?''

''No, it doesn't. I meant, are you married to anyone besides me?''

For a second he looked truly shocked. ''Where would you get an idea like that?''

''From a waitress in town. When I asked directions to Pintail Point, she made sure I knew that you were married.''

''Was she a blonde with an hourglass figure that might require more room at the bottom for the sand?''

Vicki nodded.

''A good woman, Bobbi Lee is. But she has it in her mind that every little detail of my life should be her concern.''

Vicki wasn't fooled. She'd seen Bobbi Lee's disapproval firsthand. Plus, when a man made a statement like that, he was obviously hiding something, and what Jamie was probably hiding was that he and Bobbi Lee shared more than a casual relationship.

''But back to your question,'' Jamie continued. ''Yes, indeed I have a wife, and by some miracle I've yet to understand, I'm looking at her now for the first time in thirteen years.''

''Do you tell people that you're married and I'm

your wife?'' If he did, then the honesty of such a declaration was ironic in light of Vicki's own deception.

''Not exactly. I tell people I'm married is all, and that's the God's truth. And for what it's worth, Vicki, you've been nearly the ideal mate.''

She sank into one of the leather chairs. ''That's silly. We don't even know each other.''

''Not so silly when you compare our marriage to others you know of. You never nag me. I can leave my socks in the middle of the floor. And if I want to watch a football game, you never utter a complaining word.''

He flashed her a crooked grin that under other circumstances might have been charming. And Vicki decided that Jamie Malone was not at all sinister. A man with an indolent dog, a caring mother and an ancient houseboat he lovingly tended, was strange perhaps, but not evil.

'''Course I can't really say that the lovemaking has been very satisfying over the years,'' he added.

He was, however, something of a smart-ass. Vicki's cheeks flushed as she remembered again that she and Jamie had told an INS interviewer that they made love every day. Then she pictured Bobbi Lee with the wide smile and lavender-shaded eyes. And the tapping pencil. ''I'm sure you've compensated in other ways,'' she said.

He nodded. ''A man makes do.''

The phone rang again, dispelling the very clear image in Vicki's mind of how Jamie and Bobbi Lee ''made do.''

At the same time, Jamie spoke the waitress's name out loud. ''Hello, Bobbi Lee. Yes, I heard, first on

CNN, and then Ma called to tell me.'' There was a long pause during which another of Jamie's women monopolized the conversation.

''You'll be fine,'' he encouraged. ''Make sure Charlie and Brian bring in the patio furniture. No, you shouldn't need shutters on the mainland.''

He listened more and then looked over at Vicki and grinned. ''What do you mean? Who would be fool enough to come to Pintail with a storm brewing?''

Vicki did indeed feel like the fool Jamie suggested she was, both for getting herself stuck in a hurricane and for eavesdropping on a one-sided conversation between her husband and his girlfriend.

''Yes, I'll call when I can get through,'' he said. ''But we might not talk again very soon, Bobbi. I expect I'll lose phone service if it gets bad.''

He hung up and leaned back into the sofa. ''She was fishing to know if you were here,'' he said. ''And no doubt who you are and why you've come.''

''Why didn't you tell her?''

He answered with another of those complacent shrugs that suggested nothing much bothered him. ''If I had, she would have spent hours shut in her house fretting over it. And besides, she didn't come right out and ask.''

''But if she had, would you have admitted that I'm the other half of this perfectly satisfying marriage you claim to have enjoyed all these years?''

''I would have told her you're my legal wife, yes. I don't think I could get Bobbi Lee or anyone else in Bayberry Cove to believe more than that.''

''I think your wedding license has been a convenience, Mr. Malone. I think you tell people you're married when it suits your purposes or when you have something to gain by admitting it.''

His eyes narrowed slightly. ''Like what?''

''Like protecting your independence perhaps. You don't have to commit to a relationship. A man who's already been caught can't be caught again.''

He didn't deny her accusation, and she admired the honesty in his unspoken admission.

''Why have you come here today, Vicki?'' he asked.

She walked across the room and removed the divorce papers from her briefcase. ''I've come because I see our marriage from a somewhat different perspective. I think it's time to release you back into the wild, Mr. Malone, as a free spirit for real this time.''

She shoved the document at his chest. ''These are our divorce papers. I'm here to get you to sign them.''

CHAPTER THREE

JAMIE TOOK the document Vicki held out to him and stared at the address of a Fort Lauderdale legal firm on the cover. He wasn't quite ready to open the folder just yet. He was still reeling from that unexpected bit of psychoanalysis she'd just offered to explain why he'd been hanging on to a name-only marriage for more than a decade. There was a lot of truth in what she'd said. Bobbi Lee certainly believed he'd used his marriage license to justify his not getting too involved. But then again, he'd never met a woman he'd really wanted to marry.

In fact, Jamie had never considered himself a candidate for marriage. Despite having Frank Malone, rest his soul, as a role model in the husband department, Jamie hadn't believed that a "real" marriage was essential to his future contentment. He'd spent the last thirteen years establishing his career, making friends in the only town he'd ever wanted to call home, and enjoying the independence of living by his own dictates. In a way, what he'd said to Vicki was true. She had been an almost ideal mate—primarily because Jamie had never been tested as an ideal husband.

Jamie wasn't against marriage even though he

couldn't recall his mother shedding a tear when Frank Sr. died of lung cancer. Kate Malone had been a stoic widow. Maybe she'd been nursing fresh bruises, and that had kept her eyes dry. During his long illness, Frank hadn't gotten too weak to remind his family that he was master of the household.

And Frank's three sons were still single, even if Jamie technically wasn't. Frank Junior and Cormac would likely remain so for at least another five years until their prison terms were up. And even then a woman who'd consent to wed one of the infamous Outlaw Malones would probably have to be tough as tree bark to stand up for her rights. Frank Junior was a carbon copy of his father, and years in jail might have hardened Cormac's heart, as well.

"Well, aren't you going to look at it?"

Vicki's voice brought him back from his reverie. Mostly to please her, he lifted the blue document cover and thumbed through several pages. Then he put the folder on the coffee table, leaned back and settled his ankle on the opposite knee. He noticed that Vicki's face was nearly colorless, as if she hadn't taken a breath since producing the document from her briefcase. Did she think he would throw a fit when she presented her ultimatum?

"It appears to be a lot of legal mumbo jumbo to me," he said.

"Actually it's very straightforward. I know you're probably surprised by my coming here today, but I don't think you'll find anything objectionable in the dissolution."

The truth was, her visit in the middle of a hurricane had surprised him, but he wasn't at all surprised by the divorce papers. From a purely practical standpoint, one of them should have taken care of this matter years ago. Looking at Vicki now, he almost felt like apologizing for making her be the one to initiate the inevitable.

He decided not to tell her that he'd kept track of her whereabouts through a Raleigh investigator. He'd even received pictures of her for the first few years. Lately he'd heard very little about her personal life, but had been informed of each new address she had—just in case he'd needed to find her. The latest report indicated she'd rented a classy little boutique in a posh Fort Lauderdale neighborhood. Victoria Karin Sorenson, Indiana farm girl, was doing well.

Jamie was equally surprised at the changes in the timid girl he'd promised to love, honor and cherish in an Orlando courthouse. She'd been so nervous that day, like a plump little bird facing the menacing grin of a Cheshire cat. He'd seen a multitude of emotions cross her face in the hour they'd spent sealing their agreement. Guilt, fear, embarrassment. He'd tried to make her feel better about what they were doing, but none of his efforts had helped. In the end, he'd simply repeated his vows with the same hurried indifference she had.

She was a changed woman today, however. Vicki Sorenson had lost her chubbiness and acquired the willowy stature of a new-millennium businesswoman to whom fried chicken and corn on the cob were foods enjoyed only by the non-calorie-counting masses. In her black slacks, white blouse and black leather loafers, she was a chic version of the girl she'd once been. Unfortunately he couldn't help noticing that her beauty and sophistication fell just short of confidence. Was that because she was in a little country town called Bayberry Cove asking an immigrant stranger for a divorce? Or was it just that she was windblown and wet?

She tapped one black loafer on his thick tan carpet. "Well, aren't you going to say something?"

He hunched one shoulder. "I expect I'll say plenty once I've read this document through. Right now I'm overcome with grief at the abrupt end to our thirteen years."

"Don't start with that again," she warned. "It's been thirteen years of nothing, Ja..."

She stopped, and he filled in the gap of silence. "It's okay. You can call me Jamie. People on the verge of divorce ought to be on a first-name basis at least."

She glared at him. "You can't grieve over nothing, Jamie," she said. "I really need you to sign those papers." To expedite her request, she held a pen out to him.

At the same time, a blast of wind rocked the houseboat and sent a branch from a nearby bayberry bush flying by the window. Vicki sank into the chair again. "Oh, my God, it's getting worse, isn't it?"

"That appears to be the case," he said. "And if I don't get the shutters on this boat soon, there won't be a dry line on your papers for me to put my signature.''

''Then go. Do what you have to do. I'm apparently not going anywhere for a while.''

She stood, went into the kitchen and leaned against the sink. Beasley looked up at her with uncharacteristic interest. All dogs, even those without any apparent purpose in life like Beasley, could smell fear, and Beasley sensed it in Vicki. Jamie was no stranger to the signs of it, either. He'd seen fear in the faces of his countrymen in Belfast plenty of times. He read Vicki's fear in the fix of her gaze on the dark sky, the white-knuckled grip of her hand on the edge of the porcelain.

''Don't worry,'' he said to her. ''Like I said, the *Bucket* and I have seen worse than this. And Currituck Sound is protected by the barrier islands. We'll come through all right.''

She turned to look at him. Tried to smile even, though her lips trembled at the effort. She reached for her jacket, slipped it on. ''Have you got a hat?''

''What for?''

She twisted her shoulder-length hair, pulled a clip from her pocket and held the strands in place at her crown. ''You'll need help.''

The offer pleased him, mostly because he hadn't expected it. He went into the bedroom and came back with a large-brimmed canvas hat that wouldn't do much to keep her dry once the rain started falling heavy. And a pair of galoshes. ''They're a bit big, but those fancy shoes of yours won't care. And thanks, I can use a holder as soon as I get the shutters from the shed.''

He threw on his slicker and opened the door. When he looked back, Vicki was staring out the window again. Her arms were clenched tightly around her waist.

THANK GOODNESS Jamie had enough confidence for both of them. Vicki was almost convinced that the *Bucket o' Luck* was stronger than the winds of a hurricane. At least, she was convinced that Jamie believed it. And there was comfort in that.

When she saw him come around the side of the houseboat with a load of metal shutters in his arms, she went outside. The wind was stronger now. The rain was coming in biting sheets. Vicki was grateful for the shelter of the houseboat walls as she hugged the siding on her way to the porch at the bow.

Jamie lay the shutters on the floor and picked up the one on top. It caught the wind and rattled in his hand, producing a sound like thunder in a B movie. But it looked sturdy enough. Holes in the four corners matched metal pegs in the houseboat walls. Jamie lined up the holes to the pegs, held the panel with one hand while he fished several butterfly nuts from a sack at his feet.

''Are you ready?'' he called to Vicki over the wind.

She crunched the hat onto her head, tied the chin straps and hunched into the collar of her jacket. While she held the panel with both hands, Jamie efficiently twisted each nut onto the pegs until the shutter was secure. Then he picked up the next panel, overlapped it with the first one, and the process began again.

He returned to the shed for a second and third load of shutters, and he and Vicki worked their way around the wooden catwalk to secure all the windows. The rain drove furiously, strafing the steadily sagging canvas of Vicki's hat. Rivulets streamed down her face and neck. Despite having nothing to keep water from his own eyes, Jamie worked with military precision. In less than an hour, he held up the last shutter and took the four remaining nuts from the bag.

"So, Vicki, why now?" he shouted as he twisted the first nut into place.

She kept her palms flat against the metal and wiped the side of her face on her sleeve. "What do you mean?" she yelled back.

"The divorce," he said in such a nonchalant manner they might have been sitting down to dinner, instead of gargling rainwater. "What made you ask for a divorce today?"

He turned the second nut. She wondered how he managed to concentrate on his task, much less carry on a conversation in this wind. "It's time, don't you think?"

"No doubt about that. But I was just wondering. If you let thirteen years go by, there must be a specific reason that brought you to Pintail Point now."

She waited while he finished his task. Then, seeing no reason not to tell him, she shouted above the roar of the elements. "I'm getting engaged!" For no reason she could fathom, she added, "I think."

He nodded. "We're done here. Let's get dry."

They walked around to the door and slogged inside. If it hadn't been for the glow of the TV screen and one lamp, the houseboat would have been black as pitch. No daylight, gray though it was, filtered through the shutters into the interior. She and Jamie were entombed in a cocoon, and Vicki shivered in claustrophobic reaction.

Jamie flicked switches and pulled lamp chains until soft light filled the living room. "Makes a difference having the shutters up," he said. "Boggles my mind each time I realize I'll have to get by without any daylight. You'll get used to it in a few minutes." The corners of his mouth lifted in a grin. "Of course by then, we'll probably lose power."

She rolled up her sleeves and reached for the towel she'd used earlier. "I hope you have supplies in case that happens."

"Lanterns and candles. When you live out here, you know what to expect and how to prepare."

Her shirt was soaked. She plucked the material away from her chest and arms, but it didn't ease an overall clammy feeling. And then suddenly, the dampness didn't matter. What the CNN reporter was saying took precedence over every other emotion.

"Imogene is now verging on category-two status."

Jamie stepped closer to the television and focused on the report.

"Did you hear that?" Vicki asked.

"I did. Let's hear what else the man has to say."

"The storm has slowed, giving Imogene time to

gather strength. Hurricane-force winds extend thirty-five miles from the center.''

A yellow triangle produced by the network's graphics department swept a narrow path along the northernmost North Carolina coast.

The meteorologist continued his grim forecast. ''Imogene's landfall in approximately five hours is predicted to be somewhere in this vicinity. By that time she could be a strong category-two storm.''

Vicki looked at Jamie's profile, expecting to see the placid expression of a man who faced life's obstacles with optimism. What she saw were fine lines extending from narrowed eyes. And jaw muscles clenched with tension. ''Oh, my God, you're worried,'' she said.

He glanced around the living room. ''Not worried so much as grateful we got the shutters up. I think we're going to need them. But at her worst, Imogene will still just be a category two. The houseboat can withstand that. I am concerned about the shed, though.''

Then, as if he realized in that moment that he was soaked to the skin, he added, ''No use standing here like drowned rats. And speaking for myself, hungry, drowned rats at that.''

His confidence was returning. Thank goodness. ''I should change,'' Vicki said.

Jamie took emergency lights from a cupboard and set them on a serving bar that separated the kitchen from the living room. Then he jerked his thumb at her slim briefcase. ''Did you pack a change of clothes in that thing, as well as our divorce papers?''

''Oh, no!'' Everything she needed was in the rental car—her clothes, her purse, her cell phone with the battery running down. This astounding lack of forethought sent her scurrying to the exit. ''I have to go outside.''

He gave her an incredulous look. ''I don't think that's such a clever idea.''

She flung the door open. Rain and wind pelted her face and soaked the last few patches of clothing that weren't already sodden. She fought the wind until she heard the latch click into the frame again.

Jamie chuckled and pointed to a doorway leading off the living room. ''In there. Second dresser drawer on the left. Clean T-shirts. Flannel pants. Nothing fussy, I'm sorry to say.''

''Thank you. I'll manage.''

''Do you like stew?'' he asked before she left the room.

''Love it.''

She heard the sound of a cabinet door opening and closing, followed by a pot hitting the stove burner as she walked into Jamie's bedroom. And his voice again. ''Is he anyone I know?''

She unbuttoned her blouse. ''Who?''

''This fella you think you might be engaged to. Do I know him?''

So he *had* heard her explanation out on the porch. She smiled. ''Considering that you and I have only one acquaintance in common, and I haven't seen

Kenny in years, I rather doubt you know my boyfriend.''

"You're probably right, though stranger coincidences have happened. Take today, for instance. Beasley and I got up this morning, had eggs and bacon, fertilized a few plants outside and planned on spending a quiet afternoon catching blue crabs. And now, here we are, a hurricane coming, and my long-lost wife putting on my skivvies in the next room. If that's not a corker, I don't know what is.''

Vicki couldn't argue. When she left Fort Lauderdale a few hours ago, she certainly hadn't intended to have more than a five-minute conversation with Jamie Malone. Now, two hours later, she was staring at her reflection in his bedroom mirror with a McGilley's Pub T-shirt hugging her chest. What would Graham think?

She gripped the edge of the dresser and spoke to the pale face staring back at her. "Oh, my God, Graham.'' She'd promised to call him. He thought she was in Virginia to look at some eighteenth-century antiques she'd heard about. Not only had she lied about her reason for taking this trip, but now there was a good chance she wouldn't be returning when she'd planned. And once Graham heard about the storm, he'd be terribly worried. She had to let him know she was all right.

Vicki pulled on a pair of soft flannel pants and dashed into the living room. "I have to use your phone.''

Jamie looked up from a steaming pan and motioned to the telephone. "Be my guest.''

She turned away from Jamie's direct gaze and dialed Graham's cell-phone number. He answered on the second ring. ''Graham Townsend.''

''Hi. It's me.''

He blew out an impatient breath. ''Where have you been? I've been calling your cell for hours. I've left three messages.''

''I'm sorry. It's raining really hard here. I left the cell phone in my car and now the battery's probably dead.'' Vicki glanced over her shoulder at Jamie. She figured he was listening, though he pretended otherwise. He smiled at her and set two plates on the counter. And Vicki missed most of what Graham had just said.

''Bad connection, Graham. Would you repeat that?''

''I said—'' he sounded impatient ''—we received confirmation on that container from Amsterdam. The furniture will arrive in time for the opening of your shop.''

''That's wonderful.'' It meant she'd have to rearrange everything to make room for the new arrivals, but it was good news. Graham had convinced her that he and a contact in Holland had found some fabulous antiques. The Dutch dealer was sending them via the fastest shipper.

''You can forget about those few pieces you went to Virginia to buy and come home immediately.''

''I wish I could, but—''

''You'll be the talk of the Boulevard once we get this merchandise into the shop. But there's work to be done, Victoria. You have to be here to receive the shipment.''

''There's a storm brewing, Graham,'' she said. ''Haven't you been watching the news? I can't leave right now.''

''A storm? You mean that little tropical depression?''

''That little depression has grown up.'' Vicki tightened her grip on the receiver. ''It's not like I planned it, Graham. I'll be home well ahead of the shop opening, which is still almost two weeks away.''

''Where exactly are you, Victoria?''

She stole a peek at Jamie again. He wiggled his fingers in a little wave. There was no doubt in her mind that he was listening to everything she said. ''Where am I? Didn't I tell you I was staying at the Ramada in Norfolk?'' She was becoming almost as good at evading as lying.

Graham breathed a heavy sigh. Vicki pictured him swiveling in his executive chair to face the wall of windows in his eighteenth-floor Miami office. The sight of the ocean a few blocks away might calm some people, but she doubted it was having that effect on Graham. ''Yes, I guess you did,'' he said with a deliberate show of patience. ''Just please get back here as soon as you can. You have to sign the bill of lading for customs to release the furniture.''

''I know. I'll be home as soon as the storm lets up.''

There was a pause followed by a calming breath this time. ''Of course you will, sweetheart. I know that. I'm just uptight today. The important thing is, you're not in any danger, are you?''

The *Bucket o' Luck* picked that exact moment to lurch against the dock and rock back and forth several times before finding its equilibrium. Vicki grabbed the edge of an end table to steady herself. ''I told you, I'm in a perfectly safe place. Don't worry.'' She imagined the trees swaying dramatically just outside the window. Even Mother Nature was mocking her lies.

''Okay, then. I'll call you later. I've got this number on my cell-phone call record.''

All at once Vicki hated technology. ''You're going to call me here?''

''Of course. I am worried about you, Victoria.''

''Don't be. I'll be home before you know it.''

The lights in the houseboat flickered once, twice, then a critical third time. Vicki was plunged into the deepest, darkest void she'd ever known. She squealed, reached out, but couldn't even see her hand. A second later, the glow of a fluorescent lantern outlined shapes in the living room. She saw Jamie with matches and candles in his hand, and she breathed normally again.

''Victoria, what's wrong?'' Graham asked. ''You screamed.''

''Nothing. It was a bug, that's all. Ran right across my shoe, but I killed it. I have to go now.'' She ended the connection and stared at Jamie. He'd lit candles and a pleasant scent filled the room, reminding her of Christmas in the stores of Maple Grove, Indiana.

But Vicki could not relax. Now Jamie knew what a liar she was. He'd heard her weave a grid of deceit for the man she planned to marry. She didn't know why that knowledge distressed her. After all, her relationship with Jamie was based on deception.

Jamie carried two plates to the dining table and went back for cutlery and napkins. When she didn't come to the table, he asked, "Are you all right, Vicki? I told you we'd lose power, but we'll be fine. Trust me."

"It's not that," she said. "I guess I'm not as hungry as I thought."

He brought a pitcher of milk from the kitchen and pulled out a chair. "Sit down, girl. No one can resist Jamie Malone's stew. And besides, your almost fiancé won't be calling you." He gestured toward the phone. "That's always the next thing to go."

She sat woodenly. The stew smelled delicious, and now that the power was out, it would probably be the last hot meal she and Jamie would share for hours. She should try to eat. She picked up her fork and scooped a mound of beef and potatoes. The utensil was halfway to her mouth when she realized why she was so distressed that Jamie had heard her lies.

I've just lied to the man I love, she said to herself. *The man I'm going to spend the rest of my life with.* She stared across the table at Jamie, who enjoyed his meal with all the gusto she lacked. *And then there's you,* she thought. *Once the storm is over, I'll never see you again, and everything I've told you is the truth.*

The irony of the revelation struck her with as much force as whatever bulky thing suddenly thumped and banged across the roof of the houseboat.

CHAPTER FOUR

VICKI JERKED and nearly fell out of her chair. Fear tingling in her every nerve, she looked at the ceiling. "What was that?"

Jamie glanced up, then took a swallow of milk. "A loblolly branch, I imagine."

"You mean the trees are flying?"

He gazed at her with a half grin curving his lips. "I said 'branch' Vicki. And I'm only guessing. If it had been a whole tree, I'd know for sure what kind it is because it would be sticking through a wall of the houseboat. I'm assuming it was a loblolly because the sound started here—" he pointed to the ceiling at the bow and slowly moved his finger to the stern "—and ended there. There's a thicket of loblolly trees by the front of the boat. My suspicion is that one of them is now missing a fairly good-size limb."

"It's so frustrating not being able to see," Vicki said. "We don't know what's going on out there."

Jamie cupped a hand around his ear, drawing attention to the eerie sounds beyond the houseboat walls. "Oh, I think we have a pretty good idea. Besides, there's still the door. You can have a look whenever you want."

"No, thanks. I tried that, remember?"

He smiled. "Look, Vicki, if you're going to jump at every little sound for the next few hours, you better tie yourself down. It's only going to get worse."

He was right. She took a deep breath, then dug into the tasty stew again. After a moment she heard another strange noise, a thumping coming from under the table. Forcing herself to remain composed, she looked to Jamie for an explanation.

He gestured down to a nearly hairless tail curling around a table leg. "It's Beasley. He's scratching his ear. I hear that even when there isn't a storm."

"Oh." Vicki leaned over and patted the dog's head. She expected his gray fur to be soft, but instead, each individual hair felt like a brush bristle. He lolled his head to one side and gazed up at her, his marble-size golden eyes holding something almost like adoration. "I wish I could accept this hurricane as calmly as you do," she said to the animal.

A gust of wind rattled a metal panel on the window nearest her. Vicki forced herself not to react by concentrating on Beasley. "What kind of dog is he?"

Jamie swiped at a pool of gravy with a thick corner of bread. "Nobody knows. He wandered up the causeway three years ago. I don't know where he came from or why he decided to stay. But he did. In all that time I've never spoken about his questionable parentage. I can't see making a creature feel bad over something that was none of his doing."

An image of her parents flashed through Vicki's mind. Her drab, defeated mother, whose grease-stained apron symbolized the lack of attention she gave all the details of her existence. Her indolent father, who complained of aches and pains in every part of his body while he sat in a patched recliner watching an ancient television. Nils Sorenson blamed government taxes for his inability to buy a new TV. He never once considered that he might be able to save enough money to buy a nice set if he worked as hard on the farm as he did making excuses.

Jamie was right. People couldn't change their origins. Remembering the way he'd looked thirteen years ago, she figured he'd experienced that frustrating fact of life almost as much as she had. But maybe Jamie had been lucky enough to have parents who'd encouraged him emotionally if not financially.

Jamie stood and picked up his plate. "Yep, Beasley's story is pretty much the way life is here on Pintail Point," he said.

"Why is that?"

He stacked her empty plate on top of his. "On any given day, I never know what or who is going to wander down the causeway. Or how long they're going to stay."

Vicki knew exactly how long she was staying on Pintail. Well, maybe not the precise hour she would leave, but she knew that the minute the wind stopped howling and the water receded from the causeway, she would get into her rented car, the divorce papers signed and tucked safely into her briefcase, and head back to Norfolk, where she'd catch the next plane to Fort Lauderdale. With a little luck that would happen before Graham became more impatient with her absence.

Still, if she had to endure a hurricane, she could do far worse than to be with Jamie Malone. He certainly had a calming effect in the midst of a meteorological nightmare.

They finished the dishes quickly, using hot water sparingly so there would be enough left for a couple of showers. When the supper utensils were put away, Jamie went to the living room and picked up the telephone. He gave Vicki an I-told-you-so look. ''Future husband number two won't be able to reach you tonight.''

What should have been good news was suddenly alarming. If Graham couldn't reach her here, he would probably call information for the number of the Ramada Hotel. The phones might not be out in Norfolk, and he'd discover that she wasn't at the hotel and in fact, hadn't even registered. She'd have to come up with a logical explanation for her supposed change in plans… Well, she thought, she *could* avoid the problem by contacting Graham before he tried to contact her. A good offense was always the best defense.

''Do you have a cell phone?'' she asked Jamie.

''Nope. I have a car phone in the truck, but again, that involves going outside.''

''You must have a computer. I could send an e-mail.''

''I have a laptop that I hook up to—'' he pointed to the telephone ''—that line.''

Vicki frowned. ''Great.''

"Sorry, Vicki, but until Imogene's done with us, we're not much better off than pioneers."

Okay, there wouldn't be a phone call to Graham tonight, and Vicki resigned herself to inventing a good alibi for her absence at the hotel. While she struggled to formulate a plan, Jamie worked the dials of a battery-operated radio he'd brought to the coffee table, along with a half-dozen of the scented candles. Vicki sat on the opposite end of the sofa from Jamie and said, "I'm impressed. You've reached the outside world."

He nodded. "Yep. It's an Elizabeth City station, about twenty miles from here."

As they listened to the broadcast, Jamie's expression grew serious. "You're interpreting all this as bad news, too," she said.

"Predictable, anyway. It could get rough now. The storm's just two hours from landfall."

The wind howled outside. Not a steady groaning, but a crescendo of wails and moans that made Vicki think of prowling wolves. "I think it already has gotten rough."

He managed a tight smile before scanning the four corners of the room with alert eyes. "Like I said, we'll be all right. I wish I'd done more to protect the shed, though."

It was the second time he'd mentioned the building a few yards from the houseboat. "What's in there that you're so worried about?"

He shrugged off the question with an ambiguous

answer. "Just personal items, supplies, tools, things I use in my work."

Remembering the detective saying that Jamie was an artist, Vicki asked what he did for a living.

"I make things," he said.

"What things?"

"Wooden objects, mostly. When you were in the Bayberry Cove Kettle, did you see any of those little triangles with all the holes and pegs in them?"

"Do you mean the leapfrog puzzles on the counter?"

"Yeah. I make those," Jamie said. "You can find them all over town. The local businesses put their names on the triangles. I guess they use it for promotions. There are some in the Kettle, the supermarket, even in pew boxes next to hymnals at the Methodist Church—so I'm told."

Vicki smiled to herself. Jamie made wooden puzzles. It seemed a logical calling for a man who was once a carpenter. But an artist? She hardly saw how cutting triangles and drilling holes qualified as art. But there was an appealing honesty about the pride he expressed in his contribution to Bayberry Cove society.

Vicki studied his face in the forgiving glow of the half-dozen candles. This Jamie was a more polished, confident version of the man he'd been thirteen years ago. Maybe he was no more successful than when his fingernails were stained, but the desperation in his eyes was gone. This Jamie was a man content with his life.

And though still a stranger, he was easy to be with. Comfortable. Of course Vicki could never make a life with a man like Jamie. His apparent lack of ambition was hard for her to understand. She'd come too far and worked too hard to escape her humble beginnings to settle for anything less than financial security.

When she met Graham Townsend, part of her attraction to him was his lifestyle, just the sort she longed for—stable, privileged. He, unlike her, had never known anything else. But in a way she envied Jamie Malone. She'd spent her life setting ever more challenging goals. She didn't know for sure, but she bet Jamie spent his life just living, taking each day as it came.

"I can practically see the spokes turning from over here," he said.

Vicki blinked, scattering her thoughts to the corners of her mind. "What do you mean?"

He pointed to her head and made a circle with his finger. "I can see the wheels going round in your brain. What are you thinking about?"

You. I decided your face is easy to look at.

"I was just watching the candle flames," she lied. "I'm wondering what that scent is."

He crossed one leg over the other. "You like the smell?"

She nodded.

"It's bayberry. The bushes grow wild all over the coast. In fact, it's almost time to harvest the berries."

She gave him a skeptical look. "Are you telling me that you made these candles yourself?"

He laughed. "Me? No. But thirty per cent of the working population of Bayberry Cove made them, and thousands more like them. Nearly one third of the labor force in town works at the Bayberry Cove Candle Company. Bayberry candles are made from bayberries—pretty much like they were in Colonial days, with the help of a little modern technology.''

She admired the forest-green color of the candles and the soft flicker of the flames. ''And I'll bet you know exactly how it's done, don't you.''

For the next ten minutes Vicki learned how bayberries used to be gathered in bushel baskets and how it took one full bushel to boil the berries down to produce enough wax to make one taper. When Jamie explained the candle-making process in his lilting brogue, Vicki had the impression that it was as much magic as Colonial know-how that went into each one. Maybe thirty percent of the population of Bayberry Cove made candles, but Vicki could picture a half-dozen leprechauns having a hand in the process, as well.

And she knew for sure that as the wind blustered outside the *Bucket o' Luck,* sending debris crashing into the walls, she was grateful for the woodsy-smelling candlelight on Jamie's table, no matter how it was produced. And grateful to Jamie when he opened a bottle of wine and poured her a glass. ''Go ahead, Vicki. It'll do you good.''

She took a comforting swallow and leaned her head back against the sofa. For a few minutes she listened to the static-edged voice of a radio weatherman answering questions from callers about the hurricane. Everything he advised, she and Jamie had already done. Perhaps that knowledge, or perhaps the effect of the wine, gave her more confidence. Or maybe it was a sudden intense curiosity that made her ask the questions to which she'd never had definitive answers.

"So tell me, Jamie," she said, "what were you running from that day in Orlando? Why were you desperate enough to marry a stranger? And where did you get…?" She stopped, knowing she was crossing a line that protected Jamie's privacy.

He smiled, rubbed his finger and thumb down his jaw. "And where did a fella like me get five thousand dollars?" he finished for her.

"I didn't mean…"

"Of course you did, Vicki, and it's a fair question, considering the man I was when you married me. That's why I'm going to answer it."

JAMIE REFILLED Vicki's glass. He was certain the walls of the houseboat would withstand the winds raging outside, but he'd run out of ways to convince Vicki of that. The wine was accomplishing what his logic and encouragement had not.

A kind of guarded peace had settled over her features. Her lips were soft and full, no longer defined at the corners by the crescent-shaped lines of worry. Framed by loose waves of shoulder-length hair, her cheeks had taken on a rosy blush. Her eyes, which minutes before had sparked with the icy blue of a winter sky, were now the delicate hue of Wedgwood. One blunt slam of a sea-pine branch against a shutter could fragment that calm, but right now—when Vicki wasn't afraid for her life or trying to decide if her Irish husband could be trusted—she was incredibly lovely.

And perhaps even ready to accept his reasons for marrying her. "You have to understand what Belfast was like in 1988," he began. "And then you have to know what it meant to be a Malone."

"I have a friend in Fort Lauderdale who believes you were a criminal when you came to this country," she said. "A wanted man." She stared at the contents of her glass before looking directly at him. "But I believed Kenny Corcoran when he said it wasn't so."

"I'm sorry to tell you, Vicki, but Kenny half lied back then. I wasn't a criminal. But I *was* a wanted man. It was hard to be a Malone and not be wanted by one official or another."

He glanced briefly at a photograph on the desk across the room. Three cocky young men looked back at him. Their eyes were full of hope. Their smiles were full of the devil. And their arms were wrapped around each other as if the bombs that would later tear the family apart had no chance of separating them that day. The Malone brothers. Frank Junior, Jamie and Cormac. Invincible. Proud. And two of them brimming with all the spit and fire of the furnaces of the Belfast foundry where they worked.

He returned his attention to Vicki. "Northern Ireland was a quagmire of dissent and despair in those days. Protestants hated the Catholics. Loyalists hated the followers of the Republic. It's better now since the peace accord, but back when the Malone brothers were finding their way, the young men of Belfast carried their pride and their anger in their fists.''

''I remember—the pictures on TV were very graphic,'' Vicki said. ''There were demonstrations and blockades. Children couldn't go to school.''

He nodded. ''A sad time for Ireland. And there were bombings and deaths and more heartache than a mother could measure. And through the middle of it all wound the crooked pathway chosen by Frank Junior and Cormac, my brothers. Of all the skills my poor mother imagined her boys acquiring, bomb-making wasn't even on the list.''

''What happened to your brothers?'' Vicki asked.

''They applied their talents to the destruction of Catholic churches and schools. And any number of cars and store windows, which they blew up as a sort of Malone calling card. Luckily only property was damaged, but it was enough for the Outlaw Malones to make a name for themselves.''

Vicki shook her head. ''And you, as well, I imagine. You shared their name.''

Jamie pinched the bridge of his nose. After all this time, the memory was still as painful. ''There were some problems along that line. I was questioned often by the authorities, who were trying to make an example of the Malones. But they couldn't pin anything on me, and Frank and Cormac could never be found. Most times I couldn't find them myself, the underground network was that good. Two men could bomb a market, slip down an alley and not be seen for weeks.''

Vicki shook her head, evidence that she bore some of his sadness. "So what eventually happened? Why did you leave Ireland?"

"Because Frank and Cormac came out of their dens at precisely the wrong time. They were caught in a street brawl, of all things, for once their pockets empty of explosives, though fire was in their hearts. My mother heard about the fight and knew the police were going to arrest everyone involved. She sent me to warn my brothers. The rest is a miserable piece of history. We were three Malone men with blood on our clothes and fight in our eyes. And though I hadn't thrown a punch, to the police, we were each one as guilty as the other.

"Frank hollered at me to run even as they put the cuffs around his wrists. I did. Hard and fast. The last I remember about that night was Cormac on the street, his face in the concrete, and the black boot of a policeman in the small of his back. That same night I got to know the secret network myself. Men proclaiming themselves friends of my brothers came to the door, talked to my mother and took me from the house. The next morning I was on a fishing boat to the Isle of Man where I caught a plane to the French coast. Within hours I was in the United States. And Frank and Cormac were awaiting trial."

Vicki looked at Jamie with an unexpected sympathy he found comforting. "Where are they now?"

"Still in prison, where they will remain for a good while yet." A long, low blast, like the sound a train whistle makes, snapped Jamie's attention to the worsening storm. He saw Vicki's flinch and gave her a smile of encouragement. It was the wind playing games outside the houseboat, he told her, but it was as mournful a sound as he'd ever heard.

He pictured his brothers in jail, tried to imagine how they'd changed. Frank Junior might have gray in his hair, and Cormac's would have lost its red-gold luster from years of sun deprivation. Their skin would be pasty and soft, their muscles slack, their faces lined with creases that came from knowing too few contented moments.

Fifteen years ago, Jamie accepted that he would never understand his brothers. They had been troublesome, delinquent boys who became embittered, dangerous men. To this day, Jamie didn't know what had first made them so angry. Perhaps their rage was directed at their abusive father, and when Frank Senior died, that fiery passion had nowhere to go—until the Catholics provided a target and a secret brotherhood provided the means to attack it.

But Jamie had escaped the curse of his brothers' inner turmoil, and as soon as he was able, he'd brought his mother out of her private hell and to the United States. For that he owed a young girl from Indiana whose motive had been money, but who'd kept her word to a desperate immigrant.

He realized with some embarrassment that Vicki was staring at him with a look of expectancy. Of course. He hadn't explained about the money. ''And as for the five thousand dollars,'' he said, ''that secret network I told you about extended even to America.

Through connections with my countrymen, I managed to get a respectable job that provided a room in a Rhode Island boardinghouse and enough soda bread and sausage to survive. I even had some left over for a Guinness or two on a Friday night. And when threatened with deportation, my brethren in Florida furnished the means for me to marry an American girl." He chuckled. "A girl who was scared out of her wits at the sight of me on her wedding day."

She sat up straight and set her glass on the table. "I wasn't afraid of you."

He threw back his head and laughed. "Now, Vicki, I've just poured out my soul to you on this most wicked of nights, and you dare to tell such a lie?"

She smiled. "You were different from any man I'd ever seen before, that's all," she said. "Standing next to Kenny that day, you seemed to fill the courthouse steps with your wild hair and energy. You made me nervous."

He sat back and grinned. "Ah, well, that's not so bad, then. A girl's supposed to be nervous on her wedding day."

"And how did you end up here?"

"Here in North Carolina? Or here on the *Bucket o' Luck?*"

"Both, I guess."

"I stayed in Orlando awhile, until I realized I wasn't cut out for sharing my space with an animated mouse and the million people a day who worshiped him. I'd heard about this coast and made my way here with

Ma, who'd recently come from Ireland. As for the *Bucket,* she was a gift a few years later.''

''A gift? Someone gave you this boat?''

''The mayor of Bayberry Cove himself. The old boy won her in a poker game and figured giving her to me was less trouble than having her scuttled.''

As if protesting the notion of being turned into wreckage, the houseboat lunged against its moorings in a sudden, violent gust of wind. The boat hit the dock with a force great enough to remind her occupants of the fury outside, then finally settled into a more controlled back-and-forth movement. ''I guess she didn't like that comment,'' Jamie teased.

Vicki gripped the edge of the sofa cushion. Her knuckles were nearly as white as her face. She raised her eyes to the ceiling, as if awaiting the next furious rush of wind. It came soon. The houseboat groaned, tilted and steadied. The wind answered loudly, its superior power threatening to drown out the pitiful rumblings of the beleaguered vessel.

Vicki drew her breath in sharply and bit her bottom lip. ''What do you say now, Jamie? Are we going to be blown to bits?''

''I hope not. But we're in the brunt of it. I think that while we were talking, or I was talking and you were listening, the eye of the storm passed over us. The back edge of a hurricane is always the worst.''

A strong blast of wind seemed to attack the boat at the hull. The *Bucket o' Luck* tugged viciously at its sturdy ropes and for a moment seemed about to give in. Outside the dock creaked but held fast. And Vicki slid closer to Jamie and breathed a tremulous sigh.

The next gust slid over the top of the boat, sending debris skidding across the roof and crashing into the metal shutters. It was a cacophony of wails and rends and shrieks in the night. But the single most terrifying noise came from several yards away. The sound of ripping metal sent Jamie scurrying to the door. The shed! Panic squeezed the air from his lungs. His livelihood, his art, his very existence was threatened. He grabbed a rain slicker from a hook by the door.

Vicki ran up behind him. ''Where are you going?''

He picked up a lantern. ''I've got to go outside. I think the roof's coming off the shed.''

Vicki's eyes went wide with shock. ''What? Are you crazy? You can't go out there.''

He thrust his arms through the sleeves of the slicker. ''I'll be fine. I just need to cover some materials.''

And then something happened that convinced him he wasn't the crazy one at all. Vicki reached for her own jacket, still soaked from when they put up the shutters. ''I'm going with you,'' she declared.

He froze with his hand on the doorknob. ''Oh, no, you're not!''

''I am so. If you can go out there, so can I. Two people can work twice as fast as one.''

He grabbed her arms above the elbows. ''Don't be stupid. This isn't your problem. You've no care about what's in that shed.''

She stared back at him, blue fire crackling in her eyes. ''Maybe not, but I can be just as stupid as you.''

She wriggled in his grip. "If you're going, I'm going, and that's that."

"You're not! I can't be worrying about you."

"But it's all right if I worry about *you*?"

That single moment reinforced Jamie's belief that he'd never be proper husband material. He'd never understand why a woman, even a modern one, would dispute the infallible logic of a sane man. He'd never understand women at all, and when they acted like this one, he didn't intend to try. Maybe he was old-fashioned. Chauvinistic. Controlling. He only knew that Vicki was his wife—even if only in name—and he was honor-bound to protect her if she was too stubborn to do it herself.

He scooped her up in his arms and carried her across the room. When he reached the sofa, he dumped her onto it and said, "You stay right there and behave yourself."

Her jaw dropped, and her eyes were wild, glittering. "How dare you speak to me like that!"

He glared down at her. "You don't like it? Well, let me warn you, woman, that's sweet-talking compared to what I'm capable of."

He stomped to the door but turned one more time to thrust a finger at her. "Stay put. I mean it." He stepped outside into a hundred-mile-an-hour cold shower. It was just what he needed. Vicki's body squirming against his had resulted in a totally unexpected and troublesome reaction for a man who was supposed to be signing divorce papers. He'd discovered that fighting with Vicki was more stimulating than making love to other women. Images of what it would be like to make love with her filled his head as he bent into the wind and plowed forward.

CHAPTER FIVE

VICKI BOUNDED UP from the sofa as soon as the door slammed behind him. Beasley crawled out from under the dining table and raised his pointed head to emit a huge yawn and gaze accusingly at her.

Vicki jabbed a trembling finger toward the door. "Don't blame me for waking you up, dog. Did you see what that man did? Did you hear how he spoke to me? I was only offering to help, for heaven's sake!"

Beasley snapped his jaw closed with a sound like the squeak of an old screen door. He moved a little closer to Vicki and tilted his head as if trying to understand what she said.

She crouched down to see under the coffee table but kept talking to the dog. "I'm not staying in this thirty-year-old tub with who knows what battering us from all sides. I'd rather take my chances with your irrational, ungrateful master."

She went into the kitchen and looked on the floor. "Where are those darned galoshes?" Then she remembered seeing Jamie pull the boots over his socks right after he grabbed the slicker. She looked down at her Italian leather loafers by the door and regretfully slid her feet into them. They'd cost a fortune, but that couldn't be helped now. In a few minutes they'd be wrecked.

She retrieved her coat and slipped it on. Jamie's T-shirt did little to alleviate the clammy feel of the jacket's wet silk lining.

''Don't look at me like that,'' Vicki said to the dog. ''I can't take you with me into that storm.'' She shivered as another object banged against the shutter.

She raced into the bathroom, picked up the soggy canvas hat from the floor and pulled it down over her hair. When she came back out, Beasley was standing by the door. ''What the devil is in that shed anyway?'' she asked, as she buttoned her jacket. ''It must be something pretty valuable for Jamie to risk his life to save it—something besides material to make games.''

She tried to imagine what it might be. A vintage automobile? Family heirlooms? Expensive machinery of some sort? Whatever it was, it had better be worth the sacrifice she was about to make.

Vicki wrapped her hand around the doorknob and cringed when a wretched blast of wind made the hardware tremble. She gave Beasley a last parting look. ''Wish us luck. Here's hoping we save whatever precious possessions just turned a man I'd believed to be fairly normal into a raving lunatic. And to think I was actually beginning to like Jamie Malone.''

She shouldered the door open and stepped outside. A frothy wave crashed over the catwalk of the houseboat and swamped her shoes. She tucked her head down and forged across the plank connecting the boat to the shore. Water squished through her toes with every step. "That didn't take long," she said, acknowledging the demise of her designer loafers.

She trudged forward, every step in the fierce wind a battle to gain a few inches. On a decent day, it would probably take only seconds to walk from the houseboat to the shed. But in the storm, Vicki estimated it took her well over a minute to negotiate her way around great puddles and fallen limbs to reach the building. She followed the weak glow of Jamie's lantern coming through windows streaked with rainwater. She squinted into the wind to protect her eyes from flying debris and kept her hand over her nose to avoid inhaling a foreign object.

Finally she reached the door, yanked it open and stepped over the threshold. It was drier inside, but only slightly. A gaping hole in a corner of the roof let in streams of water that puddled on the cement floor. Jamie, standing on a ladder, had looped a rope around the metal and was struggling to pull the roof back into place.

When she closed the door, he turned sharply and stared down at her. "Oh, great. Don't you remember what I said to you five minutes ago?"

"I remember," she answered. "You said, 'I'll go on out to the shed and you can meet me there as soon as you're able.'"

He tugged on the rope. The roof groaned and straightened a few inches. "Like hell!" He descended the ladder. Vicki thought he was coming after her, but instead, he continued pulling on the rope until the roof nearly covered the corner again. "Get back to the houseboat!" he shouted at her as he worked.

"I can't," she shouted back. "It's raining out there."

He pierced her with a threatening glare.

She took off the hat and wrung about a gallon of water onto the floor. "So I figure it's like this," she said. "We can argue about this for the rest of the night or you can tell me what I should do to help."

He opened his mouth as if he was about to debate with her, but apparently thought better of it and let a scowl convey his frustration. Then he secured the rope to a piece of machinery and gestured to the other end of the shed to a spool of plastic. "Start rolling that out," he said. "And get the scissors from the peg board."

In a moment he joined her and cut a length of sheeting. He rolled out another few feet and repeated the process. "We need to cover the valuables in here," he instructed. "I've only temporarily fixed the roof. It could easily blow off again."

Now was her chance to see what he meant by "valuables." Vicki looked around. Several large red-and-black metal toolboxes lined the walls. There were some electric tools, fairly standard for a woodworker, she assumed. She recognized a bench saw and a grinder. These things appeared to be indestructible. Surely he didn't intend to waste time covering them. Nor would he be concerned with a couple of heavy fiberglass tables that held cans of paint and varnish.

There was no antique auto. No ancient Irish trunk

that might contain a pot of gold or Celtic treasure. No anything. All that was left in Jamie's mysterious shed were piles of lumber of assorted shapes and lengths. Some of the bottom pieces were already lying in water, and all of them would be soaked if the roof blew off. Vicki still couldn't imagine why Jamie had rushed out in the middle of a hurricane to save something that faced the natural elements every day.

Yet when he carried a plastic sheet to a pile of cut lumber and tucked a corner under the stack, she knew that was exactly why he'd come. He gave her an expectant look, waiting for her to start tucking at the other end of the pile.

"This is what you're risking your life for?" she yelled over a wall-rattling gust of wind. "You act like a caveman with me and then charge out into a dangerous storm to cover some wood?"

He worked feverishly, stretching the plastic across the top of the pile. "Hey, I told you that you wouldn't care about what was in here."

"Well, I didn't know I wouldn't care this much!"

He stopped, dropped to his knees and stared up at her. "You're the one who disobeyed orders and came out here. Now, are you going to stand there maligning some of the most valuable timber on the East Coast, or are you going to help?"

Her breath rushed out of her lungs in a frustrated huff as she reached for the plastic and began securing it around the pile. When the next furious howl of wind swept over the shed and even ballooned the fragile roof for a terrifying few seconds, she muttered, ''I don't believe I'm doing this.''

Jamie raced for the plastic, cut another piece and dragged it to a stack of blocks. ''Hurry up. We've got to cover this black cherry and red cedar. Most of it has already been kiln-dried. If the roof goes, it'll be ruined.''

Vicki speculated that even if the wood became totally drenched, the only true catastrophe would be trying to light the wet logs in a fireplace. But she refrained from giving her opinion to the man who was intent on saving each piece. She worked as fast as he did, trying not to flinch at every roar of the elements held at bay by a thin sheet of metal.

But while she worked, she came to one irrefutable conclusion. If Jamie Malone was willing to die to save a storehouse of lumber, then he was a man who cared obsessively about triangle puzzles—and truly was a little bit crazy.

IT HAD TAKEN every ounce of willpower Jamie possessed not to climb down from the ladder and drag Vicki back to the houseboat. She had completely ignored his instructions to stay put. Did she think he'd issued those orders as a joke? Or to start a row with her? He'd been through weather like this in the past and he knew what he was talking about. Obviously he hadn't known whom he was talking *to*.

In truth, his anger had begun to dissipate before she'd started to help. She'd looked so pathetic standing there in her dripping clothes, her hat sagging like a beached water lily. Despite all that, she'd also looked determined. A smart man recognized when a woman was set on getting her way, and Jamie knew better than to try to sidetrack her from her mission.

Vicki had proved to be a good worker, even though she'd made it clear that she didn't appreciate their reason for being in a flimsy shed with a storm raging outside. She obviously didn't know much about wood and didn't believe there was a sliver of it valuable enough to justify what they were doing.

But Jamie knew it would be costly and time-consuming to replace the wood he'd acquired to produce the nautical carvings he'd promised the Boston gallery. A Celebration of Our Atlantic Heritage—that was the name of the four-month exhibit scheduled by the city for the next tourist season, and the planners were counting on museum-quality works by J. D. Malone to complete the testimonial to America's early clipper ships and seamen.

He put what remained of the roll of plastic in a corner and walked to the door. He arched his back and limped slightly when his knee joints complained about exposure to the punishing surface of the shed floor.

"How does it look out there?" Vicki asked, coming up behind him. "Can we make a run for it?"

He flexed his legs and looked over his shoulder at her. "I couldn't make a run for it if the devil himself were chasing me straight to hell."

A powerful blast blew around the door he'd opened, shoving them back a few steps. "We can't stay here," she pointed out, "and we've done all we can for your wood, haven't we?"

He scanned the interior of the shed. In the eerie amber glow from the lantern, the plastic sheets covering the wood looked like ghostly specters rippling in the strong gusts. But she was right. They had done all they could. Water still streamed down the wall from the hastily repaired rent in the roof. The structure might come loose again. But his precious lumber would probably survive the fury.

"I expect we have," he said. He picked up the lantern and reached for her hand. "Hold on to me." They stepped outside and he secured the door. With the lantern swinging in one hand and Vicki's small palm nestled in his other, Jamie lowered his head and started for the houseboat. "If we go down, we go down together," he shouted.

But it didn't happen that way.

A few yards from the shed, Vicki stepped in a storm-eroded section of the point. She yelped like a wounded puppy and fell, landing on her knees in several inches of water.

Jamie let go of her hand and grabbed her elbow. The lantern swung wildly, its light illuminating her face for seconds before arcing into the darkness. But it was enough for him to see the fear and pain in her eyes.

"Are you all right?" he asked. "Can you get up?"

She grabbed his wrist and tried to pull herself up, but her wet palm and his equally damp wrist were too slippery. "I think I twisted my ankle," she cried.

Jamie looped the handle of the lantern over his elbow and grasped her around the waist. In one fluid motion he swept her up and tucked her into his side. She bent her knee, holding her injured leg behind her. But her good leg barely touched the ground as Jamie bore her weight the rest of the way to the houseboat. When he got her inside, she collapsed on the kitchen floor and hissed a painful breath.

He knelt beside her and took off her shoe. Even that simple movement made her cringe with pain.

"This is all your fault, you know," she said through short gasps of air.

"Is it now." He began rolling up her pants leg. "And why might that be?"

She tried to smile. "You didn't make it perfectly clear that I should stay in the houseboat."

"Next time I'll make my opinions known." When he felt a slickness on his fingers, he moved the lantern closer and examined his hand. Looking directly into her frightened eyes, he said, "You can stay calm for me, can't you, Vicki?"

"Stay calm? I haven't had a calm moment since I came here."

"Well, I need you to have one now, darlin', 'cause this leg is bleeding a good bit."

VICKI STRETCHED her leg out on the floor and watched a red stain seep down her calf. "Oh, my God, what did I do?"

Jamie brought paper towels and began dabbing at

the wound. "I'd say you cut your leg when you fell into that hole."

"This is just wonderful," she moaned, leaning her head back against the wall of the houseboat. "This can't be happening. I have my store opening in a little more than a week."

Jamie lifted a towel from her leg and looked at the cut.

"How bad is it?" she asked.

"I don't think it's too bad."

Vicki wasn't so sure. Jamie reached for another towel as more blood oozed from the wound. "Do I need stitches?"

"You shouldn't," he said. "Besides, there's no way we can get you to a doctor with the causeway washed out."

She stared at the dark ceiling, the shuttered windows, anywhere but the gash on her leg. "I'll probably have a scar."

"No, I don't think so. Cuts this close to the shinbone always bleed a lot and look worse than they are."

"I hope you've got a bandage."

He studied the cut while holding the back of her calf with one hand. "Give me some credit, Vicki. I work with power tools. Next to electricity, a first-aid kit is my most important accessory."

"That's a pleasant thought."

He slipped his hands under her arms and lifted. "Let's get you over to the sofa so we can elevate your leg on a pillow."

She stood awkwardly, leaned on Jamie, and hopped

on one foot. The throbbing in her ankle convinced her that trying to put her weight on it would be a mistake. Almost as miserable as the condition of her leg was the cold, damp feel of the clothes she'd borrowed from Jamie earlier. Every inch of jersey and flannel was damp and stuck to her flesh like a second skin. "Can I get out of these wet things before you play doctor?" she asked.

He wiggled his eyebrows at her. "Play doctor? Now that truly *is* a pleasant thought."

She felt better. Obviously he didn't think her condition was too critical. He wouldn't be making jokes if he did. "Don't even think about it," she said.

He helped her to the bedroom. "Too late. My mind's already agog with the fantasy." He took a white metal box from his closet shelf. "You know where my clothes are," he said, grabbing a clean pair of jeans and a shirt for himself. "I'll see you in the living room. If you need help, call."

After he left, Vicki stripped off the wet clothes and tossed them onto the bathroom floor. Then she chose a pair of boxer shorts, which would provide easy access to her wound. She smiled at the pink-and-black Good & Plenty boxes on the material. She took the next T-shirt from a stack in the drawer—a souvenir from a U-2 concert, shed her soaked bra and slipped the shirt over her head.

She caught a glimpse of herself in the mirror as she hobbled to the door. What a sight she was. Her makeup was a complete washout, and her hair resembled thin wires sticking out in all directions. Overall, she looked as if she'd been struck by lightning in the middle of a roller-coaster ride. Oddly, though, she didn't appear tired. Her eyes practically sparkled with energy. Her nerves felt alive, her skin tingled. Stark fear did that to a person, she reasoned. Once the adrenaline wore off, Vicki figured she'd crash like a paper airplane.

She opened the bedroom door a crack. ''Are you decent?'' she called out.

''Depends who you ask,'' Jamie answered. ''But I am dressed.''

She hopped into the living room and made it to the sofa. Jamie waited for her to sit down, then settled her foot on a pillow on the coffee table. The wound had started to bleed again. Not as heavily as before, but enough to send a quiver to the pit of her stomach. The cut was at least two inches long, more than could be hidden by a simple Band-Aid. And more than could be hidden from the discriminating eye of her fiancé.

Graham! The quiver in Vicki's abdomen increased to a drumbeat. How was she going to explain the cut to Graham? And what if her ankle was broken? It probably wasn't, since it only hurt when she moved it, but she might need crutches to help her off the airplane when she returned to Fort Lauderdale.

She squeezed her eyes shut to block the image of Graham's face when he saw her. The questions he would ask! One simple lie about traveling to Virginia to look at antique furniture was fast becoming a life-altering whopper, and Vicki was being sucked into her self-made net of deceit as if she'd landed in quicksand.

She'd made this trip to Pintail Point to eliminate the one great mistake from her past and save her relationship with Graham. Now it looked as though a series of new and almost equally disastrous mistakes could put her in grave danger of ruining it.

A high-pitched whistle drew Vicki's attention away from her problems momentarily. She spotted steam coming from Jamie's kitchen, and her heart rejoiced at what appeared to be a miracle—not one that would solve all her problems, but at least one that would help her calm down enough to think about them rationally. "Is that a kettle?" she asked. "How are you boiling water?"

"Sterno," he said. "Canned heat. I never get caught in a hurricane without it." He lifted a kettle in the air. "Can I interest you in coffee? Tea?"

"Tea would be wonderful."

He brought two steaming mugs to the coffee table. Vicki grabbed hers and cradled the warm pottery between her hands. Jamie began ministering to her leg by slowly rotating her ankle.

"Ouch!"

He rested his hand on top of her foot. "Sorry, but I wanted to determine if it's broken." He looked up at her. "I don't think it is. But it is swelling and turning blue, so it's probably badly sprained."

"No surprise there."

"You'll have to stay off it."

He went into the kitchen and returned with a pot of water, a clean rag and a plastic bottle of antiseptic soap. After he'd cleaned her cut, he applied antibiotic ointment. Next he cut a two-foot length of gauze and wrapped it around the affected area. ''The bandage will be pretty tight,'' he said as he tore off a section of adhesive tape. ''The closer I can bind the cut, the less risk you'll have of getting a scar.''

"I appreciate that. So will Graham. He's so conscious of blemishes that he sees a plastic surgeon every time he gets a splinter.''

Vicki might have chuckled at her joke except Jamie made the last revolution of adhesive tape around her leg with enough force to stop blood circulation. ''Whoa!'' she cried. ''That's way too tight.''

He loosened it. ''Just trying to do a good job for Graham,'' he said. ''Wouldn't want him to have to endure the sight of your imperfection.''

If there was one skill Louise had taught Vicki, it was the ability to recognize sarcasm when she heard it. She gave Jamie a threatening look. ''That was an unkind thing to say.''

''Really? I thought it was damned sensitive.'' He busied himself with putting the supplies back into the kit and closing the lid with a snap. ''By the way, assuming you're going to see this fella you *think* you might be getting engaged to before you're ready to run a marathon, how do you plan to explain these injuries?''

Vicki regretted having made that addendum to her announcement. She knew in her heart that Graham was going to propose. ''I'll tell him I fell off a bar while I was dancing drunk.''

Jamie smirked. ''Ah, just as I thought. He doesn't know, does he?''

''Doesn't know what?''

''That I exist? That you came here to get a divorce?''

Silence stretched between them as Vicki considered her answer. Finally she decided that Jamie was not going to make her feel guilty for what she'd done thirteen years ago or for keeping it a secret. Maybe *he* didn't mind telling everyone he knew that he had a wife somewhere, but she hadn't seen any reason to broadcast that little detail about her own life.

''No, I never told him,'' she stated matter-of-factly.

''Why not? Ashamed of me? Or are you ashamed of yourself.''

''Of course not. Until today, I didn't know you well enough to be ashamed of you.''

''Then why not admit it? Especially to the guy you're going to stay married to for the next however many years.''

''He doesn't need to know. It's not important. Besides, if I'm ashamed of anything, it's the act itself. We were dishonest. You should be ashamed of that, too.''

''Why? I'm a contributing member of American society. I've never taken a handout or been on welfare. I pay taxes. As I see it, this country has only benefited by giving me my green card.''

Contributing member of society. Of course, you supply half the businesses in Bayberry Cove with triangle puzzles. How would they get along without you? Vicki looked away from him, grateful that she hadn't voiced her thoughts aloud. They were no less sarcastic than Jamie's words had been moments before.

Jamie crossed his arms over his chest and stared at her. "Look, I just think you owe someone you're going to marry complete honesty. Without that, how can you expect the marriage to last? The past is the past. Any guy who cares enough about you to want to spend the rest of his life with you will understand your motives if you explain them. The point is, he deserves to know the truth, especially about a previous husband."

He was adding fuel to her indignation with every word. How dare Jamie Malone presume to advise her on marriage? Despite her injury, Vicki stood up, grabbed the arm of the sofa for balance and faced him as squarely as her infirmity would allow. "You have no right to criticize me," she said. "Or to pretend to defend Graham. You've never even met him. You don't know how he would react to hearing news like this."

"Then tell me. How would he react?"

Vicki blew out a pent-up breath. "That's none of your business." Of course she knew exactly how Graham—and the rest of the Townsends—would react if he ever discovered her secret. Her future in-laws' pedigreed noses would be so high in the air they would need oxygen to get a breath. "Besides, all kidding aside, it's really your fault that I have to lie to him about how I got hurt."

His hand slapped his chest in a gesture of innocence. "How did you come up with *that* theory?"

"This all happened because I went out to the shed thinking I was going to help you protect some never-to-be-replaced heirloom or artifact."

"I never said that."

"No, but you were risking your life, and I naturally assumed you had a pretty good reason for doing so."

"I did. I was saving my wood."

"Oh, right. The wood. Because of those scraps of lumber, I can't walk and I have a huge gouge in my leg."

"I told you not to go to the shed. Or have you forgotten your little act of mutiny?"

"I thought I was helping! You have a hell of a way of showing your gratitude."

His hand fisted so that just his index finger punched at his chest. "That's right. I do. I'm showing it now by telling you that you owe it to this guy you fancy yourself in love with to admit that you are married. You owe it to your future together. This isn't a minor detail you should hide from your soul mate."

She wanted to erase the arrogance from his face. Just the way he'd used the ridiculous term "soul mate" and reduced her entire relationship with Graham to questionable status.

"You're trying to get rid of your first husband to make things right for your second," Jamie said. "I understand that, but I still exist, and the fact is, we've been married for thirteen years."

"This isn't a real marriage!" she shouted. "Don't you understand that? You don't even know me. I don't know you. We're strangers, for heaven's sake."

"Well, maybe we shouldn't be."

"What? What are you saying now?"

A muscle worked in his jaw. He stepped around the coffee table and stood close to her. "I'm saying maybe we should try not being strangers."

He wasn't making any sense. "And how can we do that?"

"Like this." His hands circled her upper arms and he pulled her to him. His mouth covered hers before she realized he was going to kiss her. She couldn't duck. She couldn't run. She couldn't even back up a step, since the sofa was hitting the back of her good leg. So she remained trapped, her hands clenching at her sides and her emotions spiraling out of control.

It wasn't a long kiss. It was a strike-and-run tactic that left her struggling with feelings from anger to exhilaration. Her body swayed until a dizziness that had nothing to do with the wind rocking the houseboat forced her back onto the sofa. For several seconds her heart pounded against her ribs while she stared dumbstruck into dancing green eyes. Finally she said, "Why did you do that?"

He took a deep breath. "It's been thirteen years, Vicki. I figure after all that time, a husband deserves a second kiss."

She shook her head slowly. "You're insane. I'm going to bed to try and forget what just happened."

"Good luck. You take the bedroom. I'll sleep on the sofa."

She hobbled toward the door. "Fine. And don't

even think about coming in here.'' She slammed the door.

A moment later he knocked. ''I have to use the bathroom.''

She flung back his bedspread. ''All right!''

When he was finished, he walked past her just as she was carefully levering herself onto the mattress. He stopped and looked down at her. ''You know, Vicki, all the experts say that a husband and wife shouldn't go to bed angry.''

She threw a pillow at him. He clutched it to his chest and walked out before she could throw something more menacing.

She lay down and realized for the first time that the storm had lost its fury. At least the one outside.

CHAPTER SIX

JAMIE AWOKE, as he did every morning, at seven o'clock, despite the fact that not a sliver of sunlight pierced the shutters. And despite the fact that he'd tossed and turned for a good part of the night. He sat up on the sofa, turned on a fluorescent lantern and acknowledged the long gray snout that appeared on the cushion beside his hand. "Top o' the mornin' to ya', Beasley," he said as he stood and stretched. He was rewarded with a worshipful look at the door.

Once outside, Beasley went in search of an inviting patch of grass while Jamie stood on the catwalk and did what he'd done throughout the long night—replayed the kiss in his mind. He was stupid to have done it. But last night when he put his hands on Vicki's arms, he'd felt as if his next breath depended on knowing what it would be like to kiss her. Maybe the relief he'd felt when he learned she hadn't been seriously hurt had stirred his emotions. Maybe it was because the girl he once thought looked scared but adorable outside the Orlando courthouse was now incredibly desirable. Probably both those reasons had combined to free the restraints on Jamie's urges.

Plus, he was jealous as hell of Graham, which was

stupid. He didn't even know the man Vicki was planning to marry. He hardly even knew Vicki. But from the first time she mentioned her pending engagement, Jamie had the nagging feeling that she was settling for this man. And a woman like Vicki shouldn't have to settle for anything.

A woman like Vicki. What made him think he knew what kind of woman she was? He'd kept track of her addresses through the years, and last night she'd told him she had a shop opening soon which she'd filled with antiques and delicate things like teacups and such. It was information that Jamie considered conversational fluff, the things a girl would tell a friend.

But through the hours he'd spent with her here, as bits and pieces of her personality were revealed, Jamie had a sudden intense longing to know every intimate detail about the woman he'd married—her past, her dreams, what made her sad and happy, frightened or curious.

Only now, after thirteen years, there wasn't time.

He crossed the short gangway and took a deep breath. The ground under his feet was littered with debris, but the air was crystalline cool, cleansed of all traces of the storm. Last night while the winds blew and the mortal world shuddered in fear, humanity bowed to a superior power. And today, with the danger passed, that same humanity could marvel that a force so potent would leave in its wake such purity of sky and air and silver sea.

Since the causeway was still washed out, Jamie decided to let Vicki sleep. She wouldn't be going anywhere until the road department sent trucks loaded with gravel to fill in the erosion left by the storm. He expected that to happen soon. The authorities of Bayberry Cove paid special attention to his needs.

He went to the shed to use the lavatory he'd installed there and to assure himself that his precious wood had weathered the storm. When he returned to the houseboat, Jamie poured a bowl of kibble for Beasley and made himself a cup of coffee. Then he removed the shutters from the windows leaving the ones at the bedroom to give Vicki her privacy. At nine o'clock a boat appeared on the now-calm Currituck Sound. Jamie recognized the official sheriff's department seventeen-foot Boston Whaler. Deputy Blackwell was at the helm, and he had two passengers. Jamie immediately recognized his mother's flaming-red hair, and a bright yellow scarf that could only belong to Bobbi Lee.

He walked to the end of the dock to grab the line Luther would toss to him. This visit would make for an interesting morning. Normally one woman was enough for any man to handle, but when a fellow had to deal with his mother, his ex-girlfriend and his wife all at the same time, then it was probably a good thing that an officer of the law was nearby.

"Howdy, J.D.," Luther called from the boat's console. He pulled the Whaler alongside the dock and waited for Jamie to wind the mooring rope around a piling.

Kate Malone was on her feet before Luther cut the engine. "Are you all right, son?" she asked. Her hazel-eyed gaze bored into him as if she were capable of detecting internal injuries with that special radar only mothers had.

He offered his hand and she stepped gingerly onto the dock. ''Yeah, Ma, I'm fine. It's a little messy here this morning, but no real harm done.''

Next he helped Bobbi Lee from the boat. ''Are you sure, Jamie?'' the woman said, placing her hands on his face and studying his features one by one.

He took a step back from her, an instinctive reaction. ''Of course,'' he said. ''How about the boys? They okay?''

''They're fine,'' Bobbi Lee assured him.

Luther Blackwell grabbed hold of a piling and pulled his cumbersome frame from the boat to the dock. He gave Jamie a sheepish grin. ''Sorry about this, J.D., but these women wouldn't take no for an answer. Insisted I run them out here the minute I showed up at the Kettle for a cup of coffee.''

''It's all right, Luther,'' Jamie said.

Kate Malone swatted the deputy's arm just below his official lawman's insignia. ''It's a mother's right to worry, Luther.''

Bobbi Lee looped her arm through Jamie's. ''And my right, too. Are you sure you're okay?''

Jamie rolled his eyes. ''Did the boys make it to school this morning?''

''Brian didn't,'' she said, referring to her younger son. ''School's closed. There's some mopping up to do from a leaky roof. He's at a friend's house, but

Charlie's gone off to the junior college as usual. Roads are clear around the county."

That was good news. Bobbi Lee's older son hated to miss any of his classes. "How's everybody in town?" Jamie asked. "Anybody suffer damage?"

"Nothin' too bad," Luther said. "A few uprooted trees, a couple of downed power lines. Trent Hodkins lost the roof off his toolshed." He jerked his thumb toward Jamie's shed. "I see you had a similar problem yourself."

Jamie nodded. "I'll need a roofer out here pretty quick. I made some temporary repairs in the middle of the storm."

"Saved the wood, did you?"

"Yep. Nearly all of it."

Kate pressed her hands together in prayer-fashion. "Thank God. I was thinking about you and that wood all night." She rummaged through her large shoulder bag. After a moment she produced a paper sack with Bayberry Cove Kettle printed on it. "Look what I brought. Can you make coffee?" she asked Jamie. "I had to promise Luther two chocolate eclairs to get him over here."

Jamie looked at the *Bucket o' Luck* and pictured a different kind of storm brewing. There was no avoiding the situation. Bobbi Lee was urging him to the houseboat with a series of jabs to his ribs. His mother was rustling the paper bag to get Luther's attention, and managing to get Beasley's, as well. And the deputy looked hungry enough to eat the storm-ravaged geraniums in the boat's window boxes. Jamie sighed in resignation. "Yeah, I can make coffee."

The little group was almost inside when Bobbi Lee jerked on Jamie's arm. She tugged him down the catwalk and pointed to a spot in the trees. "I've seen that car before," she said. Like a guided missile, her pink-tipped fingernail honed in on the red rental car poorly hidden in the brush of Pintail Point. "You told me nobody was here."

Jamie shook his head in anticipation of trouble. "No, I didn't. I just sort of avoided the question. It's a long story, Bobbi Lee."

"Yeah, and I know it started yesterday at the Kettle." She gave him a warning look. "It's the ending I'm worried about now."

AWAKING WITH A DEEP, contented sigh, Vicki rolled over in bed and thought about opening her eyes. Feeling refreshed and rested, she expected to see dazzling pinpoints of Florida sunlight confirming the start of a new day. She blinked, looked and blinked again. Total darkness.

Her inner clock told her it was indeed morning. But a mental alarm bell warned her that something was not as it should be. She sat up and winced when a sharp pain sliced through her ankle.

She remembered. She was in Jamie Malone's bedroom, and it was dark because she was entombed in protective shutters. She groped along the surface of the nightstand until her fingers grasped the flexible band of her wristwatch. She pressed a button on the side of the watch face and the digital readout glowed 9:48 a.m. She hadn't slept this late in years, and she was embarrassed that she'd done so this morning in Jamie's bed.

Slowly, testing the mobility of her ankle, she swung her legs over the edge of the mattress and set her feet on the floor. Placing minimal weight on her injured ankle, she realized at once that walking without an aid was still not an option. She reached for the lantern she'd left on the floor and flicked the power button to light her way to the bathroom.

She hopped to the sink and splashed water on her face. Using grooming supplies typically available in a man's medicine cabinet, she prepared herself to face the day.

She looked at her reflection in the mirror, half expecting to see a literal representation of one of her mother's favorite observations: "Guilt is written all over your face, young lady." Young Vicki used to hide in the farmhouse bathroom and try to scrub away the evidence of a crime only her mother could see.

Vicki observed her face from several angles, searching for visible proof that she was to blame for last night's kiss. She'd lain awake for some time contemplating what had happened and finally accepted that she had no reason to feel guilty about something that was clearly Jamie's doing. She had, however, reflected on the act with an undeniable sensation of pleasure. For that alone, she should feel guilty. But she would clear her conscience this morning and insist that Jamie sign the divorce papers.

Confident about the direction she would take with Jamie, she hobbled to the dresser for another pair of his boxer shorts and a T-shirt. She would ask him to bring her bag from the rental car. Then she would change into her own clothes and pray for a speedy repair to the causeway. Once she was on the way to the airport, Jamie Malone and his impulsive kiss would fade from her mind, as would her unexpected reaction to it.

Making her way slowly to the door, Vicki's resolve was bolstered when she heard voices in the living room. "The television is on," she exclaimed quietly to herself. "We have electricity!"

She opened the door and staggered into brilliant sunlight streaming into the living room, which was full of people drinking coffee and eating pastry. She hopped back a step, leaned heavily against the door frame and scanned the faces that gawked at her in obvious fascination.

She knew two of the people. Jamie, of course, and Bobbi Lee. One man wore a uniform, so he was probably the Bayberry Cove deputy Jamie knew. She had no idea who the plump little middle-aged woman with the fire-engine-red hair was.

"Doughnut, dear?" the woman offered after a moment of strained silence. She held up a pastry wrapped in bakery paper.

Dumbstruck, Vicki could not even respond to that simple question.

At last Jamie filled the void. "Good morning, Vicki. Sleep well?"

She nodded.

"This is the woman I've been telling you about," Jamie told the others. And then to Vicki, "You met Bobbi Lee..."

Vicki nodded at the Bayberry Kettle waitress, the one with the friendly smile who now regarded Vicki as if imagining a noose around her neck.

Jamie continued with the introductions. "And this is my mother, Kate Malone."

The woman who'd offered the doughnuts, narrowed her eyes and stared.

"And this," Jamie said, indicating the deputy, "is Luther Blackwell, second in command of our exemplary Bayberry Cove law-enforcement division."

The deputy lifted a pudgy hand, wiped a smear of chocolate from the corner of his mouth and said, "Howdy, ma'am."

Vicki acknowledged each person, though a genuine smile was impossible. Her mind was too busy speculating what Jamie's mother and friends must think of her emerging from his bedroom wearing his underclothes.

"This is my wife," Jamie said. "Vicki and I were married in Florida thirteen years ago and then, as you all know, we split up and lost track of each other."

Vicki attempted to lighten the effect of Jamie's words with a chuckle. Unfortunately it sounded as artificial as her marriage. "Well, there are all kinds of marriages..." she started to explain.

Bobbi Lee smirked. "But you *are* married to Jamie, aren't you?"

"Yes, but not for long."

The stony features of Bobbi Lee's face softened a little. "You're getting a divorce?"

Vicki looked at Jamie, but he remained silent, letting her address this question. "Exactly. That's why I came here. I've brought the divorce papers with me."

Kate Malone stood up and pulled out a chair from the dining table. "Come sit down, love."

Jamie walked over to help her. "You shouldn't be standing, Vicki." He helped her over to the table, where she sat down and elevated her ankle onto an empty chair. And then, hiding her expression from the others, she gave him a look that conveyed what words could not in this awkward situation.

He read her implied accusation and mouthed a response. *I didn't know they were coming.*

He brought her a cup of coffee, and she took a long swallow. Its warmth soothed her, as did the sudden presence of Beasley's head on her good foot. And then her confidence soared when she realized that if these people were on Pintail Point, the road to the mainland must be open. "Is the causeway repaired?" she asked the deputy. "Can I drive back to town?"

"Oh, no," he said. "It'll take about six loads of fill to correct that. I ordered the first truckload this morning, so I expect by tomorrow—"

"Tomorrow? How did you get here?"

The deputy explained about the women coercing him into bringing them over in the official boat. "We've got to be getting back soon. The Whaler might be needed."

"Can I go back with you?" she asked.

Luther considered her request for a moment. "I don't see why not. The boat holds six."

She looked at Jamie. "Would you please get my bag from the car so I can change into my own clothes?"

"I'd be glad to," he said, "but aren't you forgetting one little detail that might affect your escape plan?"

"What's that?"

"The rental car. Assuming you can drive—" he gestured at her ankle "—don't you have to return it to the car-rental agency?"

Vicki collapsed against the chair back. He was right. She couldn't just leave the car on Pintail Point, miles from the Norfolk airport. "I guess I'll have to stay until tomorrow then," she said. "I do have to return the car."

"I'll take the car back for you."

Everyone turned to stare at Bobbi Lee's enthusiastic expression. "It's no problem," she added. "I'm off tomorrow, and my boy Charlie doesn't have any afternoon classes. Assuming Luther's right about the causeway being fixed tomorrow, we'll pick up your car and return it." Her grin was as radiant as the sun coming in the *Bucket*'s windows.

"I couldn't ask you to do that," Vicki protested.

"You're not asking. I'm offering. I'm glad to do it." She sat forward on the sofa and met Vicki's gaze with a stubborn glint in her eyes. "In fact, I *insist* on helping you get back to Norfolk today."

Vicki wasn't fooled. She knew exactly why Bobbi

Lee was offering to give up her day off to do the neighborly thing.

But so what? Vicki *did* need to get home. ''I still have to get to the airport today,'' she said. ''And without my car—''

''You can take the shuttle,'' Bobbi Lee said. ''The driver will come through Bayberry Cove if you give him a call. It costs thirty dollars for a ride to the airport.'' That settled, Bobbi Lee produced a dazzling aqua-colored cell phone from her rhinestone-studded handbag. ''You can call information and get the number right now.''

Vicki glanced over at Jamie, who'd developed a knot of worry lines on his brow. ''What about your injury?'' he asked. ''How are you going to manage?''

''Crutches,'' Bobbi Lee answered for her. ''I'll see that Vicki gets to the clinic in town, and Doc'll give her a pair. And she'll be better off in the shuttle than driving herself, anyway.'' Bobbi Lee cast a pitying glance on Vicki. ''You poor thing.''

Jamie regarded Vicki for a moment and then raised his hands in resignation. He put the responsibility of the decision where it rightly belonged—on her shoulders.

''Well, thank you, then,'' Vicki said, taking the phone from Bobbi Lee. ''The papers for the rental car are in the glove compartment. And I'll leave you with enough money to fill up the tank.''

''Great.'' Bobbi Lee stood up and waved at Deputy Blackwell. ''Come on, Luther, let's get this lady back to the mainland where she belongs before I'm late for work."

"Just a minute," Vicki said. "I still need to change. My keys are in my jacket pocket. Jamie, would you get my bag from the car now?"

He brought her the jacket and waited while she dug out the keys. Then he went outside to retrieve her bag.

Kate Malone crumpled up the empty pastry bag and carried it to the kitchen before addressing Bobbi Lee and Luther. "You two go on outside and wait. I'll be there in a minute. We need to give Jamie and his wife a little privacy."

Bobbi Lee opened her mouth to protest. But after a stern look from Kate, she followed Luther out the door.

Kate returned to the living room and sat across from Vicki at the dining table. "I just have a minute, so I'll talk fast," she said, with her Maureen O'Sullivan accent. "Are you happy with these arrangements about leaving this morning?"

Vicki had never considered her decision in terms of whether it made her happy. Of course it did. And it should. Her true happiness was a thousand miles away from Pintail Point, and she should be delighted to be going home sooner than she'd dared to hope.

Still and all, these past twenty-odd hours would remain etched in her memory forever. And not just because of the hurricane. She'd discovered that the stranger she married all those years ago was an intriguing man. More complex than she'd ever believed—committed, determined, a bit controlling. Yet content with his simple lifestyle on Pintail Point and his career of making peg puzzles. Jamie Malone was definitely a man without airs. She had to admit she'd enjoyed seeing him again.

"It seems the most logical way of dealing with this problem," she finally answered. "As long as Bobbi Lee doesn't mind."

Kate smiled and patted Vicki's hand where it lay on the table. "Surely you could tell, dear. Bobbi Lee is only too happy to oblige."

Vicki gave Kate a knowing grin. "I'm not a threat to her, you know."

Kate tilted her head. Her bright gaze seemed to penetrate Vicki's thoughts. "Aren't you, now."

"No, of course not."

"She doesn't know the real reason you and Jamie married," Kate said. "There's only a handful of us who do know, and after all this time, I'm glad to have a chance to thank you. I wouldn't be in this country if it weren't for you. And what you did for my son was an act of kindness I'll never forget."

Vicki felt a twinge of guilt. Didn't this woman know about the money Vicki accepted to marry her son? "No, really, it wasn't—"

"I don't know what would have become of Jamie if you hadn't agreed to marry him. Did he tell you about his brothers?"

Vicki nodded.

"Somehow I thought he had. There likely would be three Malone boys in prison now if Jamie had been sent back to Ireland. But you gave him a chance in this country and saved him. Prison is no place for my Jamie.''

The door opened, and Jamie stepped inside with Vicki's bag. Kate leaned close and spoke in a low voice. ''You allowed my boy to follow his heart,'' she said. ''And it led him here to this place for this tiny ripple of time.'' She squeezed Vicki's hand. ''Who knows? Maybe your heart led you here, as well.''

Vicki's lips trembled when she tried to smile. ''Oh, no, Mrs. Malone. My heart didn't bring me here—not the way you think, at least. I came here for one reason only.''

''I know what you say, love, but smart is the man, or woman, who realizes that the heart makes its own choices.''

Jamie approached the table with her garment bag slung over his shoulder. ''Do you want me to put this in the bedroom?''

Caught in the shimmer of Kate Malone's green eyes, Vicki barely heard his words.

''Vicki?'' he prompted.

His mother stood. ''I'll wait with the others in Luther's boat. I've got a few things to say to Bobbi Lee. Good luck to you, Vicki.''

Vicki watched her walk out the door before answering Jamie. ''Yes, please, put the bag in the bedroom. I'll just take a moment to change.''

TEN MINUTES LATER, when Vicki came out of the bedroom, she was the woman she'd been when she'd arrived at Pintail Point the day before. Her dark-gray slacks had a well-defined crease. A charcoal cashmere sweater hugged her breasts. The V-shaped neckline showed off a plain silver necklace with a simple rose charm nestled at the top of her cleavage. She'd caught the soft waves of her blond hair in a silver clip at her crown. Finding her a fascinating blend of innocence and sophistication, Jamie experienced a strong desire to know which of the two characteristics was the real Vicki. He strongly suspected she was a combination of both.

He took the bag and helped her into the living room. When he noticed a sock on her injured foot and a sneaker on the other, he said, ''Sorry about those fancy shoes you arrived in.''

''It's all right. Imogene could have done worse, I guess.''

They stopped by the front door, and Vicki leaned on the kitchen counter. ''You really were a big help to me last night,'' Jamie said. ''I'm sorry, too, that it cost you a sprained ankle.''

''You did a good job of patching me up,'' she said. ''And as far as the hurricane is concerned, I don't regret being here. How often does a person have a chance to ride out a storm like that?'' She smiled. ''One thing is certain—I'll never forget my time on Pintail Point.''

''I won't forget it, either.'' He lay his palm on her cheek, testing to see if she'd flinch away from him. She didn't. Instead, her blue eyes connected with his in such a profound way it seemed he'd been looking into them for all of these thirteen years. In that moment it was as if she'd been a part of his day-to-day life since the meeting on the courthouse steps.

"I wish you the best with husband number two," he said.

Her lips made a delicate downturn. "It's Graham," she said, scolding him. "Husband number two has a name."

"And a fine one it is. It calls to mind an English country squire—a straight-backed bloke in a tweed jacket with leather patches on the sleeves." Jamie squared his hands in front of his face as if they were a frame for his imagination. "I can see him now, pipe in his mouth, fists on his hips, standing astride a wind-swept hilltop as he looks over his estate."

And such a man is about as useful as feathers on a frog, he thought.

He settled his hand on Vicki's arm and lightly rubbed his palm down the sleeve of her sweater. "Is it to be, then, Vicki, that we'll never see each other again?"

His question seemed to surprise her. A shiver ran through her. "I guess so," she said.

"I must admit, I'm finding that something of a sad thing."

"Why?"

"We're ending a thirteen-year relationship that, despite its venerable length of time, never really got started. It makes a man think of what might have been."

"Oh, Jamie, we could never have made a go of this marriage. We're from different worlds." She looked around the houseboat appraisingly, but not haughtily. ‘‘We want different things out of life.’’

‘‘Do we now? I’m thinking back on that kiss from last night. Maybe it’s wishful thinking on the part of the soon-to-be-discarded husband number one, but I am wondering if we—for that moment at least—didn’t want the same thing.’’

Her cheeks flushed a deep rose. ‘‘You’re making too much of that kiss,’’ she said. ‘‘You can’t think that it meant anything.’’

‘‘Would the same be true of the kiss I’m about to give you right now?’’

She blinked. Her lips parted, but no words came out. Jamie wrapped his arms around her and lowered his mouth to hers. He touched her lips lightly at first, testing her, ready to withdraw if she backed away. But she didn’t. Instead, he found her lips pliant and soft. Inviting. So he increased the pressure until the wariness of kissing his wife fled from his mind and he put all of himself into the joining of their mouths.

He cupped the back of her head and kissed her deeply, relishing the little moan that came from the back of her throat. After a minute he drew back and felt a surge of misery that this kiss would be as close as he’d ever get to making love to his wife.

‘‘You shouldn’t have kissed me,’’ she murmured.

‘‘Probably not. But there’s not one cell in my body that’s regretting it.’’

She swallowed, closed her eyes against the intensity of his gaze. ‘‘Please move away,’’ she said.

He did. She hobbled to the door but stopped when

she realized she was still dependent on him. ''Would you help me out to the boat?''

He picked up her bag and her briefcase and moved to open the door. Before he grasped the handle, she suddenly whirled and pierced him with a look of such shock and confusion that he grabbed her arm to keep her steady. ''The papers!'' she cried. ''You haven't signed the divorce papers!''

He'd completely forgotten. They both searched the living room. Vicki finally spotted the legal document on the floor by the sofa. ''Hurry,'' she said. ''Sign it now.''

Something—almost like panic—tightened in his abdomen. His rational side said the act of signing his name was unavoidable. If Vicki wanted him to sign, he would. But the emotional side—the part of him that had kissed her twice and longed for more—was frantically seeking a means to delay the inevitable. He picked up the document and flipped through the pages. ''I haven't had a chance to read this,'' he said.

She stared at him. ''It's just standard divorce legalese. I'm not asking anything of you. It's a clean break.'' She paused, looking at the document and then his face again. ''You trust me, don't you?''

''I suppose I do.'' He held up the document so that the page with the name of the firm was visible. ''But how do I know I can trust these lawyers? A prudent man would never sign something without reading it first.''

She leaned heavily on the counter. ''Are you saying you won't sign?''

How he wished he'd heard just a hint of hope in her question. But it wasn't hope trembling in her voice. It was fear. And bewilderment. "No, I'll sign them."

"When?"

"I'll have my lawyer look them over." When her eyes widened at the notion of Jamie having a lawyer, he explained, "My mother works as housekeeper for the mayor of Bayberry Cove. He's an attorney. It's just a precaution, Vicki."

And an absurd attempt to delay the inevitable, as if we really should explore the possibilities of this crazy marriage of ours.

"As soon as he confirms this is a standard divorce settlement, I'll sign the papers and mail them to you."

"You will?"

He nodded. "I give you my word. You'll get the divorce."

She scribbled down her address on a tablet. He didn't bother to tell her he already had it.

A horn sounded from outside. Luther hollered, "Let's go! They just radioed from the station that the sheriff needs the boat back."

"You'd better get going," Jamie said. He opened the door, and Beasley crawled out from under the table, trotted over and pressed his nose into the palm of Vicki's hand.

"He knows you're going," Jamie said. "He's waiting for you to say you'll be back in a little while. That's what I always tell him when I leave the point."

She ruffled the dog's scruffy fur, though her eyes

were fixed on Jamie. "You know I can't tell him that."

Jamie smiled at her, remembering her phone conversation with Graham and the series of lies she'd told. "So now, when the heart of a poor animal is at stake, you've suddenly developed an aversion to lying?"

"It's not that," she said. "I have too much respect for Beasley's intelligence."

Jamie might have laughed out loud at the implied comparison between her fiancé and Beasley, but he didn't feel like laughing. He shooed the dog outside, helped Vicki to the boat and handed Luther her bag and briefcase. Since the motor was already humming on the Whaler, he unwound the rope from the piling and pushed the craft away from the dock with his foot. It headed into Currituck Sound, and Jamie waved at the three women inside. But it was only one face he saw while he committed the features to memory.

BOBBI LEE CHATTED about plans that included feeding and nursing Vicki and then transporting her away from Bayberry Cove. Vicki concentrated on the houseboat sitting like an oasis on the sun-washed horizon. When Jamie was no more than a shimmering outline on the catwalk of the *Bucket o' Luck,* she turned around and stared at the approaching coastline.

She certainly hadn't expected to experience this inexplicable melancholy when she left Jamie. It had to be, she told herself, the result of meeting her husband and then leaving without accomplishing her mission.

The truth was, Jamie Malone was an even bigger

problem than he'd been two days ago. She was still a married woman lawfully unable to wed the man she loved. As far as the divorce papers were concerned, she was going home empty-handed. And yet, when she took one last look at Pintail Point and watched the houseboat become smaller and smaller until it seemed to sink into the water of the sound, her hands were not the emptiest part of her.

CHAPTER SEVEN

VICKI WAS RESTLESS, agitated, and not just because it was her bad luck to have an injury that kept her confined to an airplane seat. This feeling was worse than inactivity. Something was making her itch to crawl out of her skin. It was as if her life was in turmoil, and she would never experience a calm moment again. And this strange sensation had been with her since she'd left Pintail Point.

She wiggled her toes and stretched her legs as far as the cramped space would allow, then looked over her shoulder down two dozen rows of seats to the small lavatory at the rear of the plane. She regretted ordering a soda. Even if her crutches hadn't been stowed in the closet in front of the aircraft, it would have been too long a journey for her to consider. She'd just have to wait. It was only a half hour till the plane landed in Fort Lauderdale.

But the worst was yet to come. Not having come up with a logical explanation for her injury—she hadn't mentioned her physical problem to Graham when she'd called the night before from Norfolk. She hoped now that hadn't been a mistake. She would have to be brought off the jet in a wheelchair after everyone deplaned, and she feared he might leave when she didn't exit the walkway with the rest of the crowd. And even if he was still waiting for her, she could imagine his shock when he saw her being pushed along by airline personnel.

The plane landed smoothly and taxied to a stop at the terminal. Vicki fidgeted as her fellow passengers gathered their belongings from overhead compartments and waited for the jet doors to open. Soon she was the only one left on the aircraft. Minutes ticked by before a uniformed attendant came down the aisle with the dreaded chair. He helped her into the seat, draped her bags and crutches over the handles and wheeled her off the plane.

"Please be there, Graham," she whispered to herself, knowing the difficulty she would have handling her luggage and flagging a taxi if she had to do it on her own.

He was there, thank goodness, standing by a bank of windows. He stared alternately at the aircraft from which she'd just emerged and his watch. Vicki was struck once again at the magnificence of this man. With the afternoon sun casting highlights on his stylishly mussed blond hair, Graham Townsend was simply, irrefutably gorgeous. Tall, fair, with chiseled patrician features, he stood out from every man around him like fabled Pegasus among plow horses.

Like an English lord surveying his property from a windswept hilltop.

Vicki quickly pushed Jamie's description of Graham to the back of her mind, just as she'd tried to force images of the Irishman himself from her thoughts for the past twenty-four hours. Jamie was wrong. Graham wasn't the prototype of landed aristocracy. He was an American entrepreneur through and through, and any similarity to a stuffy British nobleman was pure fabrication.

He turned away from the window. Lines of impatience marred the perfect contours of his face as he tugged at the lapels of his camel-colored sports coat and headed for the metal detectors and the exit. Then he spotted her out of the corner of his eye. He spun around, stared for a moment in shock and hurried toward her.

"Good God, Victoria, what's happened to you?" he demanded when he reached the wheelchair.

The attendant set the brake on one of the wheels. "Hey, buddy, you want to take over from here?" he asked.

Graham seemed uncertain of how to answer at first, but quickly recovered. "Yes, of course I'll take over." He took the crutches the attendant thrust at him and tucked them under his arm. Then, releasing the brake, he pushed Vicki forward. "This is going to be one hell of a story, I can tell," he muttered. "What have you done, Victoria? Tell me you haven't broken something."

"No, Graham. Nothing is broken, except perhaps my dignity. But that will heal. My ankle is sprained, that's all."

"That's enough. Especially with the opening of the shop just a few days away. How did this happen?"

She tried to smile at him over her shoulder, thinking

the gesture would reassure him that the injury was not the catastrophe he clearly imagined. "It was the silliest thing. I was running in the rain and I slipped in a puddle. That's all it was. A nice man helped me up and took me to a clinic." It wasn't all lies. She did fall in the rain. And Jamie had been nice to her.

"That blasted storm again. First, I wasn't able to reach you by phone, and now here you are a day late returning, and practically a cripple."

Vicki felt a twinge of irritation. "I'm fine, Graham. I won't need the crutches in a couple of days. And we have plenty of time before the shop opening."

"The container from Amsterdam is arriving any day. Did I tell you that?"

"Yes, Graham, you did. Don't worry. We'll manage the customs paperwork. Everything will work out."

She heard him expel a long breath. He stopped pushing the chair, came around to the front and leaned close to her. "Of course it will," he said. "I must sound terribly insensitive, darling." He took one of her hands in his and rubbed his thumb across her knuckles. "I've just been so worried about you." He glanced down at her sock-covered foot. "Tell me how you feel. What can I do?"

"For one thing you can keep pushing me toward the ladies' room."

He looked appropriately chastened, so she refrained from telling him that she didn't appreciate his showing more concern for a shipment of antiques than he had for her injury.

SUN GLINTED off the gabled windows of the sixteen-room mansion belonging to Haywood Fletcher as Jamie drove his pickup through the open iron gates to the estate. He followed a narrow lane under overhanging oak and maple trees burgeoning with the colors of fall. Normally the russets and golds of a North Carolina autumn would capture his artist's eye for the better part of a day, but he hardly noticed them on this splendid Friday morning. His mind was focused on the legal document lying on the seat beside him.

As he followed a gentle curve in the lane, Jamie glanced down at the divorce papers and half hoped his reaction would be different this time. No such luck. He still regarded the darn things as a stumbling block to some inexplicable vision of his future happiness. Vicki had been gone for two days, and during that time he had wrestled with the unexpected feelings he'd acquired for her. Feelings that had come out of nowhere and stayed with him like the scent of wild bayberries. Or the heartburn that came from eating too many of them.

It was stupid to harbor any sort of sentiment for a woman who had openly professed her love for another man. Especially when that woman was Vicki Sorenson. She'd been a good sport about the storm and her injuries, but Vicki was clearly not a houseboat kind of girl. And she certainly wasn't interested in bonding with him.

Despite all this logical reasoning, Jamie was still hoping that Haywood Fletcher's keen legal observations would find something in the fine print of Vicki's divorce documentation. Something that might give him the time he needed to get to know this woman he'd married out of desperation.

He pulled up in front of the Tudor-style residence and walked to the door. It was opened before he'd even lifted the heavy brass door knocker, as it almost always was when anyone visited. Rudy T. Williams was finely attuned to every little thing that happened on these thirty acres of prime real estate. Haywood's butler and chauffeur for more than forty years, Rudy was as much a part of Bayberry Cove as was his employer, though no one quite understood why he kept the title of chauffeur. Haywood Fletcher drove himself where he wanted to go and had been breaking the town speed limits for as long as anyone could remember.

Rudy's milky gray eyes reflected genuine fondness when he saw Jamie on the threshold. His wide smile, centered in a smooth face the color of dark Irish ale, was bright. He was, as always, impeccably groomed, from his tightly curled white hair to the polish on his Florsheim shoes.

''Good mornin', Mistah James,'' he said in a honeyed drawl that if it could be bottled, would sell as top-shelf sipping whiskey. ''Is Mistah Fletcher expectin' you today, or are you payin' a visit to your mama?''

''I'm here to see the man himself, Rudy,'' Jamie answered. ''But if I know my mother, she'll pop into the room with a feather duster and pretend there's a speck of lint on the desk.''

Rudy chuckled. ''You surely do know your mama.''

He swept his arm toward a wide center hallway. "Mistah Fletcher is in his study. He's not due in court till this afternoon, so you go on down and see to your business."

Jamie strode down the hallway to the large room occupying the southeast corner of the house. The door was open, so he tapped on the frame and stepped inside. He focused first on the wide bay window overlooking a terraced garden. A plum orchard at the end of the garden had undergone a revival in the years since Kate Malone had been housekeeper, and due to her nurturing, fall asters and mums still bloomed between manicured bushes.

"Jamie, come on in, son." Haywood's voice boomed from the corner. His desk stood there in the angle between two floor-to-ceiling bookshelves.

Jamie crossed to it, leaned over and shook Haywood's hand. As usual, the attorney was dressed in a gleaming white shirt with a pair of wide black suspenders over the shoulders. His abundant gray hair was combed back from his forehead with enough old-fashioned pomade to hold the wiry strands perfectly in place. His dark eyes, alert under thick, straight brows, scrutinized his visitor with more than the usual interest. At sixty-eight, Haywood was still considered one of the best legal minds in the state. He motioned for Jamie to sit down. "Now, what's this about some document you want me to look over?" A little grin curled the edges of his mustache. "Somebody suing you, J.D.?"

"Nope. Somebody's divorcing me."

Clearly amused, Haywood sat back in his chair. "So, that little green-card stunt you pulled has come back on you like yesterday's chili dog."

"You might say that." Jamie slid the folder across the desk.

Haywood flipped the cover open. "She tryin' to stick it to you? If so, she doesn't have a legal leg to stand on." He angled one eyebrow with suspicion. "This marriage was never consummated, isn't that right?"

Jamie nodded. "Yes, but that's irrelevant. Vicki just wants out of the marriage. I doubt she's making any demands at all in those papers. And frankly, Haywood, that's the problem."

"You've lost me there, son. You sayin' you *want* this woman to make demands?"

"I'm saying I don't want the divorce to be as simple as that document makes it sound." Jamie rested both elbows on the arms of the chair. "Maybe I don't want a divorce at all. At least I want to buy some time to decide."

Haywood's shrewd gaze fixed on Jamie as he stroked his mustache with his index finger. "I heard this long-lost wife of yours was on Pintail during the storm."

"Yes, she was."

"She must have made quite an impression on you. I know she made one on Bobbi Lee Blanchard." Haywood chuckled. "There are rumors all over town about how Bobbi Lee gave Mrs. Jamie Malone a brown-bag lunch and hustled her outta town on her one good leg.''

Rumors were common in Bayberry Cove, and Jamie usually didn't give a second thought to the ones about him. But this—like the one ten years before about him and Bobbi Lee—was different. It mattered. ''I guess there were rumors,'' he admitted, ''but what's important to me now is having a chance to get to know this woman, my *wife,* and I want you to find something in that divorce plea that will give me that chance.'' He sat forward, placing his elbows on his knees. ''If you don't find a loophole to stall this thing, I'll have no option but to sign the document. It's what Vicki wants.''

Haywood turned the next page. ''Have you thought of telling her the truth—that you want to get to know her better?''

''Have I thought about telling her that after ignoring her existence for thirteen years and then spending one night alone with her in a raging hurricane, I'm suddenly interested?'' He shook his head. ''Somehow I don't think that would come across as overly romantic—or sincere.''

Especially when she's involved with some other guy.

''Maybe not,'' Haywood said. ''To my way of thinking, women still like to be courted these days. I don't suppose that's changed much over the years.'' He settled his fist under his chin and gave serious attention to the document. ''Let's see what we've got here.''

Jamie picked up a fishing magazine from an end

table and thumbed through it while the attorney read. Haywood's facial expression gave nothing away. He read silently and slowly turned the pages. He'd just started the last page when Jamie's mother entered the study, a silver coffee service in her hands.

"Mornin', Jamie," she said, setting the tray on a credenza. "I thought you gentlemen might like a spot of coffee and a biscuit."

Jamie wasn't fooled. He knew Kate had come into the study to find out what was going on. He was surprised that she'd managed to stay out of the room for this long.

Haywood looked up from his reading. "Blazes, woman! You only let me have one cup a day, and now all of a sudden, you're allowing me another." His eyes crinkled at the corners. "Kate Malone, you're as transparent as window glass."

Kate sidled next to the attorney's chair and looked down at him. "A man who treats his gifts lightly today, Haywood, finds himself with no favors tomorrow. Now, do you want coffee or not?"

He grunted. She poured two cups, gave one to Jamie and perched on the corner of Haywood's desk. Clearly she wasn't going anywhere.

After a couple of minutes, Haywood closed the document and folded his hands over the cover. Jamie raised his eyebrows in question.

"There's nothing, son," he said. "This document's as pure as a spinster's lips. I should be tellin' you you're a lucky man, instead of sayin' I'm sorry."

"I was afraid of that," Jamie said. "There's nothing in that document to keep me from signing it, then?"

Haywood shook his head.

Kate Malone stood up and placed her hand on the attorney's shoulder. "Tell me something, Haywood. Doesn't that paper need just the slightest bit of refinement?" She smiled at Jamie over the top of Haywood's head. "Just a tweaking, you know? Something that will protect my Jamie far into the future, not just for today."

"It's not a bit necessary, Kate," Haywood answered. "This paper is fair and complete as it stands. There's no reason the boy shouldn't sign it."

"You're a trusting man, Haywood," Kate continued. "But there are women out there, schemers and connivers... Now I'm not saying Vicki is like that, but someday she could come back and claim rights to half of everything."

Haywood held up his hand to silence her and chuckled softly. "All right, Kate. I'll tweak it for you, but only because I'll probably never lay eyes on these Fort Lauderdale lawyers in my lifetime, so they won't have a chance to make me a laughingstock." He cleared his throat dramatically and leveled a serious look at Jamie. "I'd like to keep this document a few days," he said. "For your protection there is a clause or two I might add to ensure the stability of your assets in the future. I'll need a while to make some adjustments."

"Yes, sir," Jamie said. "Take as long as you need."

Kate shot her son a look of triumph. ''The next step is up to you, James Dillon Malone. Take it wisely.''

She picked up the coffee cups to return them to the tray. But before she'd taken two steps toward the credenza, Haywood reached out and patted her behind. ''Tell me something, Kate. Do women today still like to be courted?''

She flashed him a wicked look over her shoulder. ''Indeed they do, Haywood Fletcher, and don't you be forgetting it.''

She flounced from the room without another glance at the men, and Jamie found himself suffering an unaccustomed flush of embarrassment. This was his mother, after all, acting as brazen as a barmaid. ''You know something, Haywood?'' he said to the smiling attorney. ''When a man grabs a woman's posterior in front of her son, I think that son has every right to ask when he can expect a marriage proposal to be forthcoming.''

Haywood wagged his finger at Jamie's face. ''I have no interest at all in marrying you, J.D., so you'd best look elsewhere for a mate.''

Jamie hooted with laughter, a prelude to the very real protest he intended to deliver on behalf of his mother's honor.

''Now as for Kate,'' the attorney continued, ''I'll propose when I'm good and ready, and that likely won't be until everyone in this town quits asking me when I'm going to do it.''

Jamie was still smiling when he walked down the

hallway to the exit. His mother was in good hands, and so were Vicki's divorce papers.

WHEN HE DIDN'T HAVE weighty issues on his mind, Jamie looked forward to Friday afternoons. He liked kids, still hoped to have one or two of his own someday. Which was why he donated his time every Friday to entertain and instruct the kids of Bayberry Cove—the artistically talented ones and those who just liked to fiddle around with a hammer and paintbrush. Or throw sticks for Beasley.

He was still contemplating his meeting with Haywood as he spread an oilcloth over the picnic table and wiped it free of the residue of last week's session. On his way to the shed for supplies, he spotted the red Toyota that belonged to his 17-year-old assistant, Becca Lovell. It rumbled across the newly repaired causeway and ground to a stop at the entrance to the point.

With all the enthusiasm of the lead actress in the high school plays for three years running, Becca jumped out of the little car and covered the distance that separated her from Jamie in a few playful gallops. The long hair gathered at her crown bounced like golden springs. "Hey, J.D.," she called. She scratched Beasley's head while scrutinizing the point. "I heard you stayed out here during the storm. Doesn't look too bad. A few broken tree limbs." She reprimanded him with a scowl. "You're lucky you didn't break a limb of your own."

"Not luck, my girl," he said, tapping the side of

his head with his forefinger. ‘‘Years of practice in dealing with storms and a lot of careful preparation.’’

Her blue eyes twinkled. ‘‘So how was it out here with no power, no phone and your mystery wife to snuggle with?’’

He rolled his eyes. ‘‘You heard.’’

‘‘Of course. The superintendent called off school the day after Imogene. Most of us didn’t have anything to do but go to the mall or hang out at the Kettle. I saw the very nice-looking Mrs. Malone myself.’’ She narrowed her eyes. ‘‘What’d you do to her? She was on crutches.’’

‘‘It’s a long story. One I’m not going to tell you.’’ Determined to change the topic, he asked, ‘‘How many kids are coming today?’’

‘‘I saw Luther Blackwell load about ten of them into the van. They should be here any minute.’’

‘‘Is Brian coming?’’

‘‘Nope. Bobbi Lee said he had to make up a soccer practice that was canceled because of the storm.’’

Bobbi Lee’s ten-year-old rarely missed an opportunity to be with Jamie. Even though his affair with Bobbi Lee had ended, and she’d become involved with another man, Jamie still enjoyed a close relationship with her son. ‘‘Are the rest of them all returning students?’’

‘‘Yep. You’ve got four birdhouses and six treasure chests.’’

He headed toward the shed. ‘‘Fine. Let’s get their projects and set up.’’

They had the tools on the table by the time the

sheriff's van rolled onto Pintail. Before Luther let the kids out, Becca sat down on a picnic table bench and looked up at Jamie. "Just between you and me, J.D., how'd Bobbi Lee like it when she heard you and your long-lost wife spent the night out here together?"

"You'll have to ask Bobbi Lee that question."

"Are you kidding? She'd poke my eyes out."

Jamie shrugged. Bobbi Lee just might.

"You getting back together with your wife or what?"

That was the million-dollar question. How did a guy go about getting back together with a woman he'd never been together with in the first place? And what if that woman fancied herself together with another man entirely?

"Let's just say that I'm contemplating my future in general," Jamie said. "Who knows if my wife would even want me back?"

"So what are you going to do?" Becca asked.

Jamie looked at ten kids who were running toward the picnic table. "I'm leaving town for a few days," he said. "Just as soon as we're finished here."

Becca sighed as if she'd witnessed a soap opera love scene. "You're going after her?"

"Thinking about it."

"She'd be crazy not to fall into your arms. After all, I've been in love with you since I was nine."

Jamie laughed. "Yeah. And then you turned twelve and met Charlie Blanchard." He glanced down at Beasley who had crawled from under the picnic table and was ambling onto the catwalk of the houseboat.

Smart dog. He knew if he stayed, he could expect abuse from the toes of twenty sneakers. "Hey, Beas," he called. The dog stopped and looked around. "You ever been to Florida?"

Beasley yawned once and flopped down in the sun like a rag rug. Jamie grinned at Becca. "I guess that's a yes. He doesn't look all that excited about going."

AFTER THE STUDENTS had returned to the mainland and Jamie had stored their gear in the shed, he packed a suitcase, tossed the kibble, a few sandwiches and cold drinks into a cooler and loaded his truck. He called his mother to tell her his plans and then considered calling Bobbi Lee. Knowing her, Jamie was certain she'd wonder why he hadn't called, as if their past gave her the right to know what he was up to.

In the end, he whistled for Beasley and climbed into the truck without calling. He'd take the easy way out this time and phone Bobbi when he got to Florida. He'd probably have hell to pay for the decision. As many times as he'd told her that he wasn't interested in a committed relationship with her, she stubbornly clung to the hope that he would change his mind. He supposed that wasn't so different from the way he was feeling about Vicki right now.

Jamie certainly didn't regret the time he'd spent with Bobbi Lee ten years ago, even though it had turned out that they'd each had different expectations. But Bobbi had been the best tonic Jamie could have hoped for at that time in his life. It was too bad she'd lied to him about what she wanted from him. And a damned shame she'd lied to him about Brian.

As Jamie drove along the causeway he thought about the next few days. Was he making a fool's journey or a spiritual quest? He didn't know. Either way, he was closer to finding out with each revolution of his tires.

CHAPTER EIGHT

VICKI LEANED BACK in the plushly upholstered chair behind her desk and rubbed her eyes. She'd been staring at the computer monitor for two hours and was finally pleased with the results of the six-page Web site she'd designed for Tea and Antiquities. Now that she'd done the work, she conceded that Graham had been right when he'd urged her to design the site. A Web page was a great way to advertise the shop opening.

She massaged her ankle, which was beginning to throb, stood up and stared with disgust at the crutches propped in a corner. It was Sunday night, more than four full days since the doctor in Bayberry Cove had fitted her with the cumbersome sticks. She rotated her foot, testing the flexibility. There was still a little soreness, but the swelling had gone down and the bruises were fading. If she was careful, she could probably manage without crutches now, even if it was a few hours short of the doctor's recommendation.

She rested her chin in her hand and looked out the shop window. The Boulevard was quiet. At eight-thirty, only trendy bistros and coffee shops remained open. The retail stores had closed at six. She shut down the Web design program and yawned. It would be nice to return to the two-bedroom cottage she'd recently rented in a renovated neighborhood of old Fort Lauderdale. A good long soak in her restored claw-foot bathtub would erase the stress of the past few hours—stress that wasn't entirely related to work.

In fact, Vicki hadn't relaxed since returning from North Carolina. The restlessness she'd experienced on the airplane hadn't abated, and she was beginning to wonder if she'd ever again enjoy the harmony and satisfying routine that had defined her life before that eventful trip. Getting away from the shop for a while would help, she decided, and she reached to turn off the computer.

And then she stopped and stared at the green power light. Why not? she asked herself. She was alone in the shop. Her work was finished. It was the perfect time to indulge an impulse she'd been resisting for days.

She signed on to her Internet server and typed the letters of a search engine in the address box. When the correct prompt popped up, she entered "J.D. Malone" in the blank space. Within seconds several references to J. D. Malone appeared on the screen. She scanned the first one, noting key words:

North Carolina wood crafter, advertising puzzles, original carvings...

She would have pursued the biographical information, but a tapping on the door stopped her. She whirled around as if caught pursuing a guilty pleasure and saw Louise grinning through the window. She held up a paper bag from the French restaurant a block away.

Crepes. Vicki was reminded of her empty stomach, and her mouth watered. Mindful of her injury, she got up and walked carefully to the door to let Louise in. They embraced briefly. They'd talked on the phone, but it was the first time they'd seen each other since Vicki's return from North Carolina.

Louise stepped back and looked down at Vicki's ankle. ''Okay, where are your crutches? You're still supposed to be using them.''

Vicki glanced at the things in the corner. ''I think I wore them out. Or maybe it was the other way around. Anyway, it was a mutual understanding to part company.''

Louise strode to the desk and put the paper bag on the blotter. ''Someone's got to look out for you, girl. At least I can see you get some food in you.'' She glanced absently at the computer monitor. ''What are you working on?''

Vicki quickly hit the exit prompt. The screen reverted to the ordinary desktop. ''Oh, nothing. Just surfing some antique furniture sites.'' Smiling up at Louise, she said, ''So did you come over just to make sure I eat?''

Louise spread out the selections and handed Vicki a napkin and utensils. ''Of course. What other reason would I have? Certainly not because you haven't told me anything personal about your trip.''

Vicki spoke around a delicious morsel of pastry and

cheese. "I have so. I told you I met Jamie and he agreed to the divorce."

"Big deal. Those are facts. I see enough of that kind of drivel in the office. I want the emotional, gut-wrenching details of that meeting. I want descriptions, conversations, panic attacks...you know, all the good stuff."

Vicki laughed. "Then go read a hot novel. My meeting with Jamie was brief and uncomplicated."

Louise smirked. "Which explains why you were a day late returning and why you've practically hung up on me whenever I've asked. And why you have a bandage on your leg and you're using crutches. And why you didn't come back with the document signed. And why—" she angled her head and narrowed her eyes "—you just happen to have that little tic in the corner of your eye."

"Don't be ridiculous. Are you suggesting I'm guilty of something?"

Louise nibbled on a carrot. "Not exactly. But are you?"

"Absolutely not." *And I'd cut out my tongue before I'd admit that Jamie kissed me and I didn't find it all that unpleasant.*

Louise considered Vicki's quick response. "No guilt, eh? You've told Graham everything, then?"

"Well, no." Vicki smiled sheepishly. "But I learned to handle *that* guilt a long time ago."

"So? Did he recognize you?"

Vicki grinned as she popped a raspberry into her mouth. "I should hope so. We've been dating for a year and a half, and I was only gone a couple of days.''

Louise rolled her eyes. ''Not Graham, you ninny! You know darned well I was asking about your husband, the notorious Mr. Malone. Did *he* recognize you?''

''He did, actually. Unlike you, Lulu, I haven't aged much in thirteen years.'' Vicki laughed at the expression on Louise's face. Her friend only pretended to be insulted. At thirty-five, she was a raven-haired, aerobicized knockout. Anyone who doubted that need only follow her into the Broward County courthouse and see the appreciative stares from the men in the lobby.

''I'll pretend you didn't say that,'' she warned Vicki. ''But tell the truth. How was he—on a scale of one to ten.''

''In what category? Personality? Character? Looks?''

''The important one of course. Looks.''

''I don't know how to judge that.''

''Sure you do. You obviously think Graham's a ten, right?''

Graham was definitely a ten. ''Yes.''

''Well, then, you and I have a problem with the criteria. I have to agree that Graham is good-looking, in that Matt Damon, preppie kind of way. But in my opinion, that sort of guy's not a ten.''

''No?''

''No. I give him a seven. I much prefer…'' Licking fruit sauce from her finger, Louise was silent for a few moments. Then she grinned. ''I prefer someone like that guy looking in the shop window right now. Despite the stupid shirt, he's a nine at least.'' She squinted at the window and screwed up her mouth as if the fruit had suddenly soured. ''But that dog with the yardsticks for legs is, at best, a one.''

''You're too much.'' Vicki glanced briefly at the window before returning her attention to her dinner.

Louise wouldn't let it drop. ''What's with the guy at the window, Vic? Did he follow you home? My advice is, keep him.''

Vicki took a big bite of her crepe. ''Quit looking at him. He's probably just some weirdo if he's out at nine o'clock on a Sunday night staring into shop windows—''

Recognition struck as if it had been delivered with a bolt of electricity. Pastry stuck in her throat. She struggled to get her next breath as she spun around and stared at the two familiar faces clearly visible through her shop window.

Louise stood and thumped Vicki's back. ''Are you all right?''

Vicki recovered somewhat. ''Oh, my God,'' she croaked. ''Do you know who that is?''

''No, but I'd like to.''

Vicki continued to stare at the face of Jamie Malone as his features slowly transformed. His eyes grew round and shimmered in the glow of a street lamp in front of the shop. A smile curved the corners of his mouth before bursting into a full-blown grin. He shrugged one shoulder as if marveling at the coincidence of running into Vicki and being separated by a mere quarter-inch pane of glass. Of course Vicki knew that coincidence had nothing to do with his sudden appearance.

"I think he knows you," Louise said. "And I hope there isn't lead in the paint the printer used on your shop window."

Shaking her head at Louise's odd comment, Vicki focused on the new lettering on the glass, which for some reason seemed to appeal to Beasley's taste buds. He was doing his best to lick the *s* off the word *Antiquities.*

She got up awkwardly, scowled at the window across the room and jabbed a finger at Beasley. Jamie looked down, realized what the dog was doing and tugged on the leash. The dog stopped licking, squirmed in his collar and continued looking in the window at Vicki. He seemed to be smiling.

"I think the dog knows you," Louise said. "He was trying to lick his way inside."

"Yes, they both know me," Vicki admitted as she moved around the desk and limped to the door.

Louise followed close behind. "Don't tell me you have another secret life you're hiding from your friends and loved ones."

Vicki turned the lock on her door and took a deep breath, the only immediate antidote she knew to calm the storm of emotions inside her. "No, this is the same secret life." A delicate pottery bell above the entrance jingled as Vicki admitted her visitors. "Louise, meet Jamie Malone and Beasley."

Louise stuck out her hand and Jamie grasped it.

"This is the man you're divorcing for Townsend?" She smiled into Jamie's eyes. "Oh, honey, we need to talk."

"Shut up, Lulu," Vicki said. She stared at their joined hands until Jamie pulled his back and shoved it into the pocket of his shorts. "I can't imagine what your answer's going to be," Vicki said to him, "but would you mind telling me what you're doing here?"

"Beasley and I are on vacation," he said with the nonchalance of a person telling the truth. He looked down at the dog as though the animal would actually confirm the ludicrous explanation. "I wanted to go to Wisconsin, but Beas here insisted on Florida. It really was his year to choose, so we hopped in the pickup and here we are."

"No. I mean the real reason. And I can only hope it's because you brought the divorce papers."

He blew out a breath, scratched the back of his head. "About those papers, Vicki. There's something I've got to tell you."

She crossed her arms over her chest and tried not to look directly into his green eyes. She couldn't let herself become sidetracked. She nodded toward Louise. "Tell both of us. Louise just happens to be my lawyer."

He seemed impressed. "Are you Oppenheimer, Straus or Baker?"

"I'm Duncan," she said. "A bit player. It'll be a few years before I'm up there with O, S and B. But Vicki's right. I am her lawyer and responsible for drawing up the divorce papers."

He gave her an openly admiring look. "And a fine job you did. There were just a couple of things my lawyer took exception to."

Louise glared at him. She seemed to have forgotten that she'd found him irresistible just a minute ago. "What things? That document was flawless. There's nothing objectionable—"

"Oh, right, not to me, anyway," Jamie said. "And I don't expect to hold up the divorce for very long. My lawyer will let me know as soon as he's checked the papers carefully and added a clause or two to protect me in the future."

"That's ridiculous."

"Well, you know how lawyers are..." Jamie followed the comment with a teasing grin. "You probably know better than anyone else in this room."

Vicki stopped patting Beasley's head, a gesture she'd begun automatically when the dog entered the shop and sat beside her on a Persian carpet. He immediately lay his big head against her thigh and directed his affectionate amber eyes at her. While Jamie and Louise bickered over the document that would ultimately decide Vicki's fate, her heart rate returned to something approaching normal. She was able to look at Jamie without myriad emotions sending her thoughts in twenty different directions. Okay, Jamie was a terrific-looking guy. She'd known that, but he was also the major obstacle to her future happiness.

She cleared her throat. "So if you haven't brought the divorce papers, we're back to my original question. What are you doing here?"

He raised his eyebrows before staring pointedly at Louise.

''I get it,'' Louise said. She scurried back to the desk, grabbed her purse and the remainder of a crepe. Then she skirted around Jamie and Vicki and opened the door. ''You two kids have fun now. I've got too much to do to stay here and play referee.'' In the next moment she was gone, leaving a silence broken only by the thump of Beasley's tail on the hand-woven rug.

Vicki's ankle started to throb again, forcing her to sit on the arm of a Victorian parlor chair. She stared at Jamie, waiting for him to answer her question.

He looked down at his clothes—a pair of loose-fitting navy cargo shorts and a cotton shirt with a wild Hawaiian print. ''So even in this getup, you're not buying the vacation excuse?''

''Not for a sunny south-Florida second.''

He shrugged. ''Does a man have to have a reason for wanting to see his wife?''

''Oh, yes, when that wife is engaged to marry another man, he does.''

He froze, hands in his pockets. ''He proposed?''

It would have been easier to say yes, that Graham had given her the ring, but he hadn't, and without the piece of jewelry on her finger, she had no way to back up a lie. ''Well, no, not yet,'' she admitted.

Jamie nodded. ''Ah…''

''But getting a ring is only a formality. So if you came all the way down here just to continue—''

''I wanted to know how your ankle was.''

She lifted her ankle and raised the hem of her slacks. "It's much better, see?"

"And I thought you might need some help with your shop opening."

"I don't."

"Actually I thought you might want to order some puzzles as giveaways. They really do attract customers."

"I'll call you if I do."

He rubbed his thumb and forefinger down the corners of his mouth. "I'm running out of excuses."

Vicki tried not to smile. The man had just driven a thousand miles to see her. It was hard not to appreciate that kind of weird devotion, no matter how misplaced. "Look, Jamie, I'm flattered that you put forth all this effort to visit me, but it wouldn't be fair if I let you think that this…relationship, or whatever it is we shared for twenty-four hours, would ever amount to anything more than a night in a storm. You can't possibly believe that this so-called marriage of ours is real."

"But it is. Otherwise you wouldn't need a divorce to end it."

She expelled her frustration in a long sigh. "Yes, it's real legally. But certainly not emotionally. We're two completely different people and—"

"Isn't everyone?"

She scowled at him. "Now you're just trying to make me mad. You know what I mean. We live completely different lifestyles. We have different goals. We enjoy different things."

"We both enjoyed kissing each other."

An irrefutable point she would never admit to. "That shouldn't have happened," she insisted. "I'm involved with another man! I'm attracted to another man. I'm going to marry another man as soon as you—"

"Yeah, I know. As soon as I sign the papers. And as soon as he asks you."

"Stop making it sound as if that's not going to happen. He's going to ask. And I'm going to say yes."

Jamie opened his mouth as if he might actually argue with her. But the ringing of Vicki's phone stopped him from saying anything. She didn't jump up to answer it. Part of her was inexplicably curious to know how he would react to her pronouncement.

Jamie stared at her. "You want me to get that?"

His question brought her back to her senses and she stood up. "Good heavens, no!"

She limped across the room and grabbed the receiver from its cradle.

JAMIE LEANED DOWN and scratched behind Beasley's ear. "How do you think it's going so far?" he whispered. "I think she's kinda glad to see us."

Beasley yawned, as close to a sign of agreement as could be expected. Jamie sat in the chair Vicki had just vacated, even though his artistic instincts revolted at a shirt covered in pink hibiscus blossoms mingling so intimately with classic tapestry upholstery. He shouldn't have bought the shirt at Crazy Ed's souvenir shop at the Daytona exit of I-95. But once a guy's engines started running on impulse, it was hard to settle for simple unleaded common sense.

Across the room, Vicki answered the phone and slumped into the chair behind her desk. For a woman who, just a moment before, had enthusiastically berated him for coming to see her, Vicki's voice suddenly seemed tired, devoid of inflection. "Oh, hi, Mama. Yes, I'm still at the shop and..."

There was a pause before Vicki's next response. "Everything's going well, Mama. The shop will open on time. I told you I'd call midweek and give you the latest news."

She drummed her fingers on the desk. "What do you mean you couldn't wait that long? What's wrong now?"

The edge of irritation in her voice prompted Jamie to believe that the last question must be a frequent one.

She listened for a few minutes, trying every so often to interrupt her mother's obvious manipulation of the conversation. "No, Mama," she finally said, "I don't think Elwood is a crook. He's been fixing cars in Maple Grove for years. Everybody takes their vehicles to him."

Another silent minute passed. "How much did he say it would cost to get a new transmission for the truck?" Vicki closed her eyes as if drawing upon some well of inner strength. "That much? Yes, of course I know you hate to ask..."

Vicki's eyes connected with Jamie's for an instant, prompting her to turn her chair toward the wall behind her. He couldn't see her face any longer, but he still understood most of what she said.

"As soon as I can… Yes, I suppose I could wire it… I don't have a lot right now… I won't have until the shop starts producing an income… I know you do, Mama. Don't worry about it, okay? You've got to have transportation."

She slid the chair around to face the room again. "Yes, Mama, I'll still call you Wednesday. I've got to go now." She replaced the receiver, blew out a long breath and stared at the ceiling.

Jamie sensed the change in her. The essence of that phone call had drained the pluck right out of her.

After a moment she set her elbows on the desk and leaned her chin on her clasped hands. "You heard that, right?" she said to him.

He nodded once. "It was hard not to."

"In a way I'm glad you did. It might help you to understand."

"Understand what?"

"Why I married you in the first place."

"I didn't have any illusions back then about you wanting to help a poor Irish guy escape his troubles. I know you did it for the money."

She dropped her hands and leaned forward. "That's exactly right, Jamie. Maybe it wasn't a truck that needed fixing thirteen years ago. Maybe the mortgage needed paying, maybe the river was rising and flooding our barren fields. I don't even remember, but it was something dramatic—and costly—you can be sure."

''I never blamed you for marrying for money. My motives were equally self-serving.''

''Maybe, but don't you see? That day in the Orlando courthouse, you got what you wanted. My parents got what they wanted.'' She fixed him with a penetrating stare. ''Now, all these years later, I figure it has to be my turn to get what I want.''

''No argument from me on that point, Vicki. But I'm just here to satisfy myself about what that might be.''

She slowly shook her head. ''Why, Jamie? Why do you need to know what I want out of life?''

He chewed his bottom lip, thinking carefully about his answer. ''Because I've met you again. And you made me care about you, almost like a husband should care. It might sound crazy to you, but I haven't gotten you out of my mind these past few days. I may have to. I understand that. But maybe I just need to know that the life you want for yourself is a good one, and you're as sure as anyone can be about what's in your heart.''

She blew out another long breath. This one ruffled the hair on her forehead. ''You're either unbelievably kind or unbelievably naive. Or just hopelessly weird. But since you came all this way, I'll tell you what I want. I want this shop, and nice things, and a respectable man…''

He looked around the shop, at all her pretty collectibles. ''So you think husband number two and all these fancy things make you respectable?''

''Yes. No. Not entirely. I've earned my own respectability. I've worked hard to get where I am. Graham is the perfect man to enhance my capabilities. He's a symbol of what I've struggled to become. He'll support me and encourage me. He won't let me slip back to the person I was.''

''When you married me?''

''Yes. When I married you—for money. Wait till you meet him. Then you'll see what I'm talking about.''

A pleasant little tingle made Jamie grin. It was a start. He may not have worked his way into Vicki's heart, but it seemed he'd at least found a way into her confidence. At least he mattered, or his opinion did. ''So now I'm to meet this paragon of male virtue?''

She blushed, aware of the step toward familiarity she'd just taken. ''What I meant was, if you're going to be around for a while, you'll likely meet him.''

''I'll be around,'' he said, smiling. ''If only to see how you handle the introductions. But I'll leave you alone for tonight. Can I see you to your car?''

''No. It's just out the back door. I'll lock up when you leave.''

''All right, then.'' He picked up Beasley's leash and headed for the door.

''Do you have a place to stay?'' she asked.

''Just a couple blocks away, actually. A little apartment this nice lady rents by the week. She didn't even cringe when she saw Beasley, so I'm pretty certain she's an angel.''

''Oh, that's good.''

He stepped out the door but leaned in before closing

it. ‘‘What’s truly good is that *you* didn’t flinch when I said she rents the place by the week. And by the way, Vicki, in that list of Graham’s attributes, I don’t think you mentioned that you loved him. G’night, now.’’

VICKI’S HAND shook as she aimed her keys at the ignition. ‘‘Love! How ridiculous. Jamie is trying to turn every little thing I say—or don’t say—into…’’ She dropped her forehead to the steering wheel. ‘‘Forget about that, Victoria,’’ she said. ‘‘Think about what you’ve done.’’ She backed her car out and headed toward the narrow, palm-lined street and her cottage while repeating the words she’d just spoken to Jamie. ‘‘‘Wait until you meet him’! *Good God, what was I thinking?* Nothing good can come from a meeting between Jamie and Graham.’’

The light from her porch glowed a warm welcome as she pulled into her driveway. ‘‘Maybe, just maybe, I can salvage this situation,’’ she said to herself as the initial panic began to subside. ‘‘In fact, a meeting between the two might work to my advantage. If Jamie actually sees Graham face-to-face, he’ll have to admit that Graham is a potent force in my life, one that’s not going to go away just because Jamie and Beasley have come to Fort Lauderdale.’’

Settling her purse strap over her shoulder, she locked her car and climbed the two steps to her door. ‘‘But what if something slips? What if Jamie says something? What if *I* do?’’ She stepped inside and sank into the nearest chair. ‘‘No, this meeting is definitely not worth the risk.’’

A few minutes later, she filled her kettle with water, set it on a burner and took a teacup from a nineteenth-century breakfront. Sitting at a table to wait for the water to boil, she considered another option. ‘‘Maybe they won't meet, after all. Graham is a busy man. His time at the shop is limited.’’ She chewed on a fingernail. ‘‘But then again, he's so anxious about this opening and the container arriving from Amsterdam that lately he shows up when I least expect him. In the next week, he'll probably be around more than usual.’’

A full week! Jamie had definitely said he was renting an apartment by the week. Did that mean one week? Or possibly two? No. She'd just have to convince him to leave town.

The kettle's shrill whistle made Vicki scurry to the stove. She hung a teabag over the lip of her cup and poured in steaming water. The sweet aroma of lemon-scented tea wafted to her nostrils, calming her. A week. Funny. Jamie's announcement that he'd come to stay for that length of time should have sent her spiraling to the edge of panic. Instead, the thought of Jamie living practically in her own neighborhood chilled her blood to icewater at the same time as it warmed her to the tips of her toes.

Vicki scowled into her cup. ‘‘Ridiculous. If I feel warm, it's definitely the tea!’’

CHAPTER NINE

JAMIE WALKED to the end of the block and turned off the Boulevard onto the shady street where his apartment was located. He took a deep breath, savoring the blended aromas of flowering shrubs, specialty restaurants and sea air. The shoreline of the Atlantic was less than a mile away.

"Balmy," he said aloud, and looked down at Beasley, trotting at his heels, for the moment giving in to the constraints of his leash. "This is what the word means, boy. Warm breezes, clear skies, palm leaves whispering over our heads like the hum of cicadas. I know what you're thinking, though. The stars don't have quite the twinkle of a Pintail Point evening, but they do have a certain charm."

Jamie was feeling pretty good. Vicki hadn't exactly been glad to see them tonight. But she hadn't thrown them out, either. "We still have a chance with her," he informed the dog.

Maybe sensing they were approaching their temporary living quarters, Beasley lunged forward with surprising alacrity.

"Whoa, hold on, Beas," Jamie said, quickening his own pace. He chuckled at the way the dog fought the constraints of collar and leash. "I don't think you'll ever get the hang of this 'heel' and 'go' thing."

The pair turned into the parking area of the yellow, one-story stucco building of six one-bedroom apartments. They walked past Jamie's pickup and were approaching the front door when Jamie heard the phone ring in the truck. He stopped, tugged a reluctant Beasley in the opposite direction. He reached into the cab and picked up the phone, immediately recognizing the number on the display as Bobbi Lee's. Jamie flexed his shoulders, an attempt to relax tightening muscles and pressed the connect button. "Hello."

The voice that responded was angry and impatient. "It's about time you answered," Bobbi Lee said. "I've left four messages. What the blazes are you doing going to Florida, as if I didn't know. And don't even think about lying to me, Jamie Malone!"

"I don't have any reason to lie to you, Bobbi Lee," he said.

"Oh, no? Then why didn't you let me know you were going? Or at least call me when you got there?"

"I did call you. I left a message a few hours ago with my local phone number here. You obviously got the message since you know I'm in Florida."

"You should have phoned before you left. It would have been the decent thing to do."

Jamie shook his head, looked down at Beasley with the hope of at least getting a sympathetic nod. The dog yawned, angled his large head toward the apartment—no sympathy there. "Bobbi Lee, I don't have to report my whereabouts to you. We're not married...or even seeing each other anymore.''

She responded with a squawk. ''That was mean, Jamie.''

''Sorry, but it's the truth.''

''You could have called the boys,'' she said. ''They depend on you.''

''No, they don't. They get along just fine whenever I'm out of town. And besides, Bobbi Lee, it's your job to tell them what they need to know. You're their mother.''

Her voice changed, lowered, assumed a plaintive tone. ''They love you, Jamie. You have responsibilities here.''

He leaned against the hood of the truck and massaged the nape of his neck. He was suddenly tired. ''You know I care about your boys, Bobbi, but this has nothing to do with any responsibilities I've taken on with regard to Charlie or Brian since you and I broke up ten years ago. This is entirely about what you feel I owe *you,* and we're never going to agree—''

''I can make them hate you, Jamie. Don't think I can't.''

''I suppose you could, but since that wouldn't serve any purpose, you won't. Besides, you're too good a mother. You'd only end up hating yourself.''

She sighed, a long, slow breath of capitulation. ''Damn it, Jamie. Well, then, think about me. Nearly everybody in town knows about this trip of yours. How do you think it makes me look? What will people say about our relationship?''

"What they've always said. What every last soul in Bayberry Cove knows and hasn't bothered to talk about for years now. That you and I were close at one time. Because of that, I help you with the boys, and I've always tried to be the best friend to them I can be—and the best friend to you. Nothing's changed." He steeled himself to repeat what he'd been saying to Bobbi Lee ever since Brian was born and she'd tried to make him believe that he was the boy's biological father. "And it never will."

"Maybe I'm sick and tired of your friendship, Jamie."

"It is what it is, Bobbi Lee, nothing more, nothing less. I've tried to be fair to you and help any way I could since Brian came along. You know I care about you."

Her voice was harsh. "You don't care about me. You'll always believe that I lied about you being Brian's father just so you'd marry me."

"Don't bring that up again, Bobbi."

"I honestly thought you were his father," she went on. "I was going through a bad time. I was confused. You and I were drawing apart..."

Jamie stopped listening to the excuses he'd heard countless times. Unfortunately Bobbi Lee's claims about Brian's parentage were never corroborated by medical evidence—or timing. Jamie's relationship with her had started to sour weeks before she became pregnant. "Look, Bobbi," he interrupted. "It doesn't matter. I've loved Bri since the day he was born." *Even after it broke my heart to learn he wasn't mine.*

"But you don't love me."

"No, I don't, and when we were together you claimed you didn't love me, either, and you weren't looking for a long-term relationship. But let's not go over this ground again. You and I will never be more than the good friends we are right now."

He'd missed all the signs with Bobbi Lee back then. She'd insisted that all she wanted was a casual fling, and he'd believed her. After all, she already had a kid and one divorce in her background. She wasn't looking for another entanglement.

There was an uncomfortable silence. After a moment she said, "Tell me again why you married this woman."

He'd never told Bobbi Lee the real reason he married Vicki. Too many people knew already. "We were young, Bobbi," he said. "We didn't know what we wanted." It wasn't really a lie, except that one of them wanted money and the other a green card.

"And now, all of a sudden, you've decided you want her back?"

"I don't know. Maybe. But, Bobbi, you're making canyons out of sidewalk cracks. Besides, Vicki's in love with another man."

"That's right," she said almost cheerfully. "I don't know what makes you think you can change her mind. You'll just end up looking like a fool, Jamie Malone."

"You might be right."

"Just remember, I'll be here when you come back nursing a broken heart."

He said goodbye and disconnected. All at once he didn't feel nearly so confident about his chances with Vicki.

THE DAY AFTER Jamie's arrival, Vicki tried to concentrate on decorating the shop. She removed one of several nails she'd been holding between her lips and tapped it into the wall above an eighteenth-century English sideboard. Then she hung a painting from the same era over the piece of furniture. She wanted to see if the painting was level, but from her close perspective on the third step of a ladder, it was hard to tell.

A voice from behind her settled the matter. "Lower the right side a little."

She whirled around, grabbing the backsplash of the sideboard to maintain her balance. "Jamie! How did you get in here?" Her words were mumbled. She took the nails from her mouth. "The doors are locked," she said clearly.

"Not the back one. I could be an ordinary crook come in to rob you."

"I doubt that," she said. "There's nothing ordinary about you."

He gave her that little crooked smile she'd found herself thinking about ever since she'd been to Pintail Point. She tried not to dwell on it now by focusing on Beasley. "What are you two doing here?"

"I discovered something about vacations," he said. "There's not a whole lot you can do if your only companion is a big, lumbering canine. There aren't many places that will let dogs in."

Beasley headed straight for a hand-sewn silk pillow made more than a century ago in Japan. He tramped on top and turned around several times, scratching the fabric to desirable plumpness and lay down. Vicki frowned. ''I'm not sure this shop should be one of them.''

Jamie followed her gaze and rushed over to the dog. ''No, Beas. What did I tell you about minding your manners in this store?'' He swatted the dog's hind quarters and Beasley ambled over to the rug he'd found acceptable the night before. ''Is that okay?''

''Yes, I guess so.'' Vicki smiled at the dog and wondered how Graham would react if he saw the mutt on one of her shop's valuable Mideastern imports. She lowered the right side of the painting. ''So how'd you sleep?'' she asked before slipping the nails between her teeth again and focusing on the paintings at the base of the ladder.

''Like a rock.''

That makes one of us, she thought, remembering her restless night. Pointing to the next oil painting on the floor, she muttered around the nails, ''Hand me that picture, will you?''

''Sure, but let me do that.''

''I can do it.''

He didn't argue. Instead, he studied the subject of the canvas and compared it to the similar one she'd already hung. ''Fox hunts,'' he said. ''A brutal practice, really. I hear the Brits have finally wised up and decided to abolish the barbaric tradition.''

She took the nails out of her mouth and set them

on the sideboard. ''I don't know about that, but these paintings are popular in libraries and reading rooms. Because of the debts I've accumulated lately, I can't be too concerned with their political correctness.''

''That's because you're not a fox.'' He paused, smiled, looking up at her with an intensity that put her already fragile nerves on edge. ''Well, come to think of it, you *are* a fox,'' he said. ''Isn't that a term for a pretty woman?''

She wiggled her fingers with impatience, determined to derail such personal chatter. ''Hand up the painting, please.''

He did—just as a key turned in the front door. Vicki froze, her fingers hooked around the gilded frame she'd just accepted from Jamie. Only one other person had a key to the store. She slowly turned her head. ''Graham!'' Reacting to her trembling limbs, the ladder wobbled like a living thing. One of Jamie's hands immediately steadied it while the other one closed around Vicki's calf.

She gave him back the painting, partly so she could step safely down from the ladder, but mostly so he would remove his hand from her leg. ''I...I didn't expect you till later,'' she said to Graham. ''I thought you'd be in your office all day.''

Graham's gaze was fixed solidly on Jamie's face, though he spoke to Vicki. ''I intended to be. But something came up.'' Still scrutinizing Jamie, he said, ''You're a workman?''

''Ordinarily,'' Jamie answered. ''But not today. Today I'm a vacationer.''

Graham darted a quick glance at Vicki before returning his attention to Jamie. "The shop's not open yet, you know," he said.

"That's okay. I'm not shopping."

"Then what...?"

Vicki walked over to Graham and put her hand on the sleeve of his shirt. He'd obviously left his suit jacket in his car, but he still looked boardroom polished. Almost too perfect, she thought for the first time since she'd met him. She hoped he wouldn't feel her hand trembling through the shirt fabric. "Let me introduce you," she said, and then realized she was totally unprepared.

Damn! All through her nightly tea ritual, her shower and bed preparations, and even while she'd punched her pillow and tried every sleep-inducing exercise she'd ever heard of, she'd completely forgotten to come up with an explanation for Jamie's presence. She stared at Graham. She stared at Jamie. They were both waiting for her to say something.

"This is Jamie Malone," she finally managed to mumble.

Silence. Obviously something more was needed.

Jamie walked over and stuck out his hand. "I'm her cousin. On her mother's side."

Graham frowned slightly, took Jamie's hand and shook it without enthusiasm. "Your accent. You're Irish, aren't you?"

There was condescension in his voice, as if he'd really meant to say, "You're one of Satan's minions, aren't you?"

"Born and bred," Jamie answered.

Graham withdrew his hand and studied Jamie's face. "I didn't know you were part Irish," he finally said to Vicki.

The moment's pause had been enough time for her to prepare a continuation of the explanation. "I'm not. My mother's sister married a Malone. It's my uncle who's Irish. Jamie is their son."

"Ah..." Graham nodded slowly, unaware that Beasley had stood up from his costly Persian sleeping mat and was approaching enthusiastically, ready to make a new friend. Seconds later a horrified Graham jumped back at least three feet. He stared in disgust at a pool of canine saliva in the center of his hand and then gave a venomous look at its source. "What the hell is that?"

Jamie stuck his foot in front of the dog, keeping him from continuing his tactile exploration of Graham. "Sorry," he said. "I guess you could say this is *my* cousin, Beasley Malone. So to speak."

Graham scowled. "Cute." Then he looked around for something to wipe his hand on and finally settled on a piece of paper from the tray of Vicki's printer. "Good God. That is one outrageous-looking animal."

Jamie shrugged. "Yeah, I know what you mean. I'm the brains of the family, but Beas and Vicki obviously got all the beauty."

Graham crumpled the paper and tossed it into the wastebasket. Then he whispered to Vicki, "What is that beast doing in the shop?"

"Just visiting," she said. "Don't get excited."

Hoping Jamie would take the hint and give them some privacy, she waved her hand behind her back as she led Graham to the chair behind her desk. "Sit down, Graham. Tell me what happened today." She sat on the corner of the desk and noted that while Jamie hadn't left, he was at least making himself and Beasley inconspicuous in another part of the showroom.

Graham's face paled as he reached for Vicki's hand. "It's a disaster, Victoria. I came right away to tell you."

"What? Is someone ill?"

"Nothing like that. I almost wish it were—I could call a doctor. No, this is news from our import broker."

Something must have gone terribly wrong with the shipment of antiques from the Netherlands. "Is it the container?" she asked. "It's not going to arrive on time?" She looked around the shop at all the beautiful items she and Graham had acquired, as well as the ones she'd selected herself. "That's not so bad. The store looks wonderful even without the additional pieces."

He groaned, dismissing her attempt to make him feel better. "No, no, that's not it. The shipment arrived in port yesterday."

Then what was the problem? "That's good news, isn't it?"

"It should be, but the broker called an hour ago to tell me that the container had been unloaded from the ship, but soon after, the damned customs officials hauled it off to the shed."

"The shed? What are you talking about? What shed?"

His facial muscles tightened as if it was all he could do to control his temper with a misbehaving child. "Victoria, weren't you listening when the broker explained all this to us?"

She remembered the lengthy meeting with the broker weeks before. Of course she'd listened. For the most part. But this container of antiques had been Graham's project from the beginning. He had made the contact in Amsterdam and selected the pieces. Her name was merely a formality on the bill of lading. So, yes, she'd listened, but obviously not well enough. "Perhaps you'd better tell me again, Graham," she finally said.

"When a container is sent to the shed, that's the worst thing that can happen. Ideally you want the trailer hooked up to a rig right away and delivered from the shipyard to the point of destination—in this case, your shop."

"Yes, I understand. So why wasn't our container shipped here? We did all the paperwork properly. Your man in Amsterdam listed all the items in the container and evaluated each one for import fees, right? We did everything according to the book."

"Yes, of course we did, but sometimes all the preparation in the world can't make up for bureaucratic interference." Graham clenched his hands on the desk until his knuckles turned white. "Any damned customs official can shove his weight around and have any container sent to the shed for inspection. It can be a totally random thing or based on some little detail that doesn't look right to him. Something like the seal being broken or a—'' Graham glared at Beasley ''—bloody dog sniffing around the closure. Less than ten percent of the containers get stopped this way. It's bad luck that ours was one of them.''

Vicki followed Graham's gaze and focused on Jamie and Beasley. The dog lay quietly beside him, blissfully unaware that Graham had just cursed his entire species. Unlike Jamie who, Vicki was certain, was acutely aware of everything being said.

''How long will this inspection take?'' she asked Graham.

''I don't know. The broker says it can take a few days, a week. As long as the officials want it to take.''

''But they won't find anything in the container that isn't on the bill of lading, will they?'' She leaned away from Graham when he pinned her with a threatening glare.

''Of course not. How could you even think such a thing?''

She ran a hand down his arm in an effort to soothe him. ''I'm just asking. You've got to relax, Graham. Everything will be all right. The inspectors will probably finish in a couple of days and send the container to the shop. There's still a good chance we'll have it by Saturday for the opening. And even if we don't, we'll be fine.'' She smiled at him. ''I'm very proud of all our work. You should be, too, even if the container doesn't get here on time.''

The look he gave her was blatantly patronizing.

''You don't understand, Victoria,'' he said. ''I need those pieces here. Not days from now, but today. I won't draw a normal breath thinking about those goons at customs ripping apart the valuable furniture that was personally selected for this opening.''

She withdrew her hand and threaded her fingers together. ''There's nothing we can do about it, Graham. My mother didn't teach me much, but she was fond of pointing out that if the river's rising, you may as well relax, because there's nothing you can do till the sun shines.''

''Great. Pearls of Indiana-farm wisdom. Just what I need to hear.''

Vicki glanced at Jamie, who seemed totally absorbed in a leather-bound Dickens novel.

''Frankly, Graham, your reaction surprises me,'' she said. ''For some reason you've placed entirely too much importance on this shipment and a totally random act by a customs official.''

Graham pressed his lips together, obviously trying to control his response. He stood, rolled each shoulder separately, took a long breath and faced her with a semblance of a smile on his face. ''You're right, darling. I don't know what came over me. Of course this will all work out in the end.'' He reached for her hand and held it between his. ''Forgive me, Vic? I'm just nervous, I guess. Mother and Father will be seeing the shop for the first time. I want everything to be perfect.''

She curled her fingers around his knuckles. ''It will be, Graham. Your parents will adore the shop.''

He leaned over and kissed her, a brief peck on the lips. Then he nodded toward Jamie. ''What about your cousin? Will he be at the opening?''

She pulled her hand free of Graham's grasp and stood up. ''I don't know. Maybe. He hasn't told me how long he'll be here.''

''He's not staying at your place, is he?''

She shook her head.

''Good. I'll be over later with dinner from La Maison. What do you feel like? Lobster crepes? With chardonnay or zinfandel?''

Stew. I feel like having stew. The totally inappropriate answer popped into her head and almost made it through her lips. ''I don't know. I had crepes last night. Louise brought them over.''

Graham took her into his arms. She leaned against him, searching for the comfort and familiarity of the man she knew and trusted. The confident man who didn't panic over late shipments and interrupted schedules. He whispered into her ear, ''No problem. I'll surprise you with something.''

With his confidence seemingly back in place, Graham strode to the door. Jamie acknowledged his leaving with a half smile and salute. Beasley took a few steps toward him, his toenails clicking on the wood floor.

''Hey, Jim,'' Graham called. ''Keep the beast away from me, okay?''

Jamie snapped his fingers and Beasley returned. ''It's Jamie,'' he said. ''And you don't have to worry about Beas. I don't think he particularly liked the taste of you.''

Graham slammed the door behind him, leaving Jamie and Vicki alone in the shop. Vicki stood silently for a moment waiting for Jamie to say something. She didn't have long to wait.

He nodded, chewed on his lower lip a moment and said, ''Great guy. A lot of fun.''

She frowned. ''He is. Really. Most of the time. When he's not so uptight about things.''

''Oh, sure,'' Jamie pretended to agree. ''I'm just not convinced that he's the right man for my wife...*or* my cousin.'' He grabbed the hammer and climbed the ladder. ''How's your ankle feeling?''

She squinted up at him. ''Fine. Why?''

''Hand up the rest of those paintings and let's get this job done. After that, you're taking Beas and me to the beach.''

CHAPTER TEN

JAMIE HELD UP the piece of driftwood he'd snagged and studied its gnarled appearance. Then he flung it in a beautiful arc fifty yards ahead. Beasley watched it sail and waited patiently for it to land before lumbering after it. When he had secured the wood between his teeth, he sat, his tail making a half-moon sweep in the loose sand.

Vicki, her khaki pants rolled above her knees and her sandals dangling from her hand, sloshed beside Jamie in the shallows as they followed the dog. "I don't get it," she said. "Why doesn't Beasley bring it back to you?"

Jamie grinned at her. "Don't you know by now that Beasley is the smartest dog that ever lived?" He let a smug expression take the seriousness from his next words. "And I taught him everything he knows. Like patience, for instance. See how he sits there watching us come closer?"

"Yes, I see that." She was clearly skeptical as to whether or not that constituted animal intelligence. "I suppose you're going to tell me he's being patient because he knows I have a bum ankle."

Jamie laughed. "It might be that, too. But I taught

him an important life lesson. Never risk breaking your neck chasing what's coming to you, anyway. Why should he run the stick back to me when I'm walking toward him?''

Vicki nodded, her lips pressed together to hold in a chuckle. ''Brilliant. I can believe you taught him that. From what I saw of your existence on Pintail Point, you seem to be an expert at waiting for the rest of the world to come to you.''

''I suppose, but I've done my share of chasing goals that are worth the pursuit.'' He looked straight ahead and picked up his pace as he added, ''Not too long ago I drove a thousand miles just to see a girl.''

Beasley rose to meet him, and Jamie took the stick from the dog's mouth. ''Take a breather, pal,'' he said. ''We got to give the lady time to catch up.'' Vicki had lagged behind after his last comment. When she reached them, her face was flushed. From exertion in the late-afternoon sun? He doubted it.

Tucking the driftwood under his arm, Jamie walked to the shore and stared out at the ocean. Colorful sails dotted the horizon. ''Beautiful, isn't it? Just enough breeze to kick those single-masted beauties into overdrive. Not like the power-packing gusts of Currituck Sound before the storm.''

Her gaze followed his. ''No, but those were beautiful, too. In a savage, terrifying, nail-biting way.''

He looked at her and laughed. ''You convinced me you were terrified. Even I'll admit I prefer this to the sea in advance of Imogene. So how often do you come here?''

"To the ocean?"

"Yeah."

"Almost never. I haven't walked on the beach in probably two years."

That surprised him. She seemed to belong here, her eyes bright, her tawny hair loose and dazzling in the sun. "Why not? You live so close."

She turned toward him, her features suddenly very still. "How do you know where I live?"

He winced inwardly at his blunder. Now he'd come off looking like a stalker. "I just assumed—"

"No, you didn't. You absolutely know where I live."

"Okay, I know. I've always known your addresses."

"You've kept track of me?"

"Not you exactly. Just your addresses. It seemed like information I ought to have." Her jaw dropped and he tried to put her at ease. "Don't look at me like that. You are my wife. I don't think having your address makes me a pervert."

After a moment she capitulated with a nod. "Okay. But if I hadn't come to see you, would you ever have contacted me?"

"Sure. If I'd heard you won the lottery, I'd have come to claim my half."

"And if you'd heard something terrible, like I'd ended up in prison?"

"I'd have asked for conjugal visits."

She arched her eyebrows. "That I can believe, too. May I?" She tugged at the stick of driftwood tucked under his arm, and Jamie released it. Dangling it in front of the dog's eager eyes, she said, "You ready?" She threw the stick and Beasley repeated his previous performance, waiting until the driftwood landed before he gave chase. Vicki began walking, favoring her sore ankle just a little. Jamie fell into step beside her.

"Seriously," she said after a moment, "why didn't you ever get in touch with me?"

"The same reason you didn't call me most likely. If I'd contacted you, it would probably have been to get a divorce. But until recently, neither of us ever found anybody to match that glorious hour we spent together in Orlando."

"That was one glorious hour all right. One that has haunted me more times that I'd care to admit."

He grinned. "Good. I like knowing I've been in your fantasies—even the scary ones."

She walked on, smiling slightly before she said, "Haven't you ever met someone and fallen in love? Didn't you want to marry and break the tie with me?"

It was a good question, and the answer required some consideration. They'd reached Beasley now, and figuring Vicki had walked enough for one day, Jamie took the stick, turned around and headed back toward the pickup.

"Well?" she said, keeping pace with him.

"Give me a minute," he responded. "Such a serious question deserves a serious answer."

There had been women in Jamie's life. Some of them had been spectacular. Bright, passionate, intelligent women who'd made him laugh and who'd held his interest for a while. But something had always happened. Something had always extinguished the dazzle and kept him from proposing. And before those women, there had been Bobbi Lee. And his mother when she came from Ireland. It's not like he didn't have a family of sorts to sustain him. Not the conventional family to be sure, but family nonetheless.

"Nope, never did. As I see it, there's only one reason to marry, and that's when you meet someone who fills a void you never knew was there until that someone came into your life."

Vicki looked down at the sand and smiled. "Okay. But what about Bobbi Lee? Doesn't she fill that void?"

"Bobbi's important to me," he said. "But we'll never marry."

"Oh?"

She seemed surprised. Maybe, if he used his imagination, even a little pleased. "So what about kids?" she asked. "Do you hope to have any?"

"Kids are great," he said. "Bayberry Cove's full of them. The fact is, I've never met one I didn't like. Bobbi Lee's got a couple of boys. We're close. I suppose I'm like a substitute father to them. We do a lot of things together. And I teach a bit of wood carving to some of the local youngsters."

Vicki appeared thoughtful. "You'd be a good father. Obviously you enjoy kids." She paused. "And you don't take yourself too seriously. You're fun. Kids need that from a parent." She scrunched up her nose in a sign of distaste. ''Take it from me, the daughter of Ma and Pa Dismal.''

He smiled. ''So what about you?'' he asked. ''How do you feel about kids?''

''I suppose they're okay. As long as they're somebody else's. I'm not comfortable with the thought of having kids of my own. I've never thought of myself as particularly good mother material.''

Jamie wouldn't have been more shocked at her response if she'd said, ''Kids? Why, I have five of them.''

''I don't understand,'' he said. ''Why don't you think you'd make a good mother?''

''I don't know,'' she answered. ''It's just a feeling I have. Some people are cut out to be parents, and some aren't. I've never been at ease with kids, though I haven't been around many. I'm an only child, and we lived in the country so I never had many friends my own age.'' They'd reached the truck, and she leaned against the passenger door. ''It's definitely a subject Graham and I have to discuss.''

Still dazed from the unexpected revelation, Jamie gazed at her across the hood of the truck. ''I'd say you'd better, and soon.''

''Graham wants kids,'' she continued. ''He'd certainly be a good provider.''

''A provider of what?'' he asked sarcastically. ''All that fun you recommend?''

The sarcasm was a mistake. From the look on Vicki's face he knew what was coming. She immediately jumped to her boyfriend's defense.

"Graham can be fun! He's lots of fun!"

Jamie tapped the side of the cargo area, the sign for Beasley to jump inside. Then he put his palms up in a gesture of surrender. "Okay, I believe you. Ol' Graham seems like a real good-time fella."

Vicki climbed in the passenger side. "I know you don't mean that," she said when they were both inside, "but you saw him at his worst. He was upset over that whole thing with the customs officials. You don't know how hard Graham has worked to make this opening a success for me."

Convinced there was no way to salvage the afternoon, Jamie turned the key in the ignition and blurted out the first stupid thing that came to his mind. "Maybe he's worked hard, but all I've seen so far is you on that ladder."

Vicki stiffened and stared straight ahead. "Hurry up. I have to get back. It's getting dark."

They rode to the shop in silence. When he pulled next to Vicki's car, he turned off the engine and draped his arm over the steering wheel. "I apologize," he said. "I shouldn't have made that wisecrack about Graham. I hardly know the guy."

She looked down at her hands clasped in her lap. And then surprised the hell out of him. "No, don't apologize," she said. "You're right. Graham hasn't been very involved in the physical aspect of setting up the shop. He hasn't painted or papered. I've met with the workmen and stayed on top of things. I suppose I never really thought about that until you mentioned it. But Graham has a full-time job. And he's been actively involved in acquiring inventory. So I don't mind, really.'' She sighed. ''I'm just grateful to have someone show interest in something I care about in any way at all.''

The melancholy edge in her voice touched a sympathetic chord in Jamie. ''Well, sure,'' he said. ''You know how we men are, anyway. If you hand us a roll of wallpaper, we're just as likely to use it to jot down football scores.''

She gave him a sideways glance. ''Graham wouldn't do that.''

Right. Not Mr. Perfect...

Then she giggled. ''Polo matches maybe...''

Vicki was actually poking fun at her intended. Jamie leaned back against the driver's seat and watched the play of light from a pink dusk on her face. Her skin was still rosy from the wind. Her hair was a mass of shimmering sunlight rippling to her shoulders in unaccustomed disarray. She was beautiful, and yet somehow tragic because of her lack of confidence in herself.

Her lips trembled as she smiled almost timidly at him. ''Why are you staring at me like that?''

'''Cause you look so pretty.''

She flipped a tangle of hair over her shoulder. ''I do not. I look a mess.''

He reached over and took several strands between his thumb and forefinger. ''You look like you've been having fun. Like maybe for a few minutes you quit worrying about grand openings and bothersome ex- and future husbands.''

She touched his hand. ''I did have fun today. Thanks. I've never thrown a stick for a dog on the beach before.''

He leaned closer. ''Want to try something else new?''

She squinted suspiciously. ''Like what?''

He dropped his hand to her shoulder. ''Want to see what it's like to be kissing cousins?''

Her eyes widened. She shrugged free of his grasp. ''I know what it's like to be kissed by you.''

''Yeah, and it's pretty good, isn't it. But now we're adding the illicit aspect of our blood relationship. We're pretending that your mother is my mother's sister. That's heavy. It makes kissing dangerous, as well as sensational.''

She glared at him, obviously not amused. ''Stop joking. This is my life you're making fun of, and it's no joke.''

''I know it isn't. And I'm not laughing.'' He inched to the edge of his seat. She backed up to her door. He inched closer. ''The truth is,'' he said, ''the last thing I want to be to you is your cousin.'' He reached around and slipped his hand between the back of her head and the window. Her body tensed, but just for an instant. She didn't stop him when he pulled her close and pressed his mouth to hers. She let out a breath, a kind of here-we-go-again sigh that soon mutated to a low, slow moan of pleasure.

Whatever he was doing, it was working, so he kissed her soundly, thoroughly, leaving no doubt that the kiss was not enough for him. Then he drew away.

"You'd better go. I can smell Graham's dinner from here. I think it's coming from your porch."

"Jamie—"

"If you're going to yell at me, Vicki, please don't. I've only got a few days. You're planning to give Graham the rest of your life. I've got to make use of every minute."

"You're impossible."

"No. I'm entirely *possible,* sweetheart. The most possible thing in your life right now if you only realized it."

She stared at him a moment longer as if trying to figure him out, or maybe figure herself out, and then she opened her door and stepped into the parking lot. Jamie thought she might flee to her own vehicle without a backward glance, but she didn't. She reached into the cargo section of the truck and gave Beasley a quick scratch behind his ears. After that, she climbed into her car and strapped on the seat belt. She threw Jamie a look he couldn't interpret in the darkness. "See you tomorrow," Jamie called as she backed out of the lot. And in the shadows, he detected the wild dance of her hair as she shook her head.

Jamie leaned over and reopened the passenger door. He whistled once. Beasley jumped out of the truck bed and bounded into the cab. He sat upright in Vicki's seat, waiting for Jamie to drive off.

Instead, Jamie watched Vicki's taillights disappear around a corner. He took a deep breath. "That was a revelation, wasn't it, Beas?" he said. "Can you imagine that wonderful, sensitive woman believing she wouldn't be a good mother?'' He ruffled the scruffy wires that passed for fur on Beasley's head. ''Heck, she's even good to you, and if any creature ever had a face only a mother could love, it's you, mate.''

He started the engine and backed the truck up. ''But that's not all, boy,'' he added. ''I can't shake this feeling I have about the sterling Mr. Townsend. Something's definitely going on with that shipment of antiques. Ol' Graham's too uptight even for a nose-in-the-air aristocrat.'' He looked over at Beasley. ''What do ya' say? Want to do a little sleuthing?''

The dog's answer was to twist himself into a pretzel that allowed him to miraculously fit his entire awkward body into a sleeping position on the truck seat. Then he closed his eyes and nodded off immediately. Jamie put the truck in gear and headed toward his apartment. ''I guess you'd better recover from stick-fetching before I pile on any more responsibility,'' he said.

It was dark when Jamie pulled into an empty spot at his apartment building and got out of his truck. He noticed the dark BMW parked across the street, but didn't pay much attention to the occupant until the driver's door opened, illuminating the interior of the car.

''Well, well, what's this?'' he whispered to Beasley as Vicki's friend Louise Duncan climbed out, activated her beeper car lock and walked toward him. She held out her hand and he shook it. ''And to what do I owe the privilege of this visit, Miz Lady Attorney?''

"You and I need to talk about some things," she said, motioning to his building. "May I come in?"

He shrugged. "Sure. I don't have much to offer in the way of niceties for visitors. Mostly we just have kibble."

She walked ahead of him, all slinky hips and long, shapely legs barely concealed under the short skirt of a tailored business suit. "Don't sell yourself short, Mr. Malone," she said. "You have more to offer than you think."

Jamie waggled his eyebrows at Beasley, but the gesture was lost on a creature who was basically immune to feminine wiles of the two-legged variety. He stepped around Louise at the entrance to his apartment and unlocked the door. Sweeping his arm to the inside, he invited her in. "Have a seat, Miss Duncan," he said. He went to the refrigerator and surveyed its contents. "I can give you a beer if you're interested."

She sat on the striped Danish sofa and crossed her legs. "That'll be fine. Have you got one for yourself?"

"Just so happens I do." He popped the tops off two beers and brought them to the coffee table. Louise took one from his hand, swallowed a generous amount and set the bottle down.

"So what brings you to my little vacation retreat?" he asked, sitting down on the opposite end of the sofa.

"Curiosity." She looked him straight in the eye. "I'd like to know just what game you and your attorney are playing, Mr. Malone."

He halted the rise of his own bottle to his lips and stared at her. Then he lifted it the rest of the way, took a swig and set it down next to hers. "Call me Jamie, Louise," he said. "It's all right if I call you Louise?"

She nodded.

"Good. As long as we're not pulling any punches here, I figure it's only fitting. As for what games we're playing, you're an attorney. I would assume you already know the rules."

"Oh, I do, and rule number one is, if a document is letter perfect, like the one I sent to North Carolina with Vicki, you should sign it. If you don't, then you're obviously stalling for time. Your little country lawyer appears to know this, as well. He may be adding a line or two about protecting your interests in perpetuity, but my guess is, the tactic is just to give you time to antagonize my client."

Jamie leaned back into the sofa and put his elbow on the rear cushion. "Has your client complained about being antagonized?"

"No, but she will. And if you think otherwise, you don't know her." Louise took another swallow of beer and used her finger to wipe a film of suds from her upper lip. "Vicki doesn't want you, Jamie. She's made it clear, but you don't seem to get the message." Louise reached behind her head, grabbed the mass of her stick-straight hair and twisted it into a shiny black column over one shoulder. "Frankly, between you and me, I don't get it, but that stuffy Graham Townsend is the man Vicki wants. He has been from the moment they met at an antique show last winter."

"Things can change," Jamie said.

"They won't."

''I have one distinct advantage over Graham. I'm married to Vicki.''

''You're spitting into the wind, Malone. That claim won't work, and you know it. Graham represents everything Vicki has worked for since she wised up and walked off the farm. He's a glossy, pedigreed, six-foot-two-inch package of culture and refinement. He's also an asshole, but Vicki apparently doesn't see that.''

''I can change her mind.''

''You?'' Louise scooted closer to him on the sofa and also raised her elbow to rest on the back cushion near Jamie's. Her hand dangled within inches of his. At the movement, the deep V of her blouse separated, giving him an eagle's-eye view of tempting cleavage. ''How much do you really know about your wife?''

''I'm learning.''

''Not enough, obviously.'' Louise leaned toward him. He swallowed. Hard.

''Do you know she was raised in conditions barely above the poverty line with parents who didn't have the sensitivity to raise a pig? And that because of the constant pressure and guilt they've laid on her, she's scared to death to have kids of her own for fear she'll mess up the job of raising them? Vicki lived a hand-to-mouth existence until she finally got the guts to break away from those indolent, self-serving parasites who irresponsibly gave birth to her and totally screwed up her life.''

Jamie didn't think he'd phrase Vicki's background quite that way, but he was grateful for the straightforward insight into her past. ''Actually I surmised a few of those details.''

''Then you should know that for Vicki, comparing Graham Townsend to the clod-busting Nils Sorenson, is like comparing gold to charcoal. Graham represents the life she wants for herself. His ancestors came to America on the freaking *Mayflower.*'' She took a swig of beer, draining the bottle. ''And I know how you got to America, Jamie, and we won't be celebrating any holidays to commemorate that historic event.''

He deliberately gave her an enigmatic smile. He didn't like Louise Duncan, but he had to admire her. ''You're a right hard biscuit, aren't you, Counselor?''

''If you mean that I'm tough, then yes. I have to be.'' She curled a hand over Jamie's thigh. ''But don't get me wrong, Malone. I like you. You're everything Graham is not, and while that doesn't appeal to Vicki, it's a fact that appeals to *me* enormously.''

He stared at her hand, felt the tips of her red-painted fingers flex along his inner thigh. ''Are you trying to help your client, Ms. Duncan, or are you merely coming on to me?''

She lifted a medallion from between her breasts and slid it back and forth along its silver chain. She gave him a smile that was ripe with possibilities. ''As for the first part of your question,'' she said, ''I am trying to help my client, and in so doing, I'm helping you, as well. Give the lady her divorce, Jamie. Quit stalling.'' She lifted her hand from his leg, scooted even closer to him and placed the flat of her palm on his chest. "As for the second part, if I *were* coming on to you, is it working?"

He backed away. Her hand fell to her lap. "It might be if I weren't so damned scared of you."

She smiled, stood up, hooking her purse over her shoulder. "I affect a lot of men that way...at first. Most of them learn that fear can be quite an aphrodisiac if channeled in the right direction."

She stepped around the coffee table, threw Beasley a noisy air kiss and headed for the door. "I'm not going to bill you for this session, Malone. It's on the house. Be thankful. You can't afford my rates."

She closed the door quietly on her way out. Jamie rose, took the beer bottles into the kitchen. As he passed Beasley, he said, "She may be a good friend to Vicki, Beas, but that woman's a viper. She could put a Pintail Point rat snake to shame."

CHAPTER ELEVEN

TWO DAYS AFTER Vicki's excursion to the beach, she was sitting in Tea and Antiquities folding lace-trimmed napkins and tucking them into the shelves of an antique Philadelphia linen chest, when the phone rang. She left the café section of the shop and hurried to her desk, glancing at her watch once more as she crossed the room. Noon, and still no word from Jamie. The same nagging question popped into her head again. What had kept him away from the shop all morning?

She picked up the phone, hoping to hear Jamie's voice. ''Hello.''

''Hello, Victoria. This is Susan Townsend.''

Graham's mother. Instantly alert, Vicki sat stiffly in her desk chair. This was the first time the New England-bred socialite, now Fort Lauderdale society matron, had ever telephoned. ''Mrs. Townsend, what a nice surprise.''

''I just had to call to see how everything is going, Victoria. Is there anything you need for the opening?''

An extra pair of hands, she thought, wondering again where Jamie was. He'd helped out all day yesterday, though she'd protested that she hadn't needed it. He'd changed her mind with the simple logic she'd come to associate with him.

"Look, Vicki," he'd said, "this has nothing to do with my obvious lust for you. You helped me out thirteen years ago. It's time for me to return the favor."

So she'd relented and found his assistance indispensable, his company entertaining, his sympathy genuine when she'd wired money to her parents in Indiana. Jamie was a fresh breeze in the doldrums of her responsibilities.

"No, Mrs. Townsend," she said. "Everything's under control." Vicki smiled, picturing the perfectly coiffed and manicured Susan Townsend. It was nice of her to offer her help, if that was truly what she was doing, but Vicki could hardly picture her wielding a paintbrush or hand-washing one of the dozens of authentic English teapots Vicki had chosen to use in the café.

"Well, I'm here if you need me," Susan Townsend said.

"Thank you, but everything is going smoothly."

"There is another reason I called. Richard and I are looking forward to the big event on Saturday."

"I'll be delighted to see you," Vicki said.

"We want to participate if we can, Victoria. Show our support. I was thinking of Friday night. Perhaps you'll allow us to take you and Graham to dinner as a way to alleviate your pre-opening night jitters."

"That would be lovely."

"What do you think of the Starlight Room atop the Riverview Hotel on the Boulevard?"

I think if you're willing to pick up a three-hundred-dollar tab for dinner, I'd love to go. ''That's a wonderful choice,'' she said. ''Thank you so much for the invitation.''

Quite unexpectedly an image of Kate Malone came to Vicki's mind. She remembered Kate's offer of doughnuts from a Bayberry Cove Kettle sack, and the woman's warm, welcoming manner, so different from Susan Townsend's aloof, almost rehearsed demeanor. Then she drummed her fingers on the desktop. Where *was* Jamie?

''It's our pleasure, Victoria,'' Mrs. Townsend said. ''I'd actually wanted to take you and Graham out on Saturday night—so it would be more of an immediate celebration of your success, but...'' Susan paused, sighed, indicating a hesitation to continue. ''Well, it seems Graham has other ideas,'' she finally said. ''When I suggested that date to him, he promptly informed me that he has other, more intimate arrangements in mind for Saturday night.'' Mrs. Townsend's voice lowered, became almost conspiratorial. ''Can you tell me what's going on in that gorgeous head of his?''

''I have no idea,'' Vicki said, though her stomach muscles clenched painfully. *Saturday night! Graham has bought the ring and is going to give it to me then,* she thought. It was what she'd expected, what she'd hoped for all along. And now it was actually going to happen. Vicki pressed her hand over her abdomen to quiet an escalating attack of gastric juices. She prayed that Graham's mother would fill in the conversational void, since she feared her own voice would crack if she tried to talk.

"Oh, there is one other thing," Mrs. Townsend said.

"Y-yes?"

"Graham tells me you have family in town. A distant cousin or something."

"That's right." *Distant at the moment, for sure.* Vicki checked her watch again. At this point, she could only *assume* Jamie was still in town.

"It's perfectly all right if you need…want to bring him along to dinner on Friday. I know what family obligations are like. We can make room for one more."

The lackluster invitation for her "cousin" irritated Vicki, but she experienced a shiver of apprehension between her shoulder blades at the same time. She couldn't imagine a worse social situation than trying to make dinner conversation with Susan and Richard Townsend with Graham on one side of her and Jamie on the other. Likewise, she couldn't imagine a scenario Jamie would enjoy more.

"I don't know how long Jamie is staying, Mrs. Townsend," she answered honestly. "I doubt he'll be here on Friday night, though."

Not once he hears this news. He'll finally accept that it's time for him to go back to Bayberry Cove. I'm getting the ring. This interlude of beach-going and game-playing has to end now. It's been fun, but I have to think of my future, not a fragment of a past with a pretend husband I never knew—or wanted.

"Well, he's invited at any rate," Mrs. Townsend repeated hurriedly. "I'll give Graham all the details and see you on Friday, then."

"Fine. Thank you again, Mrs. Townsend." Vicki's hand shook as she replaced the receiver. Her stomach actually hurt. She wrapped both arms around her midsection and leaned over the desk until her forehead hit the blotter. Obviously she was having this physical reaction because she had to face the facts with Jamie and make him understand once and for all that her future was with Graham.

This would be so much easier if she hadn't gotten caught up in the temporary pleasure of Jamie's presence in her life. She should have ignored the diversion he'd offered her and tried harder to make him understand that there was no future for them. She would tell him today. She would end whatever merry-go-round he'd had her on since coming to Florida. But where was he?

Vicki squeezed her eyes shut against another shooting pain that seemed determined to whittle away her resolve. All her life her stomach had been the barometer of her stress level, and today it was registering an all-out alert. She felt the same way she had as a child when she would hide behind her parents' crumbling barn after accidentally breaking a plate or deliberately sneaking a second piece of pie. She knew that her sour-faced mother would be looking for her with the key that would lock her in her room while she contemplated her sins. She felt sick, just like back then. She felt scared.

''Vic! Vicki! Open the door.''

A persistent voice coming from the background of her consciousness jolted Vicki upright. She stared at the door, amazed that her vision was blurred, almost as if she'd been crying. She blinked, refocused and recognized her best friend looking in through the shop window.

Louise mouthed her words of concern. ''What's going on? Are you okay?''

Vicki nodded, stood up and went to the door. ''I'm fine,'' she said, letting Louise inside. ''Just a little tired, I guess.''

''Well, no wonder. You've been putting in twelve-hour days here. You need a break, girl.''

''I'll catch up on my rest once the shop opens, once all the little details are taken care of...'' *Once Jamie goes home where he belongs. Once he shows up today.*

As if reading her mind, Louise said, ''So where is your soon-to-be ex?''

Another glance at her wristwatch produced more concern. ''I don't know. He was here all day yesterday helping out. I expected to see him by now.''

Louise shrugged. ''He's a big boy. I'm sure he's fine. Let's go to lunch at Flanagan's and have the Wednesday special. It's chicken pot pie.''

Vicki refused. She couldn't eat a bite, though she should be hungry. ''No, I can't.''

''Why not?''

''I'm sort of waiting...for Jamie. He brought lunch to the shop yesterday, turkey pita sandwiches.'' Vicki smiled. ''He selected that menu for me, I'm sure. Can you imagine Jamie eating pita bread? I'd more likely picture him with two slices of potato bread stuffed with anything that wasn't moving."

"Yeah, whatever," Louise mumbled. "But he's not here now, and I'm offering to buy. I have to be back in court at two."

Vicki looked out the window, scanned the sidewalk on both sides of the shop. "Let's give him a few more minutes."

Louise plopped down on an old pressed-back rocker and folded her arms over her chest. "So what's with this husband of yours, anyway? Can't the man take a hint?" She eyed Vicki over the rim of her designer sunglasses. "Or aren't you giving him one?"

Vicki nodded her head with exaggerated certainty. "I've given him lots of hints. I've told him I'm going to marry Graham, that he and I have no future, that we're completely different people..."

"That's for sure," Louise scoffed.

Taken aback, Vicki stared at her friend. "What's that supposed to mean?"

"Nothing. I'm agreeing with you, that's all. He's nothing like Graham, for instance. From what I can tell, Jamie Malone is simple, earthy, unassuming..."

"Oh, he's all that," Vicki agreed. "He makes puzzles for a living."

Louise tilted her head, indulged in a little grin. "He might do a bit more than make puzzles, Vic."

"What do you mean?"

"I've done some research on him." When Vicki gave her a skeptical look, Louise elaborated. "He piqued my interest when he showed up here without the divorce papers.''

''He ticked you off, you mean.''

Louise wiggled her eyebrows. ''That, too. Anyway, I've discovered that your little artsy-crafty hubby is an artist of some importance.''

''An artist? He paints?''

''No. He carves things.''

''What things?''

''Ducks, birds, I don't know. Stuff.''

Vicki's thoughts flashed back to the shed and Jamie's dramatic trek through the storm to save his lumber. ''Does he ever sell anything he carves?'' she asked.

''I'm looking into that. I'm doing a financial check on the mysterious Mr. Malone, hoping I'll uncover something I can use to threaten him with.''

All at once Jamie looked like a poor defenseless worm and Louise was the early bird. ''Why would you want to threaten him?''

Louise gave her an incredulous look. ''The divorce, Vic. Remember that? I'll threaten him with assuming your marital share of his financial worth. If I have to, I'll hit him with equal split of common property. With the black cloud of immigration fraud hanging over his head, he won't be able to fight back. He'll fold, and you'll have your freedom.''

Vicki understood why Louise was such a powerhouse in the courtroom. She definitely believed in winning at all costs. But in this case, her strategy wouldn't work. ''That's ridiculous, Lulu,'' she said. ''Jamie doesn't have anything. He lives on a thirty-year-old houseboat that someone gave him for nothing."

Louise shrugged off the details of Jamie's lifestyle. "Still waters, my friend. It's the quiet ones that are often hiding the most. I intend to uncover every detail about your fascinating husband." Louise rocked back in the chair and chuckled. "Don't look so shocked, Vic. This is the way things are done in my world. You do want the divorce, don't you?"

Vicki stumbled over her answer. "Of...of course. Yes. How can you ask that? As a matter of fact, I'm ninety percent certain Graham is giving me the ring Saturday night."

"Great. Then let me do my job. You'll be free to marry Mr. Too Right, and I'll have no qualms about pursuing your ex."

Vicki blinked and then stared at her oldest friend. Louise's unexpected words buzzed in Vicki's head. She swore she hadn't heard them correctly, but when the smoke in her brain cleared, she knew she had. "You're pursuing Jamie?"

"You bet. And I'm pulling out all the stops for this one. I won't have a womanly charm left untapped." Repeating her earlier appraisal of Jamie, she said, "I like earthy men."

"But...well..." Vicki didn't know how to express her shock, her outrage, her... She couldn't even find words to express her emotions.

Louise unfolded her arms and rotated her hand urging Vicki to utter something that made sense. "Well, what?"

"I'm surprised, that's all. Confused..." *Betrayed!*

"Why? I told you the night he showed up here that he got my juices flowing. Just because you don't want him doesn't mean that other women, me particularly, can't see something primal and utterly sexy simmering under that Irish charm."

"But you don't even know him," Vicki protested weakly.

"I know him better than I did Sunday night."

"What? How?"

"I stopped by his apartment Monday evening. We had a couple of beers and talked. Then I called him last night to see how he was doing. He said you wore him out putting up chair rails and installing CD speakers." She raised her eyebrows. "Maybe tonight, since you aren't working him to a frazzle, I'll get to tire him with a few little chores of my own. At least it'll keep him out of your hair...."

Louise's voice trailed off as the implications of her confession hit Vicki with a force greater than any of Imogene's winds. Louise had called him? She'd been to his apartment? Vicki hadn't even been to his apartment, and she was married to him! She'd asked him where it was, but she'd never contemplated going there. Not until today, anyway. Yes, today she'd thought she might have to stop by to see how he was, since he hadn't shown up at the shop. But she'd never in her wildest dreams imagined that he hadn't come today because he was losing interest in her.

Vicki reached under the desk and pulled out her purse. She faced Louise, who was still giggling over her plans as though she and Vicki were gabbing about boys at a slumber party. ''Get out,'' Vicki said.

Louise's mouth dropped open. ''What?''

''You have to leave.''

For once, Louise was utterly flummoxed. ''Are you mad at me?''

''No. I have to go somewhere.''

''Now? We haven't eaten. I'm hungry.''

''Lulu, if you don't leave right now, I'm going to—'' in desperation, Vicki pulled a beaded hat pin from a porcelain holder and held it like a knife ''—stab you.''

Louise stood up and backed to the door. ''Jeez, what's gotten into you?'' She twisted the door handle, but didn't step outside right away. ''Ohhh...'' The one syllable dragged for seconds as Louise slowly nodded her head. ''So that's it! You're hung up on Malone, too, but you're too chicken to admit it.''

Vicki held the hat pin in the air and made stabbing motions like a demented killer in a slasher movie.

Louise hurried outside but managed to have the last word before Vicki shut the door. ''I'm going, but Vic, you better decide what you want. If it's dessert you're interested in, then fine. Marry Graham Townsend. But you'd better realize that somebody else is going to walk away with the main course.''

VICKI PULLED UP her car in front of a sign that read ''One-bedroom apartments for rent by week or month.'' She slammed on the brakes and got out, noting that Jamie's blue pickup was parked in the middle of the lot.

She strode to the nearest door and stopped, realizing she was missing one critical piece of information. What if this wasn't his apartment? How was she to know which unit he'd rented? She went to each door, finally locating the one marked "Manager." An older woman dressed in a flowing floral caftan responded to Vicki's knock.

"Can I help you? I don't have an apartment available right now, if that's why you've come."

"No, I'm not here to rent. Can you tell me which apartment is Jamie Malone's?"

The woman smiled immediately. "Oh, that sweet young man. He's in the last unit that way." She pointed in the general direction away from her own dwelling. Keeping her smile in place, she added, "Are you his girlfriend?"

"No." Vicki started to walk away.

"His sister?"

"No."

"Then..."

Vicki marched down the sidewalk, but threw a forced smile over her shoulder to take the sting out of her abrupt dismissal of the woman's questions. "Excuse me. I really have to see Mr. Malone. Now."

She strode to the last apartment and pounded on the door.

Jamie opened it. His eyes rounded at the sight of her. He stuck his hands in the pockets of loose-fitting denim shorts and stepped back from the entrance to let her in. ''Oh, hey, Vicki, I was just—''

She stepped over the threshold. ''Why didn't you come to the shop today? I was worried sick about you.''

''I'm trying to tell you—''

''And what are you doing dallying with Louise?''

The corners of his mouth moved upward in the start of a grin. ''Dallying? You think I'm dallying?''

''Whatever. You know what I mean. Did you think I wouldn't find out? She's my best friend.''

''I know that.''

Beasley trotted up to her, cocked his head and waited for some show of affection. When none came, he stared at Vicki and emitted a sound like a wounded bird. Vicki patted his head. ''Hello, Beasley. I didn't mean to ignore you.'' Then she snapped her attention back to Jamie. ''Well?''

''I'm not doing anything with Louise,'' he said.

''Like hell. I know you've seen her. Don't you have any principles?''

Jamie's mouth transformed from hesitant movement to an unabashed grin. He was enjoying this! Vicki fumed.

She swept around him, leaving him standing near the door while she strode to the middle of the living room. ''How could you?'' she asked without looking back.

And then she stumbled. She grabbed the arm of a Danish chair and rubbed her toe, which she'd banged hard against some obstacle.

She stared down at the terrazzo floor and for the first time noticed a pile of lumber in the middle of the room. "What's all this?"

Jamie shut the door and walked over to her. "Driftwood. Dade County pine, black olive, seagrape..."

She rolled her eyes. "I know it's wood. Where did you get it?"

"Here and there. That's what I was trying to tell you. I figured since I was down here in Florida anyway, I might as well collect some local samples. I spent the morning tramping through back yards asking people if they minded if I sawed off a few limbs. Then I went to a lumber yard for the pine. I've always heard that Dade County pine is one of the most durable..." He stopped explaining.

Vicki had picked up a three-inch-thick limb. She turned it over in her hand, wondering what made it so special.

"You're not going to hit me with that, are you?" Jamie asked.

She dropped it back on the pile. "Don't be ridiculous."

"Good, because I want to get back to that thing you said a minute ago."

"What thing?"

"That you were worried sick about me."

"That was an exaggeration. But I can't help feeling somewhat responsible for you. Here you are a thousand miles from home, all because of me." She paused, reconsidering her explanation in light of recent events. ''Or what started out to be because of me. I don't know why you're here now.''

He ran his fingers through a tangle of waves that tumbled right back onto his forehead. ''Still because of you,'' he said. ''But as for you being responsible for me, you're not. I'm thirty-eight years old, Vicki. I can pretty much take care of myself.''

''Not around someone like Louise Duncan, you can't,'' she muttered.

''What's that? You think I'm no match for your girlfriend?''

She didn't answer, though she knew darned well that Lulu could eat him for lunch and not burp up as much as a bayberry.

He crossed the room, sidestepping around the lumber, and stood in front of her, mere inches away. ''Let me give you another theory, Vicki. I think it just might be possible that you're jealous.''

She shook her head adamantly. ''I'm not jealous. I'm confused, understandably so. Here I thought you came all the way to Florida to see me, and then Louise tells me you're having beers together and she's calling you.''

''That's all true enough.'' He made an X on his chest with his forefinger. ''But cross my heart and may the saints toss me in hell if there's been so much as one dally between us.''

She drew in a deep breath and looked squarely into his clear, green eyes. He was telling the truth. ''She wants you, you know. And when Louise wants a man, she usually gets him.''

"I don't doubt that. But I'm not worried, because now I know that if Louise wants me, she'll have to knock you out of the way first."

Vicki huffed. "Oh, for heaven's sake. I've told you over and over that I'm going to marry—"

"I know what you've told me, Vicki, but despite all your protestations, I truly believe that you've developed a sort of honest affection for me. You didn't want to. In fact, you fought like a demon not to, but it crept up on you, in a steady way, like the build up during the last days before Christmas."

She stared at him, tried to think of an argument and couldn't. Because he was right. Yes, having Jamie in her life was kind of like anticipating the Christmas mornings of her youth. Not that those days had ever measured up to her expectations, but the once-a-year celebrations were the only times her parents put forth an effort to make her feel loved.

A few colorful packages waited under the tree with her name on them. Maybe they were only mittens or socks, but she didn't have to do chores to earn them. And she didn't have to feel guilty when she cradled them on her lap and took precious long minutes admiring each one.

And the anticipation was the same as the way she felt at the thought of seeing Jamie each day. That was why a despondency greater than almost any she'd ever known had overwhelmed her this morning when he didn't come to the shop. It was like missing Christmas.

He was right about something else, too. All this craziness going on inside her was simply affection. Of course. Well, goodness, she could live with that notion. It wasn't love. Absolutely not. She felt affection for a lot of people, though maybe this was a bit stronger.

She released a slow sigh, letting all the stress of the day ebb from her limbs. The worry, the work, the conversation with Louise, the suspicion, the pains in her stomach. She felt weak from it all. Drained. And yet, all she had to do was look into Jamie's dancing emerald eyes, feel his confidence flow into her, and somehow, some way, she was energized anew, ready to cope. This man for whom she felt a profound affection made her strong.

He studied her expression as she stared at him with what must have seemed a childlike gratitude. He appeared a bit concerned, actually. He tilted his head first one way, then the other. He tried to smile. "Are you all right, Vicki?"

"Yes, I am." He was her friend. He cared about her. Jamie's face was suddenly so familiar, so sweet and sincere. The same familiarity encompassed his body. Lean and robust. Very masculine, but in a nice, comfortable way. Not weight-trained or sculpted in all the right places like Graham's. But natural, flowing, inviting, even soft in places. There was nothing wrong with a man being soft in places.

Without giving a thought as to propriety or rationality, she raised her hands and placed them on each side of his face. She looked intently into eyes that nearly swallowed her with their earnestness. "Affection's the damnedest thing," she said.

He appeared infinitely wise, as if all at once he understood exactly what was going on inside her head. His hands circled her waist, held her tight. He nodded slowly. ''It sneaks up on you, all right.''

She moved before he did—without warning, without thinking. She felt her mouth cover his and then they were both stumbling awkwardly, stepping around limbs and planks, searching for the nearest piece of furniture. Her purse slipped from her shoulder and fell on top of the lumber. Jamie hit the sofa and eased onto it, pulling her down on top of him. She landed between his legs, her hips wedged between his thighs. Her sandals slid from her feet and hit the terrazzo with a duet of clunks.

Every wonderfully erratic move, each mad jerk and twist of her body happened in rapid, intensely exciting succession without registering in her mind. All logic fled as her hands roamed Jamie's face with frenzied movements as if she had to memorize every detail.

His hands searched with equal desperation. One slid under her jersey top. He stroked her back, kneaded her shoulders. He fumbled for her bra hook.

''In front,'' she whispered in a voice she hardly recognized.

His hand came around and he deftly flipped the closure, leaving her breasts touching his chest. He pulled the clip that held her braid in place and twisted his fingers through her hair while his mouth ravished hers. Tasting, exploring, his tongue riding the ridge of her teeth before plunging deep inside.

Her body trembled when he covered her breast with

one callused palm. A workingman's hand that teased and tempted with gentle roughness. Vicki was overcome by sensations. Excitement, longing, desire. It was crazy. She should stop this dizzying spiral of passion before it was too late. "We can't," she croaked into his collarbone.

"I can," he said. "If you can't, tell me now."

"What are we doing?" she said, a question she would have known was stupid if she'd known anything at all beyond feelings and emotions.

"You know darned well, love," he said, "and we don't need all these clothes to do it."

He lifted her top. She fumbled with the buttons on his shirt. She moaned. He laughed in her ear, a low, wicked sound that reverberated in every nerve ending.

Her purse rang.

Her fingers stopped. Her breath hitched. Reality intruded. "That's my phone," she murmured.

"No, it isn't," he lied as the ringing repeated, a silly little version of "When the Saints Go Marching In."

She leaned over him to the edge of the sofa and reached toward the lumber. She scattered bits of it out of the way, searching for her purse. When she found it, she dragged it across the floor and sat up, digging inside for the cell phone.

Jamie covered his eyes with his arm, blew out a breath. "That had better be the president," he said.

Her words came out on shallow gasps of air. "Hello. Yes? What? Who is this?"

The voice that answered jerked her back from the

edge of madness to that place where logic prevailed. "Victoria, what are you doing? Are you running?"

"Graham! No, I'm just busy."

"Where are you? I just tried the shop."

She looked at Jamie. He raised his arm and stared at her, listening. His chest rose and fell with each labored breath he took.

"Where am I?" she repeated. "Right here, of course. Outside the shop." Thank goodness that, at least, was true.

"Oh, good. Well, stay there. I've got wonderful news."

"You do? What?"

"I've just cleared the container. It's on its way to the shop right now."

"You did? How?"

He chuckled. "The less you know, the better, my darling. Let's just say that paper talks louder than words at times."

"Graham, you didn't bribe an official? Oh, my God..."

"It's nothing for you to worry your beautiful head over, Victoria. This is the way things are done to eliminate bureaucratic red tape."

She shook her head to clear the first rumbling of alarm in her brain. "You say the container is coming now?"

"Yes. It should be at the store any minute. I'll be there as soon as I can. I've hired a couple of day laborers to unload the antiques." As an afterthought he added, ''You can get that cousin of yours to help, too. Tell him I'll give him a few bucks.''

''Oh, no, Graham, I couldn't ask—''

''Whatever. It doesn't matter. I was just trying to be nice. Look, darling, I've got to go. See you soon.''

She ended the connection and stood up, fiddling with her clothing, her hair—a frantic effort to restore some order to her appearance...and her life. ''I've got to leave,'' she said to Jamie.

''So I assumed.''

When she'd strapped her sandals back on her feet, she took a couple of steps to the door. ''Look, Jamie, I'm sorry. I acted, well, irresponsibly. I don't know what happened between us a few minutes ago.''

He rose from the sofa, buttoning his shirt. ''That's too bad, Vicki, because I see it all pretty clearly.''

She felt her face grow warm. Of course she knew what happened a few minutes ago. And she wasn't likely to forget it—ever. ''I was upset about Louise,'' she offered weakly.

''Okay.''

She opened the door. ''I've got to go. But, Jamie, about Lulu. She's having you investigated.''

''I figured she would,'' he said.

''She's got this crazy idea that you have money. I told her that was ridiculous. It is, right?''

''Vicki, everybody's got a little money.''

''Well, yes, but you do live in that houseboat, don't you? It's your main residence?''

''Yep.''

''And someone gave it to you for free, right?''

"Right."

"And you make puzzles for a living?"

"I do."

"Louise said you make ducks and things, too."

He half smiled. She hoped her little inquisition wasn't making him angry. She was just trying to verify the facts so Louise couldn't take advantage of him.

"I've been known to make ducks," he admitted. "People in North Carolina like them."

"Oh, sure. I won't let Louise threaten your income if that's what she has in mind," Vicki said. "You don't have to worry."

"I'm not worried, Vicki. But thank you."

"Okay, then."

He picked up her hairclip from the floor and handed it to her.

"Thanks. I'll see you later."

"No doubt."

And she was gone.

JAMIE TOOK a deep breath, flexed his shoulders. It had been a long time since his body had reacted so fiercely, so passionately to a woman. He reached down and patted Beasley's head. "We've got to find a way to keep her, Beas," he said.

The dog yawned, stretched out one back leg.

"I suppose I'd better get up the nerve to tell her the truth about everything. About wanting kids, about what I do for a living, the fact that I have a bit o' money. All that stuff." He shook his head, imagining her reaction when he told her he could live pretty comfortably for a lot of years on what he had in the Bayberry Cove Savings and Loan today.

Jamie parted the curtains at his window and looked out. Vicki was leaving the parking lot. "I'm going to tell her, Beasley, but not today." He looked at the old Danish sofa with the back cushions every which way and grinned. "She's got enough to deal with right now just admitting that she very nearly forgot about Graham while we were wiggling around on that couch.

"I'll tell her after she's accepted me for the man I am deep down. Then and only then will she be ready to accept whatever else comes with me." He squatted down and scratched behind Beasley's ears. For the first time he allowed himself to think positively about a future with Vicki, and he didn't want the euphoria to end. "I'll tell her soon," he said to the dog. "A day or two from now should be just about right. Vicki married me thirteen years ago for all the wrong reasons. I want her to stay married to me for all the right ones."

CHAPTER TWELVE

VICKI SWERVED around a row of holly hedges by the side of the road and sped into the parking lot behind Tea and Antiquities. She slammed on the brakes and muttered, "Thank God." The container hadn't arrived yet. She hurried to the rear entrance. Maybe she still had a few minutes to pull herself together.

She rushed into the women's lavatory at the back of the shop and immediately went to work restoring her hair and clothes to their pre-romp-on-the-sofa appearance. She brushed her hair with quick, vigorous strokes, while looking in the mirror and pretending she couldn't see the word *GUILT* flashing like a digital readout on her forehead.

"What got into you this afternoon, Victoria?" she said to her flushed reflection. "You look like you've been sitting too close to a campfire."

She tucked her jersey top into the waistband of her pants and yanked her belt closed. "Everything you've ever wanted is within your grasp, and you almost..." Oh, my, what she'd almost done! What she would have done if Graham hadn't called. "How can you jeopardize your future for one wild, irrational act of self-gratification?"

She narrowed her eyes and glared at her image. "And for what? A puzzle-maker! A duck-carver! A man who barely escaped an Irish prison and whose two brothers remain in jail to this day! You've spent years trying to escape a family without a single white sheep in it. And Jamie's family is worse than yours, for heaven's sake."

She leaned close to the glass and pressed her lips together. It didn't help. They were still swollen from Jamie's kisses, the kisses she'd all but begged for. Graham would take one look at her and be able to tell something had happened. He'd question her. He always did, even about the simplest things. What would he think when he saw her like this?

And she'd crack. The guilt would finally be too much to bear. She'd turn into a quivering mass of regret and admit everything. She squeezed her eyes shut, but when she opened them again, the same crimson-faced, puffy-lipped, sexually frustrated woman stared back at her.

She was wrong to think she could live with the guilt of her secret marriage and the lies she'd told to protect her reputation and relationship with Graham. The deceit was killing her. And now it was even worse. She'd let her *affection* for a man who was practically a stranger send her over the edge. Plunge her from her desperate climb to respectability to the depths of wantonness.

And she'd reveled in every moment of it.

That was the awful truth. She'd ridden that crazy roller-coaster of passion with Jamie as if she'd been put on this earth to experience just that. And there was another truth that was almost as hard to accept. Jamie Malone truly didn't seem like a stranger at all. Even that first night when he stood with his nose at her shop window, he seemed like someone she'd known forever.

He was someone she could confide in, complain to, laugh with, be honest with—even about that most disgraceful, unwomanly fear of having children. But the one thing she couldn't be truthful about was what she was scared to death to admit to herself. She had some very definite, terrifying feelings for Jamie. He was making her question her perfect plan, her future. He was doing it every day with an easygoing manner that made her forget her responsibilities and her goals for a few precious moments. He was doing it with a special word, a touch…

Vicki sat heavily on a Victorian wicker stool in a corner of the bathroom and put her head in her hands. "This is crazy, girl," she said. "You've built your future around Graham. Your dreams have included him as your partner, your lover, your ideal of culture and competence that is inbred, not learned." She looked up, catching her reflection in the glass once more. "You should thank your lucky stars that a man like Graham Townsend would even give you a second look—you, a woman whose lineage can't be traced beyond a few penniless immigrants."

Graham had made Vicki a part of his world, and if she was smart, she would do everything in her power to be worthy of his faith in her. So she stood and regarded her image in the mirror with a renewed sense of purpose. ''You should close your eyes to Jamie Malone and any other unambitious, charming guy who might cross your path. You should run as far and fast as the road with Graham will take you and never look back.''

She rubbed her arms, the friction reminding her of Jamie's hands on her skin. She shook her head. ''You should, Victoria. You should—''

''Anybody there?'' A pounding on the back door brought Vicki back to her current situation. She jammed her purse under the vanity and ran to the door. Through the window she saw a large brick-red container in the parking lot. A huge semi vibrated in front of it, waiting to be disconnected from its load. Graham would be so happy. He'd done it. His antiques had arrived in time for the opening.

VICKI HAD LEFT about an hour ago. Jamie grabbed the wrapped package from the top of his dresser and stuck it into the roomy pocket of his shorts. Then he left for Vicki's shop. He wasn't going to let what happened between them scare her away or make her uncomfortable. He wasn't going to pretend it didn't happen, either. He'd wait for the right time and encourage her to face her feelings. A woman like Vicki didn't stumble over lumber, fall onto thirty-year-old Danish-modern sofas and rip a man's clothes off unless some pretty darned significant emotions simmered below her surface cool. She might not want to admit it, but there had definitely been some simmering going on in his apartment.

"You stay here this time, Beas," he said to the snoozing dog, whose disappointment, if he truly felt any, was registered in a brief opening of his eyes. "I'll bring you back a hamburger."

Jamie left his pickup in the parking lot of his apartment and walked the few blocks to the Boulevard. When he approached the back lot of Tea and Antiquities, he was aware of increased activity. He wasn't surprised by the appearance of the container. He had surmised its impending arrival from Vicki's half of the phone conversation with Graham. He watched a couple of men amble up the loading ramp onto the back of the container and scoot a piece of furniture from the middle of the trailer to the exit.

"You might want to pick that bureau up and carry it," Jamie said from the opening. "Old wood tends to crack more easily than new. You could break one of those delicate legs by sliding it."

The men stared at him as if he'd spoken a foreign language. Jamie motioned for one of the workers to tip the bureau toward him. He grasped the top of the piece and indicated the worker should raise the legs. Together they walked the bureau off the container and into the rear of the shop.

Graham's impatient voice carried through the showroom to the back door. "I can't believe you were here, Victoria, and didn't let the workers inside."

"I didn't know they were out front, Graham," she said. "I was busy in the back with the truck driver. I had to sign all the papers and authorize the packing seal to be removed—''

''They claim they waited over a half hour. We have to pay their ridiculous hourly rate while they were smoking cigarettes on the front sidewalk.''

''They could have come around to find me,'' she offered.

Jamie and the worker carried the bureau past the kitchen and into the showroom, interrupting the obviously private discussion. ''So where do you want this?'' Jamie asked.

Vicki whirled around and stared at him. Caught off guard by his sudden appearance, her face became infused with the most incriminating rosy hue. She might be smack in the middle of rearranging her shop and arguing with her boyfriend, but she definitely had not pushed the afternoon's activities with her husband out of her mind.

Unaware of the intensely personal connection between Jamie and Vicki, Graham gave Jamie a condescending smirk. ''Ah, Malone. Would you like to be on the payroll, too?''

Vicki snapped back, ''Graham, don't be rude.''

''Only as a consultant, my friend,'' Jamie said, ''and I doubt you can afford my fee.'' He gestured for the laborer to set the bureau down. Jamie righted it and then surveyed the shop interior. ''But I'll advise you this one time for free. There are quite a few pieces to come off that trailer. You'd be wise to start a row of them back to back down the center of the showroom. The symmetry will give more eye appeal than taking up every inch of wall space with heavy wood.''

''I think that's a good idea, Graham,'' Vicki said. ''It puts some of the nicer pieces in the customers' direct path. And they can even see them from the tea-room.''

''Fine.'' Graham snapped his fingers at the worker who was leaning his elbow on top of the bureau. ''Go on, get another piece. We haven't got all day.''

Graham then consulted a clipboard before using a black marker to write a figure on a scallop-edged card. Using a gold tassel, he hung the classy-looking tag on the bureau handle. ''What do you think, Victoria?'' he asked. ''A fair price?''

She checked the tag and frowned. ''Five hundred. It seems a bit high.''

''Nonsense. You need some wiggle room with the customers. Most people like to haggle.''

Jamie thought the dark oak bureau was a rather ordinary piece, one that could easily be found in current use in many Irish households. Keeping his opinion to himself, he strolled around the room looking at previously applied price tags, stopping when he came to a thirty-inch-tall curio case, a small piece for mounting on a wall, made of mahogany and glass with brass fittings.

His surprise at the high price came out in a long whistle. ''What's so special about this?'' he asked.

Vicki came over and read the tag. ''Oh, Graham, this is much too high. No one will pay twenty-five hundred dollars for it.''

Graham stepped between them. ''Really, Malone, what do you know about antiques?''

Jamie smiled. ''I know a bit about wood. And I know what I like.''

''How about what you can afford?'' Graham said unpleasantly. ''Most of these items are museum quality. Do you know what that means?''

Jamie folded his arms over his chest and pretended to think about his answer. After a moment he said, ''Why, yes, Graham. I believe we have a museum or two in Ireland. I can recall my mother taking me to one dedicated to Celtic tribes who lived in the hills near our town in 400 *B.C.* I've seen an old thing or two in my life.''

Graham scoffed at Jamie's expertise. ''Celtic tribes. All they've left behind are primitive bits and pieces dug out of the earth. Tell you what, Malone. Why don't you go study pottery chips somewhere else? I think I'm the expert on fine European furniture.''

Jamie bit his bottom lip to keep from sounding as pompous as Graham by describing the intricate gold work and jewels that had also been dug out of the Irish soil. It wouldn't help Vicki if he instigated an all-out verbal battle with the supposed love of her life. He'd only force her to choose between two equally arrogant braggarts, and he might end up the loser. But it did please him to note that from the way she was nudging Graham into behaving himself, she might actually choose the Braggart Malone!

He crossed to Vicki's desk while she and Graham were occupied with placing each piece from the shipment on the shop floor. He removed the package from his pocket and slipped it into the file drawer of the desk on top of Vicki's purse where she'd be certain to find it. Then he closed the drawer and contented himself with reading more tags. Some of Graham's prices were only marginally high—perhaps a customer with bargaining skills could walk out of Tea and Antiquities with a fair-priced find—but others...well, Jamie couldn't believe he was reading them correctly.

A Queen Anne cherry vanity table. Nice, but made in the late 1920s and not all that uncommon. Priced at forty-two hundred dollars. A sixty-year-old walnut armoire, one of many just like it that he knew sold regularly at European auctions for a hundred dollars or so. Just under six thousand. Even considering the high cost of shipping, many of these prices were over the moon.

Jamie waited until late in the afternoon when the container was unloaded and Graham had left before he mentioned his concerns to Vicki. Sensing she was close to exhaustion, he poured her a cup of tea and made her sit down at one of the bistro tables in the café tearoom. He sat across from her. "So, don't you think Graham's pricing is a bit exorbitant?" he asked when she'd wrapped her hands around the warm mug.

She acknowledged the possibility with a shrug. "Yes, it seems so. But I have to trust him. He's invested some of his own money in this business, and he wants it to be a success as much as I do."

"But, Vicki, when I was a lad in Ireland, I remember pieces just like a lot of these in the houses in my neighborhood. They were nothing special then, just workingman's property, and even considering inflation, I doubt they're worth anywhere near Graham's estimates.''

Vicki swirled her spoon in the teacup. ''Maybe,'' she admitted, ''but he was quite specific about wanting me to keep to those prices. He even said I shouldn't let the customer haggle over certain pieces. Graham is certain they will bring the money, and I'm going to trust him on this.'' Then for added emphasis, she said, ''He really does know antiques, Jamie. He's read lots of books on the subject.''

''Well, that's it, then.''

Jamie let the matter drop when he noticed the tiny lines of stress at the corners of her mouth, the subtle sag of her shoulders. It was her merchandise, after all, and she had every right to do with it what she wanted—or what Graham wanted. She didn't need an argument from him.

''Why don't you call it a day, Vicki?'' he suggested. ''I'll meet you at your house, if you like, and draw you a hot bath.''

''No!'' She jerked upright in her chair. Her knee banged against the leg of the table, sending the contents of her cup over the rim. She busied herself by wiping up the tea with a napkin. ''I mean, it's not necessary for you to come over. I want to stay here a while longer anyway, and go over the broker's inventory sheet.''

She didn't look directly at him, but he could detect

a worried knot forming between her eyebrows. "My name is on those customs papers," she said. "I signed for this shipment and I want to check that everything is in order."

"I can understand that." He looked at his watch. Six-forty-five. "Have you eaten today?"

She did raise her head long enough to give him a sheepish grin. "I had a bagel at ten o'clock and a chocolate bar around two."

"That settles it. I'm going over to that cheeseburger place across the street. I'll bring you back a double decker with all the trimmings and an order of fries."

"You don't have to do that," she said, though when she licked her lips he knew the offer appealed to her.

"It's no problem. I promised Beasley a burger anyway, and if I fail to bring one home, he'll never forgive me."

He started to stand up, but she stopped him by placing her hand over his on the table. "Why are you so good to me, Jamie?" she asked.

He smiled. "You're my wife, Vicki. For now, at least. If a man can't be good to his wife, what else should he do with his life?" He layered his free hand over hers. "I may not have chosen you back in Orlando in the traditional way, but I said my vows. And now that we've met again, I intend to make them count for something while I have the chance."

He rose and headed for the door. Pausing there, he said, "Besides, love, you bring out the goodness in me."

Her lips turned up just a little. "I have a hunch the goodness in you would come out without any help," she said.

JAMIE HAD BEEN GONE only five minutes when a man entered the shop through the door Vicki had failed to lock. "I'm sorry, we're not open," she explained. "But I hope you'll come back for the grand opening this Saturday."

"I won't be in town," he stated matter-of-factly. "And I was walking by your window just now and spied a piece of furniture that would be perfect in my home."

He'd piqued her interest. He wasn't a person she'd picture as a typical Tea and Antiquities shopper. In the first place, he was the wrong sex. He was dressed Miami-style, as Vicki referred to colorful, expensive silk-blend shirts, loose-fitting trousers and leather loafers with no socks. His slicked-back hair ended in a short ponytail at his nape. He wore frameless glasses with tinted lenses and smelled of some costly cologne. He appeared to be a man who could afford to purchase a fine antique, and Vicki couldn't bring herself to turn him away. "Which piece are you interested in?" she inquired.

He walked to the lady's vanity, the one priced at forty-two hundred dollars. "This one. My wife would love it." He picked up the tag. Vicki cringed. Despite her defense of Graham earlier, deep down she agreed with Jamie's assessment of the prices. *It's all over now,* she thought, fully expecting the man to head for the door.

"I'll take it," he said, withdrawing his wallet and extracting a credit card. "My car is parked on the street outside the shop. This will fit in the cargo area."

For a moment she simply stared at the credit card the man held out to her. He flicked the corner of the plastic with a polished thumbnail, alerting her to his impatience. "Is something wrong?" he asked.

"No, nothing at all." She took the card and carried it to her desk, where her authorization machine was hooked up to a phone line waiting for the first sale. And what a first sale this was—if the credit card was good.

It was. The man signed the receipt, stuck his copy of it in his shirt pocket and picked up the vanity.

She opened the door for him and watched him slide the vanity into the rear of a luxury SUV. With a nod in her direction, he climbed behind the wheel and pulled away from the curb. In moments his taillights were lost in the busy evening traffic.

Vicki was shaking when she reentered the shop. She sat in the nearest chair and clenched her hands together to keep them from trembling. More than four thousand dollars for one piece of furniture! It was unbelievable. Spectacular. It was nothing short of a miracle, considering her tenuous financial situation. Just two days before, she'd emptied her savings account to send money to Indiana for repairs on her parents' truck. And today, after one transaction that took perhaps three seconds of high-speed wire connection, she'd transferred more than four thousand dollars to her store account. For once fate was working on her behalf. She couldn't wait to tell Jamie. She stared out the window toward the restaurant across the street. How long did it take to buy a couple of burgers?

It was while she was watching the entrance to the restaurant that she realized her thoughts were careering along a path of ironic madness. Here she was waiting breathlessly for Jamie when she should be bursting at the seams to tell Graham. After all, it had been Graham who initiated this whole success story. It was his idea to price the vanity so high. Jamie had been skeptical from the beginning.

"What is wrong with you, Victoria?" she asked herself for the hundredth time that day. Still her gaze remained fixed on the street and the man walking briskly back toward the shop, his hands grasping a sack of food. She met him at the door, the words coming from her mouth almost faster than her brain could compose them.

"You won't believe what happened. Come on, guess. No, don't. You never could." She hurried to her desk, picked up the credit-card receipt and waved it jubilantly in the air. "See this? You'll never believe how much it's for. Guess what I just sold?"

With irritating calm, Jamie carried the food to a bistro table and set it down. His sharp eyes scanned the shop for a mere few seconds. "You sold the vanity," he said.

Vicki's enthusiasm deflated like a sail at dead calm. She dropped the receipt to her side. "I wanted to tell you!"

"Oh, sorry, but I couldn't help noticing the empty spot against the wall where the vanity stood not fifteen minutes ago. It was kind of like wondering how horseshoe tracks got in the living room and then seeing a horse on the sofa.''

She was beginning to think that nothing passed Jamie's scrutiny. But no matter, his observation wasn't going to completely spoil her thrill of the moment. She shoved the receipt at him. ''Read it. Forty-two hundred dollars plus tax.''

He puckered his lips and let loose a long, low whistle. ''Impressive, Madame Saleslady.''

She took the receipt back and stared at it once more. ''That's just it, Jamie. I didn't have to sell it. The man came in and *wanted* to buy it. Didn't even examine it.''

Jamie pulled out a chair for her and gestured for her to sit. ''Have you ever seen him before?''

''No. That's what makes this so incredible.'' She sat, tapped her feet, drummed her fingers on the table. ''I've never seen him on the Boulevard before, and wonder of wonders, he picks my shop out of all the others!''

''He didn't haggle over the price?''

''Nope. He just pulled out his wallet, dug out his shiny platinum card and walked out of here with a table that, despite your previous comments, must have been worth that much money.''

Jamie rubbed his chin, looked down at her. ''Vicki, I have to ask. Don't you find this transaction a bit odd?''

''Odd? Not on your life. I find it wonderful. Beyond my wildest dreams.''

He shook his head. ''A man, a total stranger, comes into the shop before it's even open—and on the same day the container arrives. He claims he's interested in one piece of furniture from your large inventory, doesn't look around and doesn't argue over price—''

''Stop it, Jamie,'' she said. ''You are not going to spoil this moment for me. This one sale has saved me from near starvation. It couldn't have come at a better time. Can't you just accept that Graham was right about the pieces from Amsterdam? He's a very intelligent man. He knows what he's doing.''

A burst of bitter laughter escaped his lips. ''Oh, I don't doubt that for a minute. But what exactly *is* he doing? I think—''

Vicki grabbed the restaurant sack and began taking the contents out as noisily as she could. ''There are hamburgers in here, right?''

''Sure, the packages wrapped in foil.''

She picked up one shiny thick package and thrust it at him. ''Then here, stuff your face with one. You looked starved.''

He slowly peeled off the foil. Then he leaned forward and gave her an earnest look. ''Vicki, I've been thinking about this shipment from Amsterdam. Something's just not right—''

''Not another word, Jamie,'' she snapped. ''I mean it. If you can't celebrate this moment with me, then go back to your apartment. I'd rather eat alone than hear any more of your suspicions.''

Jamie stared at her a long moment as if weighing his options. Then he hastily rewrapped his hamburger, stuffed it in his pocket and strode from the tearoom.

CHAPTER THIRTEEN

VICKI STARED at Jamie's retreating back as he made his way through the showroom toward the rear exit. She expected him to turn around and head back to the table. That was the Jamie Malone *she* knew. He would stomp into the room again with an emphatic last word, which he would deliver with typical self-assurance around a healthy bite of hamburger. If Vicki understood anything at all about this man, it was that he didn't back down easily.

She waited, but he disappointed her.

In fact, seconds after his abrupt departure, she heard the back door open and close. Granted, he was only doing what she'd requested, but when had her wishes ever guided Jamie's actions before? After a couple of minutes, she unwrapped her hamburger and took a small bite, forcing herself to eat. She'd have her dinner without him if he couldn't act like an adult and share her good fortune gracefully.

She'd eaten about half her burger when the shop suddenly seemed oppressively empty. She put the remainder of her sandwich and fries into a Tea and Antiquities bag to take home and then went to retrieve her purse from her desk. She pulled out the file drawer and noticed a pink package with silver ribbon twinkling in the overhead lights. She picked it up, turned it over in her hand to examine its unusual shape and read the small tag taped to one side. "Made from Florida black olive wood. J.D.M."

She clutched the package to her chest. A gift from Jamie. When had he put it in her desk? Before she'd made him angry, she knew that much. She sat down and placed the gift on top of her desk. Then, just as she'd done all those Christmases ago in Maple Grove, Indiana, she slowly and meticulously loosened the ribbon and peeled back the wrapping.

"Oh." Just one simple syllable from her throat, but it was expressed with such reverence that she might have been staring at one of the Seven Wonders of the World. Her eyes burned as she picked up the small gray carving of a four-legged animal—a dog with a long snout, thin, awkward legs, a large dome of a head and two bits of gold paint for the eyes. Each individual hair and whisker had been carved with the precision of a surgeon.

She stood the carving on its surprisingly sturdy legs, and with her hand flat against her breast, she said, "Beasley, you are indeed one of the loveliest creatures on this earth." And remembering Jamie's words, she added, "Besides being one of the most intelligent."

Her eyes were drawn to a darker area under the dog's belly. There, carved and stained into the wood with the deftness of a steady hand were the stylistic initials of the carver—J.D.M.—the date and the simple sentiment "With affection." And for the second time that day, Vicki said out loud in a voice choked with emotion, ''Affection's the damnedest thing.''

BACK IN HIS APARTMENT with what little hamburger he'd eaten sitting like a chunk of cement in his belly, Jamie thought about what he was going to do. The plan he'd come up with was a little crazy, he supposed. For sure Vicki wouldn't appreciate it, but he'd made up his mind. He was piecing together the last details when his phone rang. He went to the kitchen to answer it. ''Hello.''

''Hey, J.D. It's Brian.''

Jamie's face broke into a grin. He couldn't have loved Bobbi Lee's young son more if he *had* been the boy's biological father.

''How you doin', buddy?'' Jamie said.

''Good. Mom said I could call you. I got the number from the message you left on her voice mail.''

''I'm glad you did. Is everything okay at home?''

''Yeah. I just wondered when you're coming back.''

Jamie had been away from Bayberry Cove lots of times to attend exhibits and gallery openings, and Brian had never called to ask this question before.

''I'm planning to leave Monday night, if not before. Be back Tuesday night for sure.''

''Okay. Mom says you'll be in big trouble if you don't start working on the stuff for that exhibit you're doing in Boston.''

Bingo. This was a Bobbi Lee-contrived excuse for a phone call, if ever he heard one.

A plaintive voice in the background interrupted

their conversation and proved him right. ''Is that Jamie? Did you reach him?''

Jamie held the phone away from his ear. Even from a thousand miles away, Bobbi Lee was a force to be reckoned with.

''Yeah, Mom,'' Brian said.

''Ask him when he's coming home.''

''I did already. It's Tuesday.''

''Ask him if he's coming back alone.''

''I already know that, too. The answer's no, he won't be alone.''

Jamie cringed. Now sparks were really going to fly. ''Brian, why'd you say that? I never said—''

''Beasley,'' the boy explained. ''You're bringing Beas back with you, aren't you?''

Jamie leaned his forehead against the kitchen cabinet. ''Oh, of course. I could never leave the Beas behind. You mention that to your mother. She could get the wrong idea.''

''What? Like you're bringing that lady back? The one who hurt her ankle in the hurricane?''

So the story had reached Bayberry Cove Elementary School. Jamie wasn't surprised, but now wasn't the time to explain the intricate relationships of adults to a ten-year-old. ''Yeah,'' he said simply. ''Let's just leave it for now that Beasley and I will be returning on Tuesday.''

''Okay, see you then.''

''Right. Goodbye, Brian.''

Jamie hung up before Bobbi Lee had a chance to grab the phone from her son. He was in no mood to go a round with her. He turned on the television and sat down on the sofa to watch something mindless for an hour or so. He'd only been back from the shop for a short time. He'd eaten, fed Beasley most of his hamburger and changed into a black T-shirt and black jeans. Thinking about it now, Jamie figured the all-black outfit wasn't really necessary to accomplish his plan. This wasn't *Mission Impossible* and he wasn't Tom Cruise. But a few minutes ago, while he was dressing, he thought the clothes lent a certain mystique to the night's coming events.

''We'll wait a little while longer, Beas,'' he said. ''By then Las Olas Boulevard ought to be nearly deserted. And Vicki should be snug in bed—alone, as I prefer to picture her in my imagination.''

At ten o'clock Jamie climbed into the pickup with Beasley and crept along the tree-lined road to the Boulevard. He turned onto it, then drove slowly past Vicki's shop. Satisfied that Tea and Antiquities was unoccupied—only the security lights were on—Jamie pulled around to the back and cut the engine. He opened his door, got out and motioned for the dog to follow. Then he went to the window of the men's rest room.

''She'd have a fit if she knew I left this window unlocked,'' Jamie whispered to Beasley. He placed his fingertips under the freshly painted bottom of the old building's original glass frame and pushed up gently. ''And she'd kick my arse all the way back to North Carolina if she knew I'd disabled the security alarm in this window.''

When he'd raised the glass, he called Beasley close. ''Here we go, boy,'' he said, wedging his shoulder under the animal's rump and hoisting him over the sill. Next he hoisted himself up and over. His sneakers landed silently on the tiled floor.

''Now for the fun part,'' he said. ''Snooping. Remember what I told you, Beas. You stay here, and if anybody drives up, you come into the shop and alert me. But no barking. I don't care if a squirrel jumps up on that window sill and does the hokeypokey on your nose, you play it cool. I'll work as fast as I can.''

Jamie took a high-intensity flashlight out of his pocket and went into the showroom. There was enough light for him to investigate the principal components of the furniture. He'd use the flashlight beam to illuminate the crevices. And since he'd already decided to take the small mahogany wall cabinet back to his apartment and give it a good scrutiny, he took it down from its hook, carried it to the rest room and lowered it carefully through the window to the ground. He'd have it back in place before Vicki opened up in the morning.

VICKI LEANED BACK in her rocking chair, put her slippered feet on an ottoman and stretched, easing her sore, tired muscles. Today had been one of the most stressful days she'd ever experienced. And as she looked at the carving of Beasley on her end table, she knew it had also been one of the most memorable.

The sale of the vanity should have made her happy. With the addition of four thousand dollars to her balance, she could look forward to the shop opening with confidence, instead of desperation. So why did she feel so despondent?

She knew why. Jamie's reaction to her good fortune was the one exception to an otherwise very satisfying day. And she hadn't been able to stop thinking about the way she'd treated him.

She was in the process of considering ways she might ease his wounded feelings tomorrow when Graham peered through the window of her front door and rapped lightly. Releasing a huge sigh, she went to let him in. Her gaze passed quickly to the clock over her fireplace mantel. Ten-thirty. It was late for Graham to come over. She wished he'd called first. Surely he must know she was tired.

He gave her a peck on her cheek. "Hi, Victoria." He sat down on her chintz-covered settee and crossed his legs. "How was the rest of your day?"

It was the first time she realized she hadn't called Graham about the sale of the vanity. She took her place in the rocking chair again and noticed that he seemed especially alert to her answer. "It was pretty amazing, actually," she said.

"Really? Why?"

She told him about the sale. He was delighted, and as she'd expected, he took credit for his expertise in pricing the vanity. He was happy for her good fortune and gratified at her renewed faith in his judgment, but—and this was the part that puzzled Vicki—he didn't seem overly surprised. He acted almost as if the sale of one of his high-priced items had been a normal transaction in a typical business day. But then, that was Graham—his confidence was always boundless. That was one of the traits Vicki admired most about him.

When the excitement of the triumph passed, Graham urged Vicki to admit anyone to the shop who might want to purchase the better pieces before the opening. Well, of course she would do that, she assured him. She wasn't a fool.

And then he noticed her carving of Beasley, and the celebration ended. He picked it up. ''What's this?'' The words spilled out on a chortle of condescension. He studied the carving from several angles, and when he recognized the subject, he laughed. ''Oh, wait, it's that stupid-looking dog of your cousin's, isn't it? Where did you get it?''

She snatched it out of his hand and cradled it in her palm. ''Jamie carved it. He's very talented.''

''Oh, right. I can see that. Imagine what he could do with corncobs. Probably whittle out miniature violins.'' He emphasized his joke by pretending to play the imaginary instrument with his thumb and forefinger.

''You're rude,'' she said, ''and unkind. This is a gift, and I love it.''

He made a halfhearted attempt to stop laughing, but with little success. ''Sorry, darling. Are you actually going to leave the thing sitting out in the middle of your living room like some prized artifact?''

''It *is* a prized artifact to me,'' she said, ''and yes, I'm keeping it here and taking it to the shop with me during the day.'' She set the carving on the end table again. ''And if you don't like it, you don't have to look at it. In fact, you don't even have to come into this room if you're so offended by my taste.''

He sobered instantly, even appeared a bit contrite, if she used her imagination. He held back the sleeve of his shirt to see his watch. ''You know, Victoria, it's late. You're probably tired. Maybe I should go.''

She stood up, waiting for him to do the same. ''Maybe you should.''

He passed by her on his way to the door without stopping to kiss her goodbye. ''See you tomorrow,'' he said. ''Congratulations again on the sale.''

Vicki was steaming—for the second time that day and at the second man. She paced the floor of the small room, trying to erase the image of Graham's smug features from her mind. Each time Graham's countenance faded, it was replaced by Jamie's easygoing smile and bright eyes, and she could barely remember why she'd been angry with him in the first place.

''Don't do this to me, Jamie,'' she said to the empty room. ''Don't make me love you. I don't want to love you. I want my life to go on just as I've planned it for so long. I'm finally where I want to be. I'm *who* I want to be. With the kind of man I've always dreamed of having by my side. Okay, he's not perfect. I see that now, but who is? Certainly not you, Jamie Malone.''

She picked up the carving of Beasley. The wood was smooth and warm to her touch. She held it next to her cheek. ''You're not going to get me to admit that I'm falling in love with you, Jamie Malone.'' A single tear slid over her bottom eyelid, and she brushed it away. ''Not to you and not to myself.''

Vicki made coffee and poured herself a cup while she tried to concentrate on Graham and their future together, but the previously clear visions of a happily-ever-after were merely hazy images now. Knowing that sleep would elude her for hours, she decided to return to the shop to pick up the inventory list of the Amsterdam antiques. She would check Graham's estimated values of the items against the retail prices she'd attached to them. She wanted to make certain she hadn't priced anything too low. Graham would be furious if she had.

She slipped on her loafers, grabbed her keys and went to her car. The Boulevard was quiet, and Vicki parked in front of her shop. She unlocked the door to Tea and Antiquities and stepped inside. The building should have been deserted, but a rustling from the back of the showroom made her heart miss a beat. The shuffling sound was followed by a loud thud as if someone had dropped a tool, and next by a mild oath. Vicki froze with her hand on the doorknob. Someone was here! She tried to scream, hoping to frighten the intruder away, but the sound was caught in the back of her dry throat and came out as an ineffective croak.

''Who's there?'' she managed to whisper in a hoarse voice.

A man dressed in black stepped into the shadows. His features blended with the amorphous gray shapes of the dimly lit room, making his face unrecognizable.

"Don't come any closer," she said, backing over the threshold.

The man held up his hands in a show of surrender. He started to speak, but before he could utter the first word, chaos erupted from the rear of the building. A large animal bounded into the showroom and ran directly toward Vicki.

She garbled another scream and raised her arm over her face. She focused a terrified gaze on the creature—a large, lumbering scruffy gray beast with a high, domed head. She dropped her arm as relief overwhelmed her. She and the intruder shouted the animal's name at the same time. "Beasley!"

The dog skidded to a stop on a rug in front of her, rippling the woven fabric like washboard. The man Vicki now knew was Jamie, charged toward them. He grabbed Beasley around the neck, preventing him from planting his paws on Vicki's chest. He then grinned sheepishly and mumbled, "Sorry."

Her breath escaped in one great, incredulous gasp. "What are you doing here?"

Jamie released Beasley and pressed down on the dog's hindquarters, forcing him to sit. Both man and dog stared at her for an interminably long moment. "Which one of us are you talking to?" Jamie finally asked.

The inane question infuriated Vicki almost as much as the obvious invasion of her property. She wound the strap of her shoulder bag around her hand several times, prepared to swing the purse at Jamie's head if he made one more wisecrack. No one would blame her. Not even the coroner. ''One more stupid question, Malone, and you'll wish you'd never left North Carolina!''

He backed up a step, dragging Beasley with him. ''Okay, okay, I get the message.''

''Then answer the question. What are you doing here? How did you get in?''

''A back window. The men's washroom. Someone left it open.''

She sputtered. ''S-someone?''

''It might have been me. I raised it earlier, thinking a little fresh air couldn't hurt in there.''

She glared at him. ''You broke into my shop?''

''No, of course not. I didn't break into your shop. I simply raised a window and climbed in. I didn't break anything.''

She stepped around him and looked to the back of the showroom where she'd first heard him swear. One of Graham's prized antique pieces, the six-thousand-dollar wardrobe, had been disassembled and was lying in pieces on the floor. Its twin doors leaned against a wall. The small attached mirror that used to be on top of the cabinet lay beside them. Four interior drawers were scattered around the empty framework.

She marched to the pieces and pointed. ''What do you call that, if not breaking something?''

He went to her and waved his hand, dismissing her concern. ''It can be put back together.''

''It darned well better be...''

He picked up a drawer, tapped the bottom panel of

wood lightly. ‘‘But, Vicki, listen to this. See how hollow it sounds?’’

She couldn’t detect any sound over the roar of fury in her head. ‘‘Of course it’s hollow,’’ she snapped at him. ‘‘It’s a drawer! And all I hear is your ridiculous tapping.’’

‘‘All I have to do is pry off these under panels with a screwdriver—’’

‘‘No.’’

He stared at her as if he hadn’t heard her correctly.

‘‘You’re not prying anything else from this piece of furniture. I don’t know what you think you’re going to find—’’

‘‘I don’t, either, but I have a hunch that maybe—’’

‘‘Stop right there, Jamie.’’ Vicki stared at the sections of the valuable wardrobe scattered around her feet. She looked back at Jamie. ‘‘You’ve done enough. And frankly, I’ve had all I can take of your suspicions and your pranks. It wasn’t enough that you belittled the importance of that sale today. You had to take it a step further by implying that Graham is some kind of a crook. And now you’ve broken into the shop.’’ She swept her arm from his black T-shirt to his black jeans. ‘‘You’re sneaking around like some sort of special agent, taking apart furniture that’s worth thousands of dollars…’’

‘‘But Vicki, it isn’t worth that kind of money. Something just doesn’t add up.’’

‘‘Maybe not to you. But all the proof I need is in that credit-card voucher in my desk drawer.’’ She looked away from him, knowing it was the only way she could summon the strength to say what had to be said. ''I want you to leave. Go back to your apartment and leave me alone.''

She sensed that he was looking at her probably hoping she would change her mind. When she remained impassive, he reached down to retrieve a flashlight and a few tools from the floor. He'd just stuffed them into the back pocket of his jeans when an automobile braked to an abrupt halt in front of the shop. Revolving lights on its roof illuminated the sidewalk in brilliant hues of blue and red.

Vicki spun around. ''Oh, no. When I came in I forgot to turn off the alarm.''

An officer entered the shop with his weapon drawn. ''Nobody move,'' he ordered.

Vicki took one step toward him but his glower prevented her from taking another.

''What's going on here?'' the officer demanded.

''It's a mistake, Officer,'' she explained. ''I'm Victoria Sorenson, and this is my shop. I came in late to do a little work. I guess I forgot to turn off the alarm.''

''I'll need to see some identification, ma'am.''

Vicki took her license from her purse and handed it to him. Satisfied, the officer nodded toward Jamie. ''And who's that guy? Is he supposed to be here?''

Vicki glanced over her shoulder at Jamie. He bit his bottom lip and waited, watching. A wrinkle of worry formed between his eyes. She turned back to the policeman. ''He's my cousin. Coincidentally he showed up here tonight, too. He's been helping me during the day, and he forgot something and came back to find it.''

To validate her story she spoke to Jamie. ''Did you find what you were looking for?''

He had the nerve to grin just a little. ''No, not yet, but I'm sure I will. I just need more time.''

If he expected this little aside to amuse her, he was mistaken. ''You're not going to get any more time,'' she muttered between clenched teeth. ''We've caused the Fort Lauderdale Police Department enough trouble for one night.'' She smiled at the policeman. ''I'm sorry, Officer. As you can see, this is just a misunderstanding.''

''All right, then, ma'am,'' he said, returning his revolver to its holster. ''You have a good evening now.'' He joined his partner, who'd been observing the scene from the sidewalk. They returned to the squad car and pulled away.

Jamie spoke to her back. ''Thanks, Vicki. For a minute I thought you might actually tell them I was a burglar.'' He laughed nervously. ''You had a right, I guess, but even as mad as you are, you couldn't leave Beasley orphaned while I was hauled off to jail.'' He moved around her so he could look directly into her face. ''I'm sorry,'' he said again. ''I went about this all the wrong way. But I'm asking you to trust me. I have the strongest hunch that your boyfriend—''

''I don't want to hear it, Jamie!'' she said fiercely. ''Ten days ago I expected to go to North Carolina and get a simple divorce from a man who, if he were the least bit reasonable, would have simply obliged. But no. For some reason you got it into your head that this ridiculous marriage of ours has a chance.''

She shook her head sharply, a feeble attempt to keep her eyes from tearing up. Why was it so incredibly difficult to explain her feelings to this man? ''It *doesn't* have a chance, Jamie. I had a life before I went to Pintail Point. Included in that life is a man with whom I've had a relationship for eighteen months. And then you come along and try to force me to accept your doubts about him. You've made me question my feelings, my decisions, my plans for the future.

''I can't take any more, Jamie. My life is here, with Graham. My future is with him and this shop. It's not that I don't care about you.'' The first tear slid down her cheek. She dashed it away as if it were acid burning her skin. ''I can't deny what happened between us this afternoon. I can't deny feeling something for you. And the longer you stay...'' She couldn't finish—the conclusion of the statement scared the hell out of her.

Silently she implored him to understand. Then she said, ''Don't you see it's not what I want? *You're* not what I want.'' She looked down at the floor, the drawers, the doors, the mirror that once sat on top of the wardrobe, and she felt like that piece of furniture. Torn apart, in pieces that could only be put back together if she resumed the life she'd planned for herself before Jamie Malone had caught her in a windstorm and scattered the well-ordered parts of her every which way.

She couldn't take the risk of never feeling whole again. She couldn't risk everything she'd worked for, everything she'd become, on a humble artist, a simple wood-carver who lived on a houseboat and took in strays. Victoria Sorenson wasn't a stray. She'd spent years convincing herself of that.

"You're making me crazy, Jamie," she said softly. "And I want you to go. Go back to North Carolina. And please, I beg you—" her voice hitched on a sob "—send me the divorce papers."

HER MISERY touched him as profoundly as it baffled him. He didn't have the slightest notion how to deal with it. He started to speak, but no words came. He wanted to reach for her, but his arms felt made of lead. So he picked up one drawer and slid it into the cabinet. When he reached for another, she shook her head. He understood. She didn't want his help.

He snapped his fingers and Beasley trotted over to him. "It'll be all right, Vicki. You'll be all right," he said at last. "I'll do what you want. I'll send the papers."

She closed her eyes. Moisture glistened on her lashes. He resisted the urge to wipe the dampness away with the pad of his thumb. "Let's go, Beas," he said. "We've got a long drive ahead of us tomorrow."

When he turned away, he heard her whisper his name.

He stopped, looked back at her. "What is it, love?" he asked.

Her bottom lip trembled. "I...I want you to know this is hard for me. I wish I'd never gone to North Carolina, that I'd never seen you again."

It was a strange irony, but this powerful confession

brought a bit of cheer to Jamie's heart. She only wished it because she was so close to admitting that the exact opposite was true.

"You know where to find me—tonight at least," he said, and patted Beasley on the rump. The two of them strode to the short hallway that led to the rest rooms and kitchen, then entered the men's bathroom and climbed out the window, the same route they'd taken before. Jamie shut the window and headed to his truck. He'd only taken one step before the toe of his sneaker collided with something. He looked down and saw the wall cabinet he'd lowered from the window earlier.

He considered opening the window and returning the piece. Instead, he spoke softly to his dog. "I know what you're thinkin', Beas. I'd be a thickheaded gob-shite for sure if I borrowed Graham's fine European museum piece overnight."

Then he picked up the cabinet and tucked it under his arm. "What difference will a few hours make?" he said to Beasley as he hurried to the pickup. "Will she scorn me twice as much for bringing it back in the daylight? With a bit of luck, she might never know it was missing at all."

Back at his apartment, ten minutes later, Jamie had scrutinized the cabinet with a powerful magnifying glass and the trained eye of a man who understood the grain and fabric of wood. He tapped his index finger up and down the spine of the cabinet, listening for the ping that would indicate a hollow area. When he was convinced, he lay the piece facedown on his coffee table and pulled a screwdriver from his back pocket.

He winked at Beasley, curled up on his pillow. "I think we're about to discover why this little knick-knack shelf is a bargain at twenty-five hundred dollars."

Carefully he leveraged the corners of the back panel until the thin wood separated from the cabinet. A new sheet of white pine was exposed.

But it wasn't the false back that intrigued Jamie. It was the canvas carefully rolled and stuffed in the narrow space between the two panels. Carefully he spread the painting on his table.

It was a pastoral landscape twenty-four inches wide and eighteen inches tall. Trees in the full dress of summer shaded stone pathways and a brook running alongside. Sheep dotted the hills where a lone shepherd stood in front of a thatched cottage. The edges of the canvas were ragged as if torn from a frame, but the painting was intact. As was the name of the artist in the lower right corner. Jamie grabbed a pencil and wrote it down. Henrik Petrovich.

He rolled the canvas and carried it and the cabinet into the bedroom. Then he took the telephone book from a nightstand drawer. "I knew I should have brought my laptop," he said to himself as he flipped through the pages to the Broward County listings. "It would make researching this a whole lot easier." He dialed a number and listened to a recorded message. "But since I didn't, I guarantee I'll be the first customer at the library when it opens tomorrow."

CHAPTER FOURTEEN

THE NEXT MORNING, Thursday, just two days before the grand opening of Tea and Antiquities, Vicki rolled over in bed and made the discouraging discovery that the headache she'd had at three in the morning was still with her. She squinted one eye open enough to read her digital clock before flopping onto her back and covering her face with her arm. Eight-thirty. Damn. She had to meet with Hazel and Marcia Huggins, the mother-and-daughter team she'd hired to help in the shop. She hoped their customary enthusiasm for Tea and Antiquities would compensate for her strange indifference.

This was the second time since she'd encountered Jamie Malone that she'd overslept. The first time, on the houseboat, she'd lain awake in his bed fretting the hours away because he'd made her so angry. Last night, she'd lain awake in her own bed because he'd made her so miserable.

And now he could be gone. He might have taken her commandment to heart, packed up his lumber and his dog, and headed his pickup back to Bayberry Cove.

Vicki groaned, threw off her covers with a violent

kick and swung her legs over the side of the mattress. She pinched the bridge of her nose and sat up. ''It's what you want, isn't it?'' she asked herself. ''You want him out of your life so you can go back to the way things were. So that, once again, your future will be exactly the way you've envisioned it—you, Graham Townsend and an elegant little shop where vanity tables sell for over four thousand dollars.''

So why was it that these very things that had promised her a full, rewarding life now made her think of only lonely days ahead?

She stumbled into the bathroom, but refused to look at her reflection in the mirror. She knew that crying half the night would have left her eyelids as swollen as soaked sponges. She knew that tossing and turning on a mattress that seemed too hard one minute and too soft the next would have made a tangled mess of her hair. She didn't need the cold hard evidence staring back at her.

She yanked the first pieces of clothing she could find from her bureau and pulled them on. Then she went to the kitchen and switched on her coffeemaker. Without waiting for the brewing cycle to finish, she pulled out the pot, poured the contents into a mug and returned the glass container to the heating mat, now puddled with coffee. Her first few swallows provided the jolt of caffeine she needed to face the responsibilities of her day. Unfortunately the return of logical thought only made her question the events of the day before.

All last night she'd tried to ignore her doubts about

the sale of the vanity. Had she been so grateful to replenish her dwindling checking account that she'd pushed all sense of reason aside? What was it her mother used to say? "If a thing seems too good to be true, Victoria, it usually is—especially for us out-of-luck Sorensons." That sale had definitely been too good to be true. Still, the man's credit card had been good. Whatever his reason for buying the piece, it wasn't her problem.

Not the way Jamie Malone was her problem. Her doubts about him far outweighed the ones about the vanity. Her feelings for him were mystifying. He was an uncomplicated man who made puzzles and created beautiful remembrances out of blocks of wood. He was nothing like Graham, and Vicki feared now that she'd sent him away, that Jamie was immeasurably more noble.

When she finished her coffee, she went to the bathroom, swiped the mascara wand across her eyelashes, applied strokes of blush to her cheeks and headed for her car. There were important matters to take care of, yet her thoughts kept returning to one simple question: *What if he signs and sends the divorce papers?* She was still asking herself this question as she drove to the shop. And each time she told herself that it would be for the best if he did. But her heart refused to believe it.

The Misses Huggins, both bundles of energy and brimming with ideas, were waiting by the back door when Vicki pulled behind the shop. She took a deep breath and got out of the car to greet them. She was back in business mode and reminding herself that soon her old habits of perseverance and dedication would feel as comfortable as the worn sneakers she'd put on this morning. But she still wasn't convinced an hour later when the women had gone and she went to check her phone messages. There was only one. It was from Graham, and he was telling her she just might have another big sale, another super day. With a sputter of bitter laughter, she erased the message.

JAMIE PULLED his truck alongside Vicki's small car a little after ten. "You have to stay here, Beasley," he instructed the dog. "She might just bite my head off when she realizes we haven't left. Or she might break into a bout of hysterics. Either way, I don't want you witnessing what could be the most humbling moment of my life."

He took the cabinet and the canvas from behind the front seat and walked to the shop's rear entrance. He'd debated his decision from every angle and had come up with the same answer each time. He had to show her what he'd found. As she'd said, it was her name on those customs papers, her shop's reputation on the line. She might not care enough about Jamie to change her mind about divorcing him, but she did care about her shop. He'd show her the evidence and say goodbye. A real goodbye this time. What she did after that was up to her.

The back door was open, so he went inside. He walked past the kitchen to the entrance to the showroom, but stopped when he heard Vicki speaking to someone. He waited just out of sight and listened.

"You want to buy *this* piece?" she asked incredulously.

"I said I did, didn't I?" the man answered.

Jamie wondered which item the customer was interested in, and Vicki's next words clearly identified it as the wardrobe Jamie had taken apart the night before.

"But it's in pieces," she pointed out. "I'm planning to have someone put it back together."

"Never mind," the man insisted. "I'll take it just as it is and do the repairs myself."

"Are you sure you want to do that?" Vicki asked. "Have you seen the price?"

After a short pause Jamie heard the distinctive sound of individual bills being peeled off a roll. "That ought to cover it," the customer said with a cocky assurance that Jamie found irritating.

Vicki's voice became more persuasive. "Look, I don't feel right about selling you this piece. I think you should reconsider your interest in light of the condition of the wardrobe..."

Aha! Jamie smiled grimly. Vicki wasn't taking the money as she'd done the night before. She knew something didn't make sense.

The customer became noticeably impatient. "Lady, are you crazy? I'm standing here waving six thousand bucks in your face, and you're trying to talk me out of giving it to you. Write up this sale now, miss. I don't have all day to wait for you to come to your senses."

Jamie's instincts went on red alert. Setting the cabinet and painting out of sight, he plastered a huge grin on his face and strode into the showroom. "Top o' the mornin' to you, cuz," he said to Vicki. He planted a little kiss on her cheek next to her open mouth. "What's brewin'?"

Without waiting for her to gather her wits, he tapped the top of the wardrobe. "I see you noticed my little work in progress. I left it in a shambles last night, but I've come in this morning to fix the damages."

The customer glared at him. "You did this to this piece?"

"Guilty," Jamie said. "The doors weren't closing properly. Thought I'd sand them down a bit. And then one thing led to another—"

"Well, don't bother putting it back together. Like I was telling the shopkeeper here. I'll take the piece as it is."

Jamie chuckled. "I can't let you do that, my friend. My cousin and I have the shop's reputation to consider. You come back in a few hours and this ol' cupboard will be firstrate and worth every penny of its—" He pretended to look at the price tag for the first time and shook his head in amazement "—nearly six thousand dollar price." He snickered and nudged his elbow into Vicki's ribs. "Got yourself a live one, haven't you, cuz."

He then threw an arm around the man's shoulders and led him toward the front door. "I'm just kidding, you know. It's a fine piece you've chosen here. I'll plane the doors, clean the rust off the squeaky old hinges, reattach the mirror, and she'll be good as new—or good as old as the case may be. This cupboard will be a right fine showpiece when I finish with her, befitting the prestige of this fine establishment.''

Jamie swung the door wide and pushed the man through the opening. Winking at Vicki, he added, ''Just a few hours, wouldn't you say, cuz?''

''Y-yes! Right. Come back this afternoon.''

The man's face had turned an alarming shade of pink. But finding no appropriate response to the crazy Irishman's domineering tactics, he stuffed his money into his pocket and wagged a finger threateningly. ''I'll be back, young lady,'' he called to Vicki. ''I'm going to have that piece!''

She smiled at him and gave him a friendly wave as if everything was fine. The smile remained frozen on her face and her hand stilled its movement as if chiseled out of granite until the man moved off down the street. Then she turned toward Jamie. Her eyes widened. She blinked rapidly several times and said, ''You're still here.''

''Yes, I am, and you don't have to remind me that I should be about two hundred miles up the road by now. I got your message loud and clear last night.''

Her lips trembled, almost as if she was trying not to smile. Jamie was just thankful she hadn't picked up the nearest antique item suitable for head-cracking and come after him.

''But why?'' she said after a moment.

''I've got something to show you. I'll say my piece and you can do what you want with it.'' He headed for the spot where he'd hidden the cabinet, but stopped and turned back to her. "Beasley's in the truck outside. My packed suitcase is waiting by the door of my apartment. I won't bother you again once I've had my say."

She nodded. "Fair enough."

He picked up the cabinet and the canvas and brought them to her. She looked at the cabinet and then at the wall where she'd hung it the day before. "Oh, my gosh," she said. "I never noticed until now that it was gone. You took it?"

"Yes. Last night. I told you that I couldn't shake the feeling that something was strange about the way Graham was pricing certain items from the container."

Her brow knotted in a frown. "I'm starting to think the same thing myself. Especially now after that customer tried to buy the wardrobe this morning."

The phone on Vicki's desk rang. She looked at Jamie as though expecting him to instruct her what to do.

"Answer it," he said. "I'm pretty sure it's Graham, and he's heard all about what just happened here."

SHE PICKED UP the receiver slowly. "Hello." When she heard Graham's voice, she nodded at Jamie. "Hi, Graham." She twisted the phone cord around her finger while he questioned her. "Of course everything's all right. Why wouldn't it be?"

"I was hoping you might make another big sale like you did yesterday," he said. "You know, that you might find a buyer for another of the container pieces."

He was definitely on a fishing expedition, but Vicki wasn't taking the bait. ''No, nothing like that has happened yet.'' She pointed to the phone and then to the wardrobe so Jamie would understand that Graham was talking about the piece. Then into the phone, she said, ''Actually, I did have some interest in the wardrobe.''

His voice rose a notch. ''Really? Did you sell it?''

''No. I noticed this morning that it needs a little work. I'm arranging to make the appropriate improvements. I wouldn't feel right selling it in its current condition.''

Any hold Graham might have had on his patience snapped. ''What? Are you kidding? Sell the damn thing, Victoria. That's what it's there for.''

''But it's such an expensive item, Graham. A person who pays that much should at least walk out of here with something in excellent condition, don't you think?''

''Hell, no. It's 'buyer beware' in this business. I think you're out of your mind if you don't take the money when you can get it. Where is this guy? Is he still there?''

''How did you know it was a man?'' she asked, winking at Jamie.

''What? I didn't, of course. Why are you concerned about such insignificant details when thousands of dollars are at stake?''

Jamie had settled on the corner of her desk and was listening intently. She mouthed the words *He's upset* before speaking into the phone again. ''I suppose you just made a lucky guess about the customer's gender, but anyway, he's gone. Don't worry, though, Graham. I told him we'd fix the wardrobe and he could come back and get it later."

"We?" Graham fairly screeched the word. "I suppose you've got that moronic cousin of yours in the shop with you again. I thought he was leaving."

Obviously Graham had been informed of Jamie's interference. Vicki abandoned her attempt to keep her own voice calm and level. She was truly angry. "What right do you have calling my cousin moronic? He's been a lot more help lately than you have." She smiled at Jamie and was rewarded with a thumbs-up sign. "Frankly, I'm glad he didn't leave last night."

Like a metronome, she turned her head back and forth in time to Graham's incessant grumbling. "We'll talk about this later," she finally said. "But I don't appreciate you implying that I'm incapable of making decisions in this store. Everything is running splendidly, if you want to know the truth."

She ended the call on that lie. Things were not running splendidly at all. She'd just turned down six thousand easy dollars. There was some sort of mystery about the items from the container and she had no idea what it was. And the only really honest thing she'd just said to the man she thought she loved was that she was glad Jamie hadn't left.

Vicki replaced the receiver and looked at Jamie. He hissed out a breath between his teeth and said, "I take it Graham's not happy."

"That's an understatement. He thinks I'm a complete incompetent and probably a little bit insane. He's got a meeting this morning, but he told me to sit tight and wait for him to get here around noon. I think what he really meant was I shouldn't make any more decisions on my own."

She leaned over the desk and gave Jamie a hard stare. "So, about that wall cabinet, what did you find? Since I just royally screwed up my relationship with my future fiancé, it had better be something spectacular."

"I think you'll agree that it is." He picked up the cabinet and set it on her desk. "Notice that the corners of the back panel are loose."

She tested them. "How did that happen?"

"I took the panel off last night." When he saw her expression, he quickly added, "I can fix it, don't worry. The thing I want you to know is that I wasn't the first person to take off that panel and replace it."

"You weren't?"

He showed her the canvas. "This was inside."

She unrolled the painting and lay it beside the cabinet. After studying it for several seconds, she laid her palm flat against her chest and released a long sigh. "It's beautiful. I feel as if I'm in that place, walking along that lane. The colors are so true."

She looked over at Jamie. "But how did it get into the cabinet? Do you suppose someone left it there years ago, forgot where they'd put it?"

The look he returned was pained, remorseful, as if it hurt him to answer her question—or as if he knew the answer would hurt her. And suddenly, before he uttered the first word, she understood what he was going to say because she recognized how naive her question was. She stepped away from him, stared at the painting again and back into Jamie's eyes.

"You think Graham..." She leaned heavily against the desk and fought a wave of dizziness. It couldn't be. "You think he put it there?"

Jamie pulled out a chair and forced her to sit. "I don't know about that, Vicki. Graham had contacts in Amsterdam who could have physically placed the painting in this cabinet. But I'm fairly certain he knows it was shipped to your shop."

She reached for the painting, held it up in front of her eyes. "Is it worth anything?" She knew the answer, knew the implications, as well, but deep inside, because her fragile self-esteem was shattering like fine old glass, she prayed the opposite was true.

Jamie took several sheets of folded paper from his jeans pocket and handed them to her. "I copied this in the library this morning. We can do more research on your computer, of course, but this is pretty conclusive."

Setting the painting in her lap, she unfolded the papers. The top one contained publication information of a reputable artist catalog. Then she read a lengthy biographical sketch of a Polish artist named Henrik Petrovich, a nineteenth-century painter noted for his canvases of the Polish countryside.

There was also a listing from the Art Loss Register, a national compilation of stolen or lost treasures. There, mentioned among several paintings missing since the German occupation of Poland in the Second

World War was a photo of the painting in her lap and the words *A Shepherd's Dusk* by Henrik Petrovich. Its value—two hundred thousand dollars.

Jamie spoke softly and calmly as she continued to read. "It was stolen from the National Museum of Warsaw during the war. No one has come forth with any information about it since then, but I read articles about officers high up in the Third Reich who confiscated the art of conquered countries. Many of the works are only now finding their way out of cellars and attics where they've been hidden for decades."

When she'd read all she needed to know, Vicki set the papers and the painting on the desk and covered her face with her hands. "Oh, dear God, what have I been party to?"

Jamie put his hand on her shoulder. "You didn't know. You can't blame yourself."

But the signs had been there. Maybe if she hadn't been so dazzled by Graham's sophistication, his good looks, his *pedigree,* for heaven's sake, she would have seen through the false trappings to the man he really was—an opportunist consumed by greed.

"How could I have been so stupid?" she said. "Why wasn't I suspicious when Graham called me in North Carolina and was so anxious about the arrival of the container? Why didn't I question him when he freaked out about the shipment being delayed a few days by customs?"

"I guess you can understand why he overreacted now," Jamie said. "To keep from alerting customs to a smuggling operation, Graham had to get the items sent to your shop with as little red tape as possible. Tea and Antiquities was the legitimate business he used as the point of destination so he wouldn't raise any eyebrows with officials. I can imagine that when the container was going to be searched, he panicked."

"And bribed someone to have it released," Vicki added.

"That would be my guess," Jamie said. "I suspect that the delay was truly a random act, however."

Vicki nodded as all the evidence flooded her mind, followed by the inevitable guilt. "Why did Graham price the pieces so high?"

"Probably because he couldn't risk having anyone but his own 'selected' buyers purchase the items that concealed the smuggled art. He set the exorbitant prices so no one else would be interested. He knew they would be out of the shop before the official opening. You would be happy with the prices, and he would be enormously wealthy."

She'd never felt so betrayed. "He used my shop—the fulfillment of my life's work—as a front for smuggling! I've poured everything into this business, my money, my labor, my knowledge… And for what? So he could risk it all to satisfy his own greed?"

She wanted to break something, throw something. Her stomach hurt. She wanted to strike out with her hands, but the only targets were the things she loved.

And then, by degrees, an overwhelming need for revenge replaced the shock and humiliation. She was sick with bitterness toward Graham and wanted to fight back. She stared at Jamie. ''What am I going to do now?''

He took her in his arms and held her. She pressed her face into the comfort of his worn denim shirt. ''I believed in him—in us.''

''I know.''

''I thought he loved me.''

''Maybe he does,'' Jamie whispered. He tilted up her head and smiled down into her tear-filled eyes. ''You're not very hard to love, you know.''

''Maybe for my gullibility,'' she said. ''He never thought I'd find out about his scheme. And he was probably right. If it hadn't been for you…''

''You'd have caught on, love,'' Jamie said. ''Just as you've known for days that I could have brought those divorce papers with me if I'd wanted to. Your friend is a topnotch attorney. It took a crafty old North Carolina lawyer and a feisty redheaded Irish mother to finagle a way for me to stay married to you for a few more days.''

Vicki stopped sniffling, lay her forehead against his chest. ''I might need both those lawyers to keep me out of jail,'' she said.

''I don't think that's going to happen,'' Jamie said. ''But we do need a plan, and luckily I've got one.'' He stroked the back of her head. ''Are you ready to see your blue-blooded intended sent up the river, Vicki? Can you watch that happen?''

''You bet I can. What's your plan?''

''I'm going to give that wardrobe a good going over. If I don't miss my guess, there are a few more works of art tucked away in the linings of the drawers. But first we make a phone call. The local police will know who to call in on this case. I hope I can convince the authorities that there's a way to catch Graham in his own trap. But we'd better hurry. Something tells me Graham is going to rush through his meeting and get to this shop as fast as he can."

Vicki picked up the telephone to call the police. Jamie had been right about everything else, so she was confident he was right about this, too. She hesitated before punching in the number and looked at him. "Jamie, I'm so sorry about…"

He waved off her attempt to apologize. "There's no need to say anything, Vicki. You were just being loyal."

"Well, then, there's something else I want to tell you. I said it to Graham, but now I'll say it to you. I'm awfully glad you didn't leave."

He smiled. "Now *that* you can say for the rest of the day, and I won't tire of hearing it."

With a determination she never thought she'd feel for such a task, Vicki dialed the number to the police. In a moment she would incriminate the man she'd just discovered she had never truly known at all.

CHAPTER FIFTEEN

FOR THE NEXT HOUR and a half, events progressed rapidly, and the tensions in Tea and Antiquities escalated. Within the first few minutes, Jamie had returned Beasley to the apartment and had taken apart the drawers of the wardrobe. He discovered four eleven-by-fourteen portraits by the Polish artist Josep Lonz. Vicki searched the Internet and found Lonz's paintings in the Art Loss Register. They were the last missing works from a series of twelve portraits entitled *Faces of Poland.*

Once that discovery was made, the detective, who'd been dispatched by the police, called in a special agent from the U.S. Customs Service. The agent arrived at the shop twenty minutes later.

"I'm Special Agent Mark Ford," he said to Vicki. "You must be Miss Sorenson."

She nodded and shook his hand, then introduced the tall, burly man to Jamie, who stopped working on picture frames he was constructing out of strips of pine to explain what he knew about the paintings so far.

Taking notes, the agent asked, "Where is the furniture used in the smuggling?"

Jamie took him to the women's rest room, where

he'd moved the pieces of the wardrobe and the wall cabinet. He and the detective explained the scheme they'd devised to force Graham Townsend into admitting his involvement in the art smuggling. Vicki listened again to the details and tried to keep her anxiety to a somewhat reasonable level. They were running out of time. If Jamie was correct in his prediction, Graham could show up at any minute.

"I think it just might work," the agent said. "And there will be four witnesses who can vouch for Mr. Townsend's culpability."

Mr. Ford regarded Vicki with concern in his eyes. "Are you all right with this, Miss Sorenson?" he asked. "Your personal risk should actually be quite minimal, but I can't tell you that there isn't a slight possibility that something could go wrong."

"I'm ready," she said. "I want to get it over with."

"We'll be right here—just out of sight," the agent said. "Detective Brightman, myself, and..." he looked at Jamie for a clarification of his relationship to Vicki.

"Jamie is a close friend," she said.

"Okay, then." The agent ran his hand over his graying brush cut. "We won't let anything happen to you."

His coat fell open and Vicki saw the shoulder holster under his arm. She hoped this plan wouldn't end in violence. She couldn't believe she was plotting to trap the man she'd hoped to spend the rest of her life with. But she knew it was the right thing to do. She smiled at the agent. "I'll be fine."

"I want you to know, Miss Sorenson, that your government appreciates what you're doing to apprehend Mr. Townsend. I specialize in international trade fraud and money laundering, and so often the cases we investigate are never prosecuted due to a lack of concrete evidence." He nodded once decisively. "I feel pretty good about what's happening here today. I think we're going to nail your partner and retrieve even more valuable art treasures."

Vicki tried to share his enthusiasm, but obviously the agent didn't know the depth of her involvement with Graham. That would come out, of course, but for now only Jamie and she understood how difficult this charade was going to be for her.

Ford suggested she call Graham to determine if he was en route to the shop. She reached him on his cell phone. He sounded angry and explained that his meeting had finally ended, and he was driving on the I-95 and just crossing the Dade/Broward County line. He would arrive at the shop in a few minutes. He warned Vicki again not to make any more decisions about the Amsterdam antiques until he arrived.

"You know what you're going to say to Mr. Townsend?" the agent asked Vicki when she had disconnected.

"Pretty much." She'd rehearsed her responses to anything Graham might say in the limited time she'd had to prepare.

As the minutes ticked by, Jamie and Agent Ford tacked the Josep Lonz portraits into the makeshift pine frames and hung the artwork on a wall of the shop.

Vicki stood watch at the front door while Detective Brightman covered the rear.

Ten minutes after all preparations were in place, Graham's BMW swung into a vacant parking place a few doors down from the shop. Vicki saw him get out of the vehicle. "He's on his way."

Ford gave her an encouraging nod as he and the detective exited the showroom to wait in the hallway in the rear. Jamie wrapped his hand around hers long enough to give her a supportive squeeze. "You'll be all right, love," he said. "It'll all be over soon." Then he joined the other men in the hallway.

She tried to smile, but her lips felt like cement. Her mouth was so dry she wondered if she'd be able to speak. To alleviate her escalating panic, she picked up a paper from her desk and pretended to read it, looking up only when Graham entered the shop.

"Hello," she said coolly. She had to force herself to keep her gaze steady on his face as she would any other day. He looked like the same man she'd thought she loved, but he'd become a stranger, a menacing presence that threatened her livelihood and possibly even her life. But she could keep up the pretense for a few more minutes because she had a job to do. And when she was done, Graham would know what it felt like to be nothing more than an instrument for someone else's objectives.

She moistened her lips and formed them into a smile. "You look tense, Graham. Bad traffic? You needn't have come at all, you know."

He gave her a look more appropriately reserved for

a naughty child. "How could I stay at the office with all hell breaking loose around here?"

She affected surprise. "What do you mean? Everything's fine."

"No, it isn't. Not when you turn down a guaranteed six-thousand-dollar sale." He paced back to the door and looked out. "How could you let that man walk out of here, Victoria? How could you be so..." He stopped, apparently thought better of what he was about to say and whirled around to face her again. "I couldn't let that happen again, so I'm here now, and when the customer comes back, I'll sell him the damned wardrobe myself."

She set the paper down, picked up a crystal vase and pretended to wipe fingerprints off the glass. "Well, you didn't need to come here, Graham. I've taken care of the problem with the wardrobe."

He narrowed his eyes and glowered at her. "What do you mean?"

"Jamie fixed it. The wardrobe looked wonderful when he was done. In fact, someone came in right after he finished and made an offer on it."

Graham appeared thoroughly agitated now. He strode from one end of the showroom to the other searching for the wardrobe. Vicki watched his movements with a swell of satisfaction.

"Where is it?" Graham asked. "Was it the original buyer who came back for it?"

"No, it was someone completely different." Vicki set down the vase and moved so that the desk separated her from Graham, anticipating his reaction to her next statement. "I didn't get quite as much for it, but I thought it wise to take a sure offer rather than take the chance the first customer wouldn't come back."

Graham's jaw dropped. His eyes widened in horror. "You sold it to someone else?"

"Yes, but don't be concerned." She gestured toward another wardrobe that she'd had in stock for several weeks. "I'm sure I can interest the other man in this piece. It really is in better condition than the one from the Netherlands, and it's priced much lower."

She could barely comprehend Graham's words when he screeched, "Do you have any idea what you've done?"

Vicki continued to ignore Graham's anger, though her heart pounded in her chest. She clasped her hands behind her back so he couldn't see them shaking. "Yes. I made a pretty good deal," she said.

He leaned over the desk, his gaze contemptuous. "Who bought the piece? Do you have his name? How did he pay?" Graham rifled through the papers on her blotter, picking up scraps and tossing them on the floor. "You do have records, don't you?"

"He paid cash," she said. "I gave him a receipt, he took the wardrobe and left. There was no reason to request his name and address."

"No reason? My God, Victoria, you've given away a fortune. Why didn't you just sell the piece this morning when you had a chance? How stupid can you be?"

She placed her palms flat on the desk and drew in a long, quivering breath. She was no longer frightened. She was mad as hell and experiencing a strange delight in delivering the final blow that would crush this man. "Stupid? Let me tell you something, Graham. There was something hidden in the bottoms of the drawers of that piece."

His face paled. He ripped open the top button of his collar and ran his finger around the edge. "What do you mean, 'hidden'?"

"Paintings," she said, edging her way down the wall to where Jamie had hung the works of art. She pointed at them, noting how the panic in Graham's eyes changed to relief when he saw them. "Aren't they nice? I found them when Jamie was repairing the wardrobe. We framed them and hung them here. I think I can get fifty dollars apiece for them."

He collapsed into a chair, sputtered a few incoherent syllables and stared at the paintings, then gave a burst of hysterical laughter. When that subsided, he made no attempt to hide his scorn for her. "You stupid, ignorant plowgirl. It's my good fortune that you haven't learned a damned thing about this business."

She pretended to be hurt. "Why are you being so mean?" she asked. "I thought you'd be pleased that I found the paintings."

"Oh, I am, Victoria. I'm probably the happiest man on earth, and despite your ignorance, or more accurately, because of it, I have you to thank. You've saved my hide, darling. Fifty dollars apiece! These paintings are worth a small fortune." He rose and began taking the paintings from the wall.

"Put those back," she ordered. "They belong to the shop. I'm going to sell them."

"Like hell you are." He tucked them under his arm and looked down at her, his eyes hard, cold. "For your information, these paintings are already sold. They were sold before they ever left Amsterdam."

"What do you mean?"

"Wise up, Victoria." He laughed as he looked around the room at all the treasures Vicki had amassed. "Do you think people actually make money importing all this crap? No, darling, the money is where you can't see it, in drawers and hidden compartments. And if you aren't able to accept that, then you'd better tuck your tail between your legs and go back to planting soybeans in Indiana."

"She'll be far better off planting soybeans in the open air than you will be behind bars, Mr. Townsend."

Graham's face turned into a mask of shock as the three men strode into the showroom. "What the hell?"

Agent Ford stepped forward. "I'm with the U.S. Customs Service, international trade fraud division," he said.

Graham laughed nervously. "Trade fraud? Look, there's been a mistake."

"I don't think so, Mr. Townsend. I think you made everything quite clear." He took the paintings from Graham and handed them to the detective.

Graham tore his gaze from the treasures leaving his possession and looked at each man. He appraised the situation and immediately took his anger out on Vicki. "You witless little tramp."

Jamie stepped between them. "Ah, come on now,

Graham, let's not sink to name-calling. You'll hurt the lady's feelings."

"To hell with the lady's feelings." Graham's eyes blazed. "I was going to ask you to marry me, did you know that, Victoria? You, a nothing little girl with cowpats stuck to her shoes. But I knew before I came here today that you would never be Mrs. Graham Townsend. I knew it the minute I found out you lied to me. I knew it was over then."

His words confounded her. "*I* lied to *you?*" She had, of course, several times today as a matter of fact, but that wasn't what he was talking about now. "When?"

Switching his venomous gaze to Jamie, he said, "Just who is this guy? He sure as hell isn't your cousin."

Vicki kept silent and simply stared at the hatred for her in Graham's face.

Agent Ford attached a pair of handcuffs to Graham's wrists, but that didn't stop him from lashing out. "Surprised, darling, that I found out your little secret? Your mother was only too happy to tell me that there are no Irish relatives on either side of your family. And no cousin named Jamie Malone."

"You called my mother?"

"Brought her in from plucking the feathers off dinner, I suppose. She doesn't know any Jamie Malone. So as long as we're airing all the dirty laundry today, why don't you tell everyone here who this clown really is?"

Agent Ford took Graham's arm and attempted to

turn him toward the front door. "Let's save it for the trial, Mr. Townsend. Right now the detective has to read you your rights so we can take you down to the station."

"Wait a minute, Mr. Ford," Jamie interrupted. "I'd like very much to tell this man who I am."

Keeping a firm grip on Graham's elbow, the agent said, "Make it quick."

Vicki's breath caught in her lungs. Her gaze snapped to Jamie. Surely he wasn't about to admit…

"Oh, I will," Jamie said. "You're right, mate, I'm not Vicki's cousin. I'm the real stumbling block to that proposal you were about to give her. I'm her husband."

OKAY, HE SHOULDN'T have said it. And once he had, he should have regretted it. But he didn't. Jamie was damn glad to have Graham Townsend know that the woman he'd just scorned as being not good enough to share the Townsend name had already been selected and wed by someone long before he came along. Maybe not selected in the usual way, but Graham didn't need to know that.

And the look on the blue blood's face was ample reward. Even if he'd made Vicki angry, it was worth it. Seeing Graham's jaw drop, hearing the croaking noises from his throat were priceless. Seeing his complexion turn as gray as the underside of a beached flounder was best of all.

Intelligent syllables finally found their way out of

Graham's mouth. "Victoria, is this true? You're married to this goon?"

She looked at Jamie. She looked at Graham. She arched her eyebrows and took a deep breath. And then she said, "Yes, it's true. We've been married for thirteen years. Did I forget to tell you?"

A vein pumped hard in Graham's temple. "I can't believe I wasted more than a year of my life on you."

Agent Ford actually had to hide a grin behind his hand as he pulled Graham away. "Let's go, Mr. Townsend. You can say whatever you want to this lady later—in about twenty years." Then he instructed the detective, "Would you take the paintings? We'll send a team of inspectors later this afternoon to go through the rest of these imported items."

"You probably don't have to check them all," Jamie said. "Just the ones with prices high enough to give a bargain-hunter a coronary."

FINALLY HE AND VICKI were alone, and Jamie sensed that caution was the best way to approach the rest of the afternoon—assuming he was still welcome.

"Are you okay?" he said to her stiff figure.

She moved to her desk. "I guess so. It was a shock, of course. And I'm hurt. I never knew Graham harbored such resentment of me and my background." She was pensive for a moment before she said, "Maybe I should have, though. Truthfully I think I was already starting to have doubts about Graham and me. I certainly didn't have reason to believe he was a criminal, however."

"Yeah, that was something, wasn't it?" Jamie said. "About those doubts you were having about you and Graham..." He paused a moment and then plunged ahead. "Did you start having them about the time I came to Florida?" When she didn't answer immediately, he studied her expression and added, "Or is this a bad time to ask?"

Vicki sat at her desk and began reorganizing the mess Graham had made of her papers. Several seconds passed before she stopped fussing and looked up at him. "Maybe I did," she said, "and yes, this is a bad time to ask, since I'm still reeling from what you just did."

"What's that?"

"You just had to come right out and say it, didn't you."

He knew what she was referring to. That husband announcement had hung in the air ever since he'd said it. She didn't sound exactly angry, but neither did she seem ready to come over and pat him on the back. "Yes, I felt I did," he said.

"Why?"

"Why? Because it's true."

She gave him a forced smile. "No. Really why?"

"Because he pissed me off."

She shook her head slowly. "Ahhh..."

"For the love of God, Vicki, the man put your shop in jeopardy, he committed international trade fraud, and he continued to put you down even while his neck was practically in a noose. I think that calls for someone to stand up on your behalf and declare himself on your side. You are someone's wife, you know, and that someone is desperately trying to get you to at least think of the advantages of this union and about the pretty spectacular days we've spent together before you throw everything we have away.''

She put her elbows on the desk and threaded her fingers together. ''Okay, but you think about this, Jamie. If this whole mess hadn't happened, I would have accepted Graham's ring. And I probably would have married him some time in the near future. I've known Graham Townsend for a year and a half, and even after all that time, I think it's safe to say that if I had married him, it would have been the worst possible mistake I could have made.''

Now she was making sense. ''You're right. That's what I've been trying to tell you ever since you came to Bayberry Cove. I knew that guy wasn't for you—''

She continued as if he hadn't spoken. ''And yet you want me to stay married to you, a man I've known for...what?'' She untwined her fingers and counted on them. ''Six? Seven days?''

''Thirteen years!'' He stopped, rethought his answer. ''At least two weeks, anyway. Besides it's the quality of time that matters, not the quantity.''

She conceded his argument with a nod. ''Still, my success rate for marriage isn't much to brag about. I married you to get five thousand dollars. And then I almost married an international art smuggler to gain respectability. What a laugh! I wonder if there's a course in how not to bungle a marriage.''

He smiled. ''Yeah, it's right after the prerequisite

how to believe in yourself. Once you ace that course, the rest is easy."

"You make it sound simple, but it isn't."

"I know it isn't. But I can help. I think you're terrific. You're smart and warm and funny despite being raised by people you affectionately call Ma and Pa Dismal."

She smiled at his reference to their talk on the beach.

"And you're not half-bad to look at."

She made a circular motion with her hand, encouraging him to continue. "I'm listening."

"But the first thing you should do to gain self-confidence is not send me up the road today."

Her smile broadened. "Oh, that. I've already decided to ask you to stay. I was going to do it right after I thanked you for saving my shop and keeping me from ruining my life." She opened a drawer, removed the wood carving he'd left for her yesterday and set it in a place of honor on her desk. "And I especially thank you for giving me this."

Suddenly that carving of Beasley was the greatest achievement of Jamie's career. "So you like that little critter."

"I love it. Please, Jamie, stay for the shop opening. I need you. I want you to be here."

He whistled through his teeth. "Whoa! I may not be husband material, but I think I've just jumped right up to best-friend category."

"Oh, you have, Jamie. You definitely have."

He pulled up a chair and sat across the desk from

her. "Then tell me, Vic, what can your best friend do to make you feel better about all this?"

She folded her hands on her blotter. "You can talk to me, Jamie. Tell me about yourself—the things I don't know. I'm tired of men with secrets, and I think you might have some."

"Me?" He slapped his palms on his chest. "Vicki, love, what you see is—"

"—what I get?" she inserted. "I doubt that. Tell me about Bobbi Lee and her sons and your relationship with them. Tell me what you want out of life. Kids? Success?" She smiled. "Bigger and better puzzles? Tell me about your mother. I like her, but I want to know more about her life in Bayberry Cove."

Vicki leaned back in her chair and looked at him. "I've got plenty of time, Jamie. The Misses Huggins will be in this afternoon to do a final dust and primp. The pastry chef has the kitchen in sparkling good order. And my former boyfriend is on his way to jail. For however long it takes, I'm all yours."

FOR THE NEXT two hours Jamie talked and Vicki listened. She seemed to find the simple details of life on Pintail Point the most fascinating things she'd ever heard. He told her about Bobbi Lee and how they'd once had an intimate relationship, but it had ended before her second son, Brian, was born.

He admitted that he chipped in a little on her son Charlie's college tuition and he never missed Brian's soccer games. And when he told her that although he wanted kids of his own, he wanted a woman he loved by his side even more, her cheeks flushed.

When Vicki asked if Bobbi still loved him, he confessed that she believed she did. And he promised Vicki that he would set things straight with Bobbi, especially if it looked as if he and Vicki would make a go of their marriage.

And when he was through talking, Vicki knew that Bayberry Cove was more than candles and Currituck Sound. It was kids and dogs and simple people. And Kate Malone and the seasoned attorney Haywood Fletcher, who wasn't above a little tweaking of a document when a friend's future was at stake.

Vicki smiled when he told her how Kate had "insisted" that Haywood find a loophole in Louise's flawless divorce document. "I thought it might have been something like that," she said.

"You're not mad that I resorted to a bit of trickery to keep you tied to me a while longer?"

She tried to hide a smirk behind a stern expression, but Jamie could tell she wasn't truly angry.

"I should be," she said, "but considering the way things turned out, I'm going to forgive you."

"Saints be praised," he teased. "You're a good woman, Vicki Sorenson Malone. And as long as you're in the forgivin' mode, I probably should tell you something else."

She leaned over the desk and fixed him with a hard stare. "What now?"

He grinned to put her at ease, and himself as well. Admitting he had some money shouldn't be a difficult confession, but since he'd concealed the fact for so long, it suddenly was. "Nothing that warrants a face as serious as that," he said. "It concerns those bigger and better puzzles you asked me about."

"What about them?"

It was time to tell her something about his talent and success and have faith that she would judge him for the man he was inside, not for his bank account or reputation.

"A few of my wood carvings have sold for a tidy sum," he admitted. "There are people who, for whatever reasons, seem to like what I create."

She looked at the carving of Beasley. "That's easy to believe. Louise thought you might have some assets. But why the houseboat?"

"It's a place to live, that's all. It suits my purpose. It has until now, at least."

"Why didn't you tell me this before?"

"I was fearful that knowing I've had a bit of success might influence your opinion of the man, Jamie Malone. I don't believe that now, but before, the way you talked about Graham..."

She held up her hand. "It's okay. I used to be the kind of woman who was impressed by money and privilege. But so much has happened to change what I used to believe in..." She smiled. "Mostly getting to know you."

He stood up, confidence straightening his spine. "I'm going to stay this afternoon until the agents have searched the rest of the pieces from Amsterdam," he said. "And I'll probably stop by in the morning to see if there's anything you need me to do before the opening on Saturday. But then Beas and I are going off alone, maybe to scout up more wood or toss a limb on the beach."

He reached over and covered her hand with his. "But mostly I want to give you some time to yourself to sort things out. You know where to find me if you need me. Otherwise I'll be at the opening of the shop day after tomorrow. I'll be the one looking very much like the proud husband of the shopkeeper, even if the position's only temporary."

He let his fingertips linger on her wrist where her pulse beat strong and fast. "And, Vicki, if you decide it's the divorce papers you want, I'll head quietly north to Bayberry Cove and put my name and a stamp on the document. That will be the end of it. You have my word." He stared into her blue eyes. "You and I, like all things in life, are a risk. I know that. But I hope you'll decide that we're one that's worth taking."

He stood up, placed his hand under her chin, leaned over the desk and kissed her. "You have to take the risk, love, in order to have the dream." And then he walked away from her.

CHAPTER SIXTEEN

VICKI STEPPED out of the shower and into a terry-cloth robe. She rubbed her hair with a towel and blew it dry. After plugging in her electric curlers, she went into the bedroom and removed the plastic bag from the new dress she'd picked up that afternoon. The simple sequined black sheath was perfect for the shop opening. And the single-hook closure and smooth-gliding zipper made it perfect for anything that might occur later.

A flush of desire warmed Vicki's body just as it had for two days whenever she fantasized about one sexy Irishman who just happened to be her husband. A knock at her door reminded her that she still had some important business to take care of—the opening of her shop in two hours.

She opened the door to Louise, who sailed inside on dangerously spiked heels. ''You look smashing, Lulu, as always,'' Vicki said, admiring the midthigh spaghetti-strap dress that fit Louise like gold foil on an almond kiss.

''It's all for you, friend,'' Louise said. ''I don't want anyone at the opening wondering what kind of riffraff you run around with.'' She went into Vicki's small kitchen and called out, ''Don't you have an open bottle of wine?''

''No, but help yourself.''

''I will, but only because I can see you need it.''

''I do?''

''It's not every day a woman has to give up the most eligible bachelor in the state penitentiary.''

Vicki listened to the rustle of kitchen gadgets in her utensil drawer. ''I suppose not,'' she said, knowing Louise was probably rejoicing at the latest turn of events.

Louise walked into the living room with two glasses of cabernet and handed one to Vicki. ''Mrs. Townsend was in the office today,'' she said.

Vicki nearly choked on the first sip of wine. ''Really? She's hiring you to defend Graham?''

Louise hooted with laughter. ''Me? Right! Come on, Vic. When a woman can afford filet, why would she settle for ground beef? No, Mrs. Susan Townsend spent two hours in the office of Mr. Oppenheimer himself.''

Oddly, Vicki experienced a sense of relief at hearing this news. She felt sorry for Susan Townsend having to deal with the arrest of her only son. ''At least Graham will have competent legal representation,'' she said to Louise.

''The best money can buy. Even so, Mrs. T. still looked distraught when she left Oppenheimer's office. As I see it, this is an open-and-shut case. The only variables are how much time Graham is going to have to spend behind bars and how many appeals we'll have to go through.'' She took a sip of wine and looked at Vicki over the rim of her glass. ''It won't be easy for you when this case goes to trial,'' Louise said.

''I'll be fine,'' Vicki responded, knowing she wouldn't be going through the ordeal alone. Jamie would be with her, lending his support in that quiet, self-assured way he had.

Louise stood up from the sofa. ''Okay, then, enough about that. Look at the time.'' She held Vicki's shoulders and turned her toward the bedroom. ''Let's see what a self-respecting antiques-shop owner is wearing to her opening these days.''

Louise appraised the sequined dress from its choker-style neckline that bared the shoulders to its ankle-length skirt. ''Good choice,'' she said. ''Obviously expensive. Elegant to be sure. Yet it screams, 'Take me, right here. Right now.''' She waved her hand with impatience. ''Well, come on, let's get you into these clothes so the cream of Fort Lauderdale can ogle you even if Townsend can't.''

Louise plopped down on the bed and set her glass on a strip of paper on Vicki's nightstand. Noticing the distinctive plum-colored receipt, Louise slid it out from under the glass. ''You bought the dress and shoes at Maxine's. I'm impressed.''

Vicki went into the bathroom and wound a strand of hair around the first heated curler. ''Don't be. I think I can write it off as a business expense. Besides, nobody said I had to give back the four-thousand on the vanity, so I splurged.''

"Good for you." Louise remained silent as Vicki continued to set her hair. After a few minutes she said, "By the way, Vic?"

"Yeah?"

"When exactly did you decide you wanted Jamie Malone, after all?"

Vicki sputtered, coughed, dropped a hot roller. "What are you talking about?"

"This receipt. It's a dead giveaway. You didn't buy this outfit for Graham. You bought it today to impress Jamie. It's his eyes you hope will pop out of his head."

Vicki didn't bother to argue. She had thought of Jamie with every swish of the hangers at the exclusive shop.

Louise came to the bathroom door. "Look, honey, if you want him, he's yours. You've already got the best claim on the guy anyone can have. But you've got to admit it to me, because I'll tell you straight out." She ran a fingertip along the revealing neckline of her own dress. "I wore this for Malone, and I'm not afraid to admit it. So if you don't want him, I'm pulling out all the stops to make this a Lulu night. But if you do..."

Vicki slumped against the sink. "I do want him, Lulu. But it's so soon after Graham. I'm very confused. But I think about Jamie all the time. I have these incredible dreams about him..."

Louise smiled. "You're smitten for sure, Vic. Consider me out of the game. Now which is your underwear drawer?"

"Panties are there—" Vicki pointed "—and my strapless bra—"

"Forget the bra."

"What? Forget the bra?" Indiana farm girls didn't forget their bras.

Louise waltzed over to Vicki's full-length mirror, put a hand under each of her own breasts and admired the look. "Victoria, you and I only have a few more good years for these puppies of ours to do their jobs. Play 'em up for all they're worth while they're still working for you. No bra."

Vicki bit her bottom lip to squelch a giggle. "You're the expert. No bra, it is."

THE SCENT OF Tropical Rum Spice followed Jamie out of the swanky men's salon on Las Olas Boulevard. He ran his hands through his cropped locks and marveled at how a man could get so caught up in the atmosphere of a place that he'd willingly hand over fifty bucks for what cost twelve dollars in Bayberry Cove. But he'd been pleased when the stylist told him he looked quite dashing. "Dashing" ought to do for the opening of Tea and Antiquities this evening.

Next he walked to the men's store a block from Vicki's shop to pick up his new suit. Jamie normally didn't need a suit. He already had one in his closet on the *Bucket o' Luck.* He'd bought it three years before when he'd been given an honorary degree from the Humanities Department of Duke University. That same suit had served him well through weddings, funerals, christenings and many other notable events in Bayberry Cove. Unfortunately a suit in North Carolina wasn't much help when the man who needed it was in Florida.

Ten minutes later Jamie left the men's store with a charcoal-gray garment bag over his shoulder and a shoe box under his arm. The phone was ringing when he entered his apartment. He deposited his purchases on the nearest chair.

''What good are ya', Beas?'' he said to the dog who stared at him with an aloofness that said he wasn't impressed with Tropical Rum Spice. ''Can't even answer the phone.''

He picked up the receiver while he reached under the counter for the bag of kibble. ''Hello.''

''Jamie, darlin',' chimed his mother's voice.

''Hi, Ma. How's everything in the Cove?''

''It's all fine here, son, though folks at the Kettle say Bobbi Lee's been in a mood.''

If Bobbi was grumpy, Jamie knew he was the reason. He poured some kibble into a bowl and coaxed Beasley over. ''She and I spoke last night,'' he said. ''Have you seen her today?''

''This morning at the supermarket.''

''How did she seem to you?''

''Actually, she seemed resigned. She said you two had a talk and she was accepting the situation.'' Kate sighed. ''It's a hard thing for a girl to give up her hopes, Jamie. You be kind to her when you get back.''

''I will, Ma.''

''Now then, how are things going with you and Vicki?''

How could he answer truthfully? Kate didn't even know about Vicki's relationship with Graham.

"Things are going well, Ma," he answered. "I think Vicki's starting to adjust to me."

"Do you mean like a wife adjusts to a husband?"

"Maybe. I hope so."

"I liked her," Kate said. "I sensed an earnestness in her, a softness of heart and a yearning, too. And it made me think that there was a reason you never divorced her, never found another woman to marry."

There was a pause, but Jamie knew Kate wasn't finished, and he waited for her to continue.

"So do you think you'll stay married to her, then?" she said.

He chuckled. "I think *I* would right enough, but I'm only half the equation. It's still too soon for you to start planning on grandchildren."

The instant the words were out of his mouth, he regretted them. Vicki may never want a child, and if that was the case, then Jamie was prepared to accept her terms.

"Ah, a grandbaby." Kate practically crooned the words.

"Don't get your hopes up, Ma," Jamie said. "Vicki's somehow got it into her head that she wouldn't be a good mother. Truth is, she's half-scared of kids."

"Scared of them? The poor darlin'. Being a mother is the easiest thing in the world. Even when your babes break your heart, it's still worth the risk to see them grow."

Jamie smiled, thinking about how Kate never gave

up on his brothers, still hadn't to this day. "It was easy for you, Ma, but it's not for all women. I'll see you in a couple of days, okay?"

When Jamie hung up, he went to take his shower. So much had happened in the past few days, but he didn't yet know how it would end. He'd understated his reputation as an artist, but Vicki knew everything else there was to know about him. "I hope she wants the man that I am." He stood under the spray, letting the water sluice over his body. "Even after I wash off all this fancy Tropical Rum Spice."

VICKI AND LOUISE arrived at Tea and Antiquities half an hour before the opening was scheduled to begin. There was little for Vicki to do at this late date. The shop looked beautiful, from the pale lavender paint to the tasteful floral wallpaper trim around the ceiling and chair rails. Each piece of china inside cupboards and on shelves gleamed with personal attention. From the CD player Jamie had recently installed, the muted strains of Pachelbel lent a relaxed, dignified ambiance.

Dressed fashionably and eager to begin work, Hazel and Marcia Huggins entered the shop a few minutes early. After greeting Vicki, Hazel buzzed around the showroom looking for any specks of dust left from her inspection the day before. Marcia busied herself in the kitchen with the chef.

Vicki unlocked the front door just before five o'clock. She was talking to Hazel a few minutes later when the first visitor came in. Hazel stopped talking, touched her eyeglasses and stared over the rims. "My goodness, Vicki, is that Jamie, the fella who's been helping around here?''

Vicki turned to answer Hazel's question, and her whole body went limp for a few seconds as she looked at Jamie. The man who'd entered her shop was Jamie, but he was almost unrecognizable, so totally different from the man she'd married thirteen years before. Except for those dazzling green eyes and that brilliant smile, both as captivating as always.

He stood just inside the door, his gaze on Vicki as intense as hers was on him. She noticed that he actually seemed a bit self-conscious.

He shuffled his feet and looked down at his chest before giving her his familiar crooked grin and saying, ''What? Do I have mustard on my tie? I stopped at that street cart on the corner on my way here and had a couple of hot bangers.''

Relief, as warm and comforting as the first sip of fine wine, swept through Vicki. She shook her head slowly and smiled at him. ''No, you don't have mustard on your tie. You are, every inch, magnificent.''

He blushed, the first time she'd ever seen that happen. ''Oh, well, then, that's good, I guess. Let's see how long I can pull it off.'' He leaned slightly to see around Vicki and said, ''Good evening, Louise. How's everything in the legal trade?''

Louise emitted a little growl ripe with sexual frustration. ''I'm not sure I care,'' she answered sharply.

Hazel engaged Jamie in conversation while Louise remarked in Vicki's ear, ''You'd better get a happy ending out of this, because I already regret that promise I made to you.''

Vicki inclined her head and whispered, ''He does look good, doesn't he?''

''Good? Honey, that's what you say about a piece of chocolate cake. Malone's in another realm altogether.'' She skirted around Vicki and dragged Jamie away from Hazel. ''So what do you think of our shop proprietor?'' she said. ''Vic looks pretty sensational, don't you think?''

''Don't listen to Lulu,'' Vicki said to Jamie. ''She gets this perverse pleasure out of embarrassing me.'' Vicki tried to laugh off Louise's obvious efforts at matchmaking, but she was suddenly incapable of any sound other than a long, deep sigh. She returned Jamie's fervent sexual gaze and knew that at this moment words were unnecessary.

''Very nice, Vicki,'' he said.

And then they were swept up in a tide of people.

''BRILLIANT, MALONE,'' Jamie muttered to himself as Vicki scurried off to answer questions and offer refreshments. '''Very nice, Vicki'? Nice? That was all you could think to say?'' He watched her glide gracefully through the crowd making each person feel welcome. ''Good God, you idiot, she's spectacular.''

The high-collared dress exposed enough of her creamy skin to send a man's fantasies soaring to new levels while maintaining a refinement appropriate for the occasion. Her hair tumbled in bouncing curls from a glittering band across the top of her head. She was a vision of sequins and sparkle all the way to the thin sandal straps showing off rosy pink toenails.

She was angelic and seductive. Innocent and sensual. Sophisticated and erotic. For a man who just a few minutes ago could only say, "Very nice, Vicki," adjectives were suddenly popping into his brain like lottery balls.

The opening only lasted four hours, but to Jamie it was an eternity. He mingled with the Fort Lauderdale Downtown Improvement Committee. He chatted with the mayor. He discussed the fine points of antique collecting with people whose knowledge was far greater than his own. He even credited himself with coaxing a few hesitant buyers into purchasing a treasure or two.

But through it all, his gaze kept going back to the woman who managed her store and the people in it with grace and style. His libido kept fantasizing about the woman under the shimmering dress. His mind kept imagining the possibilities of bedding his wife. His ego prompted him to believe that Vicki was thinking the same things about him. And his heart dared hope for a future.

And then, at last, everyone was gone. Even Louise had found a board chairman to take her to dinner. Vicki's chef accepted praise for his delicacies and quietly slipped out the back door. And after congratulating Vicki on the all-important bottom line for sales while no doubt calculating their commissions, Hazel and Marcia complained of sore feet and bid their employer good-night.

Vicki carried a tray of pastry crumbs to the kitchen. Jamie took off his jacket, slung it over a chair and went to a back closet where cleaning supplies were located. He was reaching for a broom when she called him.

He found her leaning against a kitchen counter. She had a flaky pastry of some sort between her thumb and finger. "You were wonderful tonight," she said. "Did you get something to eat?"

"I'll eat later. Right now I thought I'd—"

He never finished telling her he was going to sweep, because she popped the fruity confection into his mouth. He chewed while she wiped a bit of powdered sugar from his upper lip and slowly licked her finger clean. After that, it took Herculean effort to swallow the soggy dough that stuck in his throat.

She rubbed her hands down his upper arms, stopping at his elbows and coaxing them toward her. "How can I ever thank you?"

He raised one eyebrow. "I think there's still a bit of sugar on my lip, and since your hands are busy..."

She smiled. "I can do that." She pulled his hands around her waist and leaned into him. Her mouth was warm, soft, tasting vaguely of wine. He tried to follow her lead of gentle seduction, but his instincts put him into overdrive.

His arms tightened around her. His hands clutched her bottom, and he crushed her against his groin. His erection was immediate and intense. She flattened her breasts against his chest and arched her neck to give him access to the flesh he'd admired from a distance all evening.

His lips left a moist trail down her throat to her shoulders. When he returned to her mouth, she drew in his tongue and closed her lips firmly around it, teasing and tantalizing him with seductive images. He moved his hand to cover her breast, leaving nothing between it and her skin but silk and sequins. Her nipple responded instantly and peaked against his palm. He slipped his hand inside the garment and held one soft, rounded globe. She moaned and cuddled closer to him until they were joined even more intimately.

Too soon, she disengaged the kiss and leaned away from him. Her lips glistened with moisture. Her face was flushed with the heat of desire. "Do you know what I want?" she asked.

He blew out a long breath. "I'd be the biggest dolt in the world if I got this one wrong."

She laughed. "I want to go to Flanagan's, grab a couple of Guinnesses and two shepherd's pies and go back to my place."

He nodded. "So you've a yen to eat Irish tonight?"

She placed her hands on each side of his face. "I've a yen for *all* things Irish tonight," she said.

For the first time in his life, Jamie knew how it felt to have your heart threaten to jump from your chest. "What an amazin' coincidence," he said in his thickest brogue. "Did ya' know, now, that I happen to be Irish?"

"Of course. I was once married to an Irish fella. You can spot an Irish guy even when he's standing on a rooftop. Now what do you say to my suggestion?''

What did he say? What could he shout? What silly romantic lyrics could he sing? She was offering herself to him, and accepting him for who he was. She loved him, truly loved him, in a way she'd never loved Graham. And so tonight, Jamie knew he had everything that had been missing in his life.

''I say that you have a special gift, Vicki,'' he said.

''I do?''

''All my mates in Bayberry Cove complain that after thirteen years their marriages have gone stale. Yet you find the most entertaining ways to keep ours fresh.''

She smiled. ''Good. Let's get those Guinnesses.''

He linked his arm with hers. They walked out of the kitchen and into the showroom—and realized they were not alone. A customer was still in the shop, a nicely dressed, middle-aged woman.

She looked at Vicki. ''I know the opening is over,'' she said. ''I hope you'll forgive me for lingering, but there is one piece I just noticed, and I must have it.''

Vicki saw the carving of Beasley in the woman's hand and went to retrieve it. ''I'm sorry. This piece is not for sale.'' She set it back on her desk where it had been for two days.

''Are you sure you won't change your mind?'' The woman pointed to the underbelly of the carving, to the initials. ''This artist is one of my favorites. I know the money his pieces fetch. I'll pay a fair price to add this to my collection.''

Vicki glanced at Jamie. His gaze was focused on the ceiling. With the tips of his fingers, he attempted to hide a smile lurking at the corners of his mouth.

''Your 'collection'?'' Vicki said. ''You must be mistaken. The man who made this is a North Carolina local artist.''

''There's no mistake,'' the woman insisted. ''He signs all his pieces with these initials, and he's known nationally. This is definitely the work of J.D. Malone.''

Vicki grabbed up the carving and studied it closely, appreciating the details of Jamie's talent in the chiseled angles and fine cuts. Snatches of familiar conversation came to her mind once more. *''Everybody's got a little money, Vicki,''* he'd once said to her. Beginning to grasp the magnitude of Jamie's reputation, she turned to face him. ''What do you know about this artist?'' she asked.

He met the challenge in her stare with guilt-edged teasing. ''I've heard of him,'' he answered. ''They say he lives in an old houseboat with a good-for-nothin' dog. He's a simple man, appreciates good wood. He's fairly talented at what he does, they say. Oh, and he's married, has been for thirteen years. And he's very much in love with his wife.''

She fought unsuccessfully to hide a grin. ''My, you certainly know some intimate details about his life.''

He shrugged. ''He and I know some of the same people.''

''I see.'' Vicki smiled at the woman, who waited expectantly. ''I can't sell you this piece, ma'am,'' she said, handing the woman a sheet of paper and a pen. "But if you'll leave me your address, I'll contact the artist and insist that he send you a similar carving at no charge."

The woman beamed. "You can do that?"

Vicki looked over her shoulder at Jamie, who was blushing for the second time that night. "Oh, I can do it."

The woman quickly jotted down the information, thanked Vicki and left the shop. When the door closed, Vicki folded her arms across her chest and stared at Jamie. Her toe tapped against Beasley's favorite Persian rug. "Is there anything else you've neglected to tell me, Jamie?"

He shook his head. "I think that's about it. Oh, wait, there is one other thing."

"I can only imagine."

"Do you remember that rise of land across from the point on Sandy Ridge Road?"

She recalled the gentle hill sloping down toward Currituck Sound. "Yes, I remember it."

"Well, I own that bit. Before I made this trip to Florida, I had a notion one night standing on the catwalk of the *Bucket o' Luck* and looking out at that land. I was thinking about you. I thought that if you should decide to throw all good sense to the wind and stay a renegade Malone, I might want to build a right proper house on that hill. One that would shimmer under the stars and laugh at the winds of Currituck Sound.

"And if it should happen that your heart suddenly

yearns for motherhood, I could picture a nursery in the southeast corner.'' He shrugged. ''If not, it would make a fine sunroom where the lady of the house could put her feet up and wrap her hands around a warm mug of tea on a winter's afternoon.''

Vicki pictured Jamie's house, and dreams she'd never allowed herself to have swelled inside her heart. ''You've thought of all this?''

''What's the use of having a fantasy if you keep it small?''

''I think I like your fantasy.''

''But what about you, Vicki, and your dreams? Your shop?''

She walked over to the only dream that really mattered and nestled into the protection of his arm around her shoulders. ''The Hugginses have practically taken over the running of Tea and Antiquities,'' she said. ''I would want to keep it, though, buy stock, spend some of my time here.''

''Thank goodness for that!''

''You don't mind?''

''Mind? You've seen Beasley on Fort Lauderdale beach. He's practically taken up surfing.''

She laughed. ''But what about Ma and Pa Sorenson? What will you say when the roof blows off the chicken coop and the hens stop laying?''

''That's an easy one. I'll tell Pa that his daughter married a guy who's somewhat of an expert with wood. I'll offer to repair that coop, and I'll suggest he sharpen up his tools so he can lend me a hand. We'll have those hens back laying in no time, he and I.''

Vicki smiled at the thought of her father hammering and sawing under Jamie's direction. "And knowing he has to help, he might even keep things in better repair."

Jamie nodded sagely. "Ahhh... I told you once that you were a clever girl. Now, have we missed any other important details?"

"I don't think so."

He turned her in his arms and gave her a long, passionate kiss. "Then I suggest we start the honeymoon. I've waited thirteen years for it. Tomorrow we'll head back to Bayberry Cove together. And I guarantee you that if it's nurturing you think you've missed in your life, you'll get your fill of it there."

* * * * *

Watch for Louise's story in
Cynthia Thomason's next Superromance
coming in late 2004.

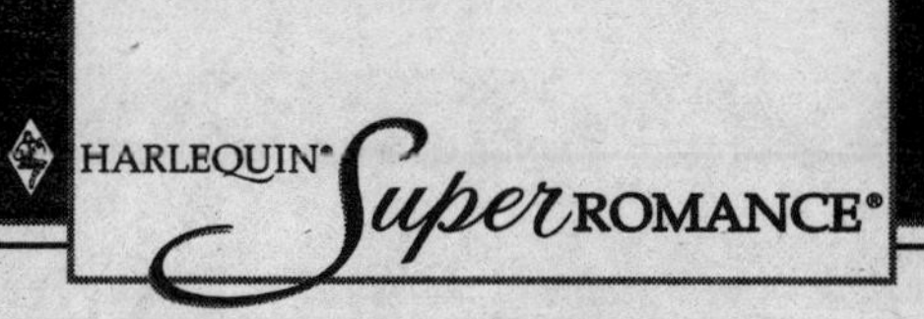

Sea View House in Pilgrim Cove offers *its residents the sea, the sun, the sound of the surf and the call of the gulls.* But *sometimes serenity is only an illusion...*

Pilgrim Cove

Four *heartwarming stories by popular author*

Linda Barrett

The House *on the* Beach

Laura McCloud's come back to Pilgrim Cove—the source of her fondest childhood memories—to pick up the pieces of her life. The tranquility of Sea View House is just what she needs. She moves in...and finds much more than she bargained for.

Available in March 2004, *The House on the Beach* is the first title in this charming series.

Available wherever Harlequin books are sold.

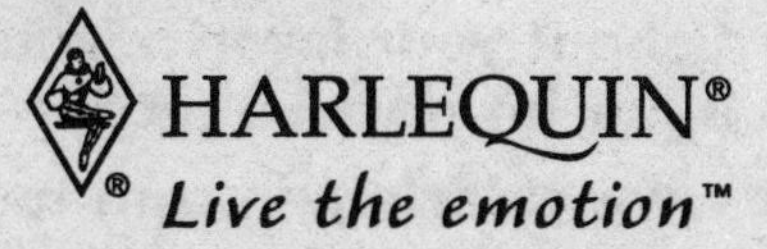

Visit us at www.eHarlequin.com HSRPC1